# Corrupted Lies

## JANE BLYTHE

# Acknowledgments

I'd like to thank everyone who played a part in bringing this story to life. Particularly my mom who is always there to share her thoughts and opinions with me. My wonderful cover designer Letitia who did an amazing job with this stunning cover. My fabulous editor Lisa for all the hard work she puts into polishing my work. My awesome team, Sophie, Robyn, and Clayr, without your help I'd never be able to run my street team. And my fantastic street team members who help share my books with every share, comment, and like!

And of course a big thank you to all of you, my readers! Without you I wouldn't be living my dreams of sharing the stories in my head with the world!

# CHAPTER *One*

October 13<sup>th</sup>
12:45 P.M.

"I've hardly seen you in months. I've missed you."

The words, softly spoken though they'd been, had Jake Holloway stiffening. If there was one thing the woman standing in front of him knew without a shadow of a doubt it was that for him, family would *always* come first.

No exceptions.

These last three months he'd barely had time to breathe, let alone make time for anything outside of protecting his family from threat after threat.

The blows just kept coming.

First, his stepbrother Cooper was almost killed in Egypt after chasing down a lead on who was involved in setting up Jake's step-mother to look like a traitor. Then his stepbrother Cole's neighbor was targeted after someone wrongly assumed the two were a couple, although they were in fact now dating. Then, his stepbrother Connor brought danger right to his ex-girlfriend's door when he traveled to

Cambodia to attempt a reconciliation. Then finally, last month, his last stepbrother Cade's four-year-old daughter and her nanny had been abducted.

With all that going on in his family, how could he possibly have time for anything other than keeping the people he loved safe?

More than just safe, this was literally a matter of life and death, he'd been focused on keeping his family alive.

In comparison to that, nothing else mattered.

Certainly not him taking time out of his day to do something fun that he actually enjoyed.

And spending time with Alannah Johansen was *always* something he enjoyed.

"Family first, Alannah. You know that," he snapped a little harsher than he should have, then again, if anyone was used to his grumpy attitude, it was certainly his best friend since childhood.

"Course I know that, grumpypants," Alannah shot back with a laugh that to anyone else would sound completely natural. But he'd known this woman since they were small children. In fact, he'd met her when he'd been five and playing in his backyard and heard someone crying. When he squeezed himself through a hole in the fence, he'd found four-year-old Alannah curled up in a ball in the middle of a flower bush crying her little eyes out.

From then on, the two of them had been best friends.

Which, after almost thirty years, meant he knew how to read Alannah.

Knew that she was covering her hurt at not being included as a member of his family even though she technically wasn't. May as well be though, they'd grown up together, she'd been there for him when his mom died, and then his dad remarried out of the blue only to be accused of treason six months later and committed suicide. She'd been his rock, and throughout the years he'd been her protector. Making sure no one teased her on the playground because of her lisp when she was little, then making sure no boys took advantage of her as they got older and both started dating.

Truth was, Jake did consider Alannah family, but right now, it was pretty dangerous to be part of his family.

"I didn't mean it how it sounded, sunshine," he assured her. "You're my best friend and have been since we were in kindergarten. It's just this stuff with my family is messed up, and I don't want you involved in it."

Alannah's golden-brown eyes softened, and she set down the dumb-bell she'd been lifting as he gave himself an hour off to work out at the gym with his best friend, and stepped closer. "Jake, I don't know the details, and I'm not asking you to share. You're right, I'm not family, but I am your best friend, and I care about you. If you need help, I'll do anything I can to give it to you."

That was absolutely true.

No one had as good a heart as Alannah. Despite an entire lifetime of constantly being put down and told she wasn't enough by her parents as they favored her older sister, the family's golden child, she loved and cared about everybody she met. She was bright, bubbly, and sunshiny, and it seemed like nobody but him realized that was just a shield she used to mask her pain and fears.

Reaching out, he took her hand and gave it a squeeze. "I know you would, sunshine, but unfortunately this is one thing I can't bring you in on. Please understand, it's not because I don't respect the hell out of you, you have always had my back, I just don't want you getting dragged into this and hurt."

Because he'd been keeping what was going on with his family quiet, Alannah had no idea the extent of the danger he and his family were in. She'd been around when his dad remarried, and they'd both been upset when his dad made them move into his new stepmother's house. But their friendship had continued, and Alannah knew about his dad and stepmom getting arrested, knew that he and all his brothers believed the marriage was fake, knew that for the last almost twenty years he and his brothers had been searching for the truth.

She just didn't know how close they were to finding it, or the lengths the people responsible for framing his dad and stepmother would go to cover it up.

"Grumpy, are you in danger? Are you safe?" she asked, her voice dropping to a whisper because at least two dozen other people were inside the gym that Alannah owned and ran.

A familiar smile tugged at the corners of his lips. Grumpy and sunshine had been their nicknames since they were in middle school. The other kids always thought it was hilarious that the angriest kid in the class was best friends with the happiest.

Kids had always thought they were going to wind up a couple too.

But it had never happened, never would happen. They were best friends, and he had no intention of messing that up.

Because they were best friends, he couldn't lie to her when she asked point blank. "No, sunshine, I'm not safe. No one in my family is."

Fear filled her eyes. Although Alannah had a family, she'd been virtually no contact with them for years given the way they continued to treat her, and although she had plenty of friends, and was more often than not dating someone, he was the closest person in her life, and he knew he probably should have clued her in on what was going on.

Raking his fingers through his hair, he nodded to the stairs at the side of the large open space. "Can we go talk in your office?"

It was time to tell his best friend what was going on. Jake realized this was exactly what he'd needed. While it had felt selfish to take a little time to himself, everyone else was safe and being watched. Cooper had Willow, Cole had Susanna, Connor had Becca, and now that he'd gotten his head on straight, Cade finally had both his five-year-old daughter, Esther, and the former nanny Gabriella.

This was what *he* needed.

"Of course we can," Alannah readily agreed.

Without another word, they packed away the weights they'd been lifting and headed for the stairs. Alannah's gym was broken down into multiple floors. Top floor was a men's only space, then came a women's only space, the unisex space they'd been using, then a seniors space, a teen space, a kid's space, then the ground floor was used for classes, and the basement was office, storage, and a childcare area.

Since he knew this place like the back of his hand, had encouraged her to follow her passion and start the gym, Jake led the way down the several flights of stairs and past the playroom where there were a handful of toddlers building with blocks and banging on some instruments while the carer sat on the floor playing with them, down a hall, and into Alannah's office.

"I'm really worried about you, Jake," she told him as soon as he closed the door behind them.

Like it always did when he was in Alannah's space, whether it be there or at her apartment, Jake felt peace and calm flood into his soul as he settled beside her on the couch. No wonder he'd caved and said yes today when she called and asked if he wanted to do a workout session with her. His body and his mind knew what he needed, and it was a couple of hours recharging his batteries with his best friend.

"I didn't keep any of this from you to hurt you or shut you out, but these people are targeting anyone they even suspect of being connected to us," he told her.

"What people?" Alannah asked. "Did you get a lead on the men who had your dad's team killed and then set him and your stepmom up to take the fall? Last I heard, Cooper was going to Egypt to try to get answers from some Egyptologist, but when I asked you about it after the news broke that he'd died, you told me it was nothing."

Of course, he didn't miss the tiny thread of hurt in her voice even though he was sure everyone else would have.

Before he could open his mouth to assure her once again that he hadn't shut her out on purpose, he smelled something that had the hairs on the back of his neck standing up.

Smoke.

~

October 13th
1:01 P.M.

Alannah Johansen was about to open her mouth to ask Jake what was going on with his family and why he kept talking about danger and not wanting to get her involved, when she froze.

Was that ...?

Startled, her gaze snapped from Jake to the door to her office, which they'd walked through no more than two minutes ago, and then back to Jake again.

"Do you smell—?"

"Smoke?" he inserted, saying exactly what she'd been about to.

Both jumped up off the small couch in her office where she'd spent more than the occasional night sleeping when she'd first been starting up her gym. It had taken a lot of time, a whole lot of hard work, and every cent of the inheritance she'd gotten from her grandparents.

Which she'd had to fight to maintain after her parents tried to have it taken away from her and given to her sister instead.

But that was not what she should be thinking about right now.

Smoke.

They'd both smelled smoke coming from the other side of the door, only when they'd walked through the area to get to her office, there had been no indication of a fire or anyone about to start one.

What the heck was going on?

Right as Jake's hand reached out to grab her door handle, the shrill sound of the fire alarm began to shriek through the building.

There was no doubt about it, there was definitely a fire out there.

Faulty wiring or something?

No.

That couldn't be it.

She'd only just had an inspection of the building done to ensure everything was in tiptop working condition, and that had included the entire electrical system.

"Open the door, Jake," she said urgently when he didn't fling it open so they could figure out what was going on and get out.

"Can't."

The simple word shot like an arrow of fear straight through her chest, sending icy tentacles throughout her body.

"Wh-what do y-you mean?" she asked, her voice shaking as her entire body trembled.

It wasn't like she couldn't figure that out on her own.

What else *could* he mean?

Can't meant he couldn't open the door, only neither of them had locked it when they came in. She hadn't thought it was necessary, and she was anxious to help her best friend carry the burdens that were clearly weighing heavily upon him.

"I mean, someone locked us in here and started a fire to kill us," Jake said.

Kill them?

Wasn't that quite a leap?

There could be any number of reasons why the door wouldn't open, and while she had, of course, assumed someone must have started the fire, she hadn't been thinking deliberately. She'd assumed someone had burned something in the kitchen, it was only right next to her office, so it was the most logical conclusion.

Who would want to kill her?

Her gym was successful. They ran a fabulous in-person as well as online do-at-home sessions. They had a great reputation, a wonderful clientele, they catered to everyone, and people could choose how to use the spaces there. There was no reason that anyone should want to hurt her.

Then it dawned on her.

The men Jake had spoken about. The ones he was clearly afraid of, and she wasn't used to seeing Jake afraid of anything. He'd always been her big, strong protector. Ever since she was four years old, and he'd come wiggling through a hole in their joined fences because he'd heard her crying. That day, he'd made her feel special when he'd picked a dozen flowers from her garden and somehow managed to weave them into a crown. When he'd placed it on her head and declared her the flower garden fairy queen, he'd forever earned himself a place in her heart.

Today, he hadn't brought smiles and peace into her world. It was the opposite in fact.

He's brought danger right to her door.

Not that she blamed him. It wasn't his fault that someone had targeted his dad and stepmom, and he and his brothers deserved answers, they deserved the truth.

She just didn't want to die for them to get that truth.

It wasn't until she saw Jake putting his cell phone back in his pocket, then reaching out to clasp her shoulders, giving her a gentle shake, that Alannah realized she'd been panicking.

Now that she did realize it, she found her breath was sawing in and out of her chest, and the trembling in her limbs had morphed to full-on violent shaking.

"Come on, sunshine, stick with me," Jake soothed in a voice she rarely heard him use. He was her best friend, but he'd come by the nickname grumpy honestly. His face always looked like it was scowling, although she knew, in fact, he wasn't actually frowning at anything, and he had a gruff, no-nonsense way of speaking.

Usually.

But not today.

"I know you're scared, Alannah, trust me, I'm terrified having you in here with me, but I will get you out, I swear."

"H-how?" she managed to force the word out past her chattering teeth.

"I'll figure something out, but I need you to trust me, okay? I need you to calm your breathing down. Can you do that for me?"

It wasn't really a matter of if she could or not.

She had to.

If she wanted to live, she had to help Jake, not work against him by becoming dead weight.

Dragging in a shaky breath, she nodded. When he released his hold on her, she wanted to call him back, insist that he never let her go because he made her feel safe.

But she didn't.

She got her breathing under control while he prowled around her office looking for ... something.

A way out, she guessed, only the door was the only one. This was the basement. There were no windows and only one set of stairs up to the first floor.

Only they couldn't get to the stairs if they couldn't get out of the office.

*Focus, Alannah.*

*You're not the weak, pathetic, waste of space your parents are always insisting that you are.*

*Help Jake.*

The pep talk worked, and she managed to calm both her breathing and the shaking. "What do you need?" she asked Jake.

"Something to break down the door. It's locked. I called my brothers, so they'll get here as quickly as they can. Firefighters will check the building, too, but I don't want to count on someone else getting us out. Not when you're here."

His words made her smile, her protective grumpypants was there, and somehow in her mind that meant everything would be okay.

Running over to a corner where she had a stack of new weights she'd been going to think about stocking in the small shop on the ground floor, she ripped it open and grabbed two. "Here, Jake, we could use these."

"Perfect." He took one, she kept hold of the other, and they both headed for the door.

While she hammered on it with her weight along with Jake, Alannah knew he was the one making progress. She was like the toddler who you allowed to help but really only wound up getting in the way.

Making his way methodically up the door, when he got near the top, he began to hammer in earnest, and soon he was able to smash right through her door.

Immediately, smoke billowed into the room, making Alannah choke as all the oxygen seemed to disappear.

"Damn," Jake muttered as he grabbed hold of the hole he'd made and lifted himself up enough to see out it.

"What is it?"

"Someone has shoved one of those metal storage shelves you have up against the door."

"So we're trapped?" Try as she might to remain calm, Alannah could feel her heart hammering in her chest. They might be found in time by either Jake's brothers or firefighters, but they also might not.

It didn't take long for smoke inhalation to take effect.

"The hell we are," Jake snarled. Dropping back down, he picked up the weight he'd set down and hammered at the door again, stopping only once he'd made a bigger hole. "I'll give you a boost."

"We're going to climb through the hole?" As badly as she wanted out of the room, they didn't know what was out there. Maybe they were safer inside.

"I've got you, sunshine." For a second, Jake palmed her cheek, his fingertips feathered across her cheekbone, and Alannah got the weirdest desire for him to lean down and brush his lips across hers the same way his fingers had just caressed her cheek.

It must be the smoke affecting her brain combined with the fear of dying.

"Okay," she agreed. Jake had been in Delta Force like his dad, before going to work for Prey Security's Charlie Team. He knew what he was doing, and she had to trust him to make the best decisions for them both.

Grabbing her hips, he did more than just give her a boost, he lifted her so she could grab onto the edges of the hole in the door and then kept a hold of her as she pulled herself through it. The air was thicker outside the office, the smoke hanging heavily in the room, and she choked on it again as she quickly climbed down the shelves so Jake could get himself out.

Already her eyes were stinging and watering badly, and it was difficult to breathe.

Reality was quickly sinking in.

They were on the opposite side of the basement to the staircase that would lead them to safety, and she wasn't sure they were going to make it.

Jake barely paused when his feet hit the ground. He just grabbed her hand and tugged her down to the floor.

"Less smoke and more oxygen down here. We'll crawl to the stairs, I want you to hold onto my ankle and not let go. If we get separated down here, I might not be able to find you."

His warning hung heavily in the air as he guided her onto her hands and knees, placed one of her hands on his ankle, and started moving. The last thing she wanted was to be alone in the thick smoke, fighting to breathe, confused and turned around. With Jake, she was safe.

Always safe with Jake.

It was awkward crawling with one hand on Jake's ankle, but she wasn't letting go of him for anything.

Blocking out everything else, Alannah focused just on crawling, getting closer to the stairs, closer to safety and fresh air.

While it felt like it took them an hour, it was probably more like a couple of minutes at the most to work their way through the corridors and into the open space where the stairs were, and when they did, all the air left her lungs in a rush.

The entire childcare area at the bottom of the stairs was alight.

Flames danced everywhere.

Consuming everything in their path.

There was no way through them.

They were trapped.

They were going to die.

# CHAPTER

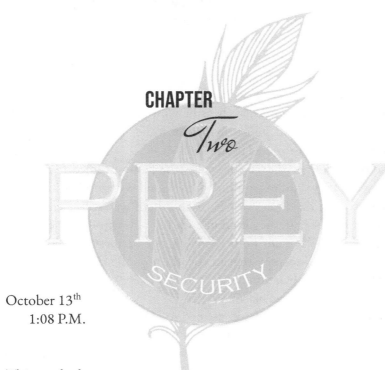

## Two

October 13<sup>th</sup>
1:08 P.M.

This was bad.

Really bad.

The kind of bad you didn't always survive.

Jake stared in horror at the ferocity of the flames dancing about in front of him and Alannah.

Blocking their only exit.

There were no other ways out of the basement.

It was go up the stairs or nothing.

And it couldn't be nothing.

Not while he had his best friend with him.

This was exactly why he'd been keeping his distance from Alannah. It wasn't to hurt her feelings, it wasn't because he didn't miss her, it wasn't because he wanted to shut her out of his life, and it wasn't because he didn't think she was strong enough to handle his family's mess and stand beside him offering him her support.

It was because he hadn't wanted to put her in danger. Didn't want to put her life at risk the way he was doing right now.

He never should have come.

Only it was too late to take it back now.

"We're going to die," Alannah whimpered beside him, and her terrified words ripped him out of the panicked stupor he'd slid into.

"No," he said the word fiercely as he whipped around and grabbed Alannah's shoulders and pulled her up onto her knees. "No," he said again, only this time he roared it out.

Like they smothered everything else, the flames seemed to dampen his words, but they didn't—couldn't—dampen his determination.

They weren't dead yet, which meant there was still a chance he could get them out. If they couldn't find a way through the flames, they'd go back to Alannah's office since it was furthest away from the fire, hide in there, and pray that his brothers or the firefighters got to them before smoke inhalation did.

"Don't give up on me, okay?"

Alannah's golden-brown eyes seemed to glow in the dancing orange light of the flames. They locked onto his and stared at him with an intensity he hadn't felt in a long time. Maybe ever. It was like she was reaching down into his very soul to see if he honestly believed they stood a chance.

After a moment, she gave a small nod. "Okay. I won't give up. What do we do?"

Fear for his best friend and the very real possibility of death he'd brought right to her doorstep almost impeded his ability to think clearly and logically.

The thick smoke slowly filling up his lungs didn't help.

But he needed a clear head.

Alannah needed him to have a clear head.

Forcing himself to focus, to shove away the fear like he'd learned to do when he joined the elite Delta Force, Jake fell back on his training. After so many years working in Delta and then for Prey Security, this should be natural, and he allowed his instincts to take over rather than his fear.

"We need something to cover us so we can make a run for it," he announced, scanning the room that was quickly being destroyed by fire. "The flames haven't taken over the whole staircase yet, they're mostly in the childcare playroom. If we can get through them and onto the steps, we stand a good chance at getting out of here."

It was a long shot. The flames were already devouring the room, and the fire was only growing stronger with each passing second. But the fire alarm had gone off, so he knew firefighters were on their way, and he'd called his stepbrother Cade and told him what was going on, so he also knew that his brothers were on the way.

He couldn't give up hope yet.

All he had to do was trust that his team would have his back and do his part.

"There are blankets we have for the doll's crib," Alannah suggested. "They're not that big, but they'd at least cover our heads and shoulders. Oh and there's a fire extinguisher in the kitchen. Its small but better than nothing."

Perfect.

They could grab them, take them to the kitchen, run them under water, then cover their faces, grab the fire extinguisher, and make a run for it.

A risky plan, but all they had right now.

"That'll work," he told Alannah, and she offered him a small smile. Scared as she was, she was doing her best not to let panic consume her, and he was so proud of her. "You stay here, and I'll go get them."

"I know where they are," she countered. "It'll be quicker for me to grab them."

No way was he allowing them to get separated because, in the thickening smoke, he might not find her again. Leaving her in a spot he could backtrack to was one thing, but they weren't splitting up like that.

"Together. We'll go together," he declared. Not sure if it was his imagination or not, but he was sure Alannah relaxed at that suggestion, and he realized she felt safer with him around. Not surprising since he'd always been her protector, but something that he was positive was going to change once she learned that all of this was absolutely his fault.

Then she'd hate him.

If they survived.

His best friend hating him but alive and safe was infinitely prefer-able to her dying with him powerless to stop it from happening.

"Tell me where it is, and I'll lead. Same as before, you'll hold onto me," he instructed.

"We have a storage cabinet right over there." Alannah pointed back toward the way they'd come, further away from where the fire was claiming everything in its path.

If they didn't get out of there sooner rather than later, it was going to claim them too.

Shoving that horrific thought out of his mind, Jake began crawling toward the storage cabinet. The reassuring feel of Alannah's small hand clutching his ankle was the only thing that kept him grounded.

Being in danger wasn't what had him so close to losing control, he'd been in situations worse than this over the years, it was that this time Alannah was with him. She was so sweet, bubbly, and loving toward everyone. Sometimes he worried she cared too much because there was no shortage of people who would take advantage of someone with such a giving heart.

A lesson Alannah had learned several times over even though it never seemed to sink in.

They reached the storage cabinet, and with Alannah's help, Jake quickly located and retrieved a couple of the blankets. She was right, they weren't that large, but they would cover their heads and hang a little way down their backs, and that was probably the best he could hope for.

After that, they trailed their way down the hall to the kitchen. "Where's the fire extinguisher?" he asked.

"Under the sink."

Staying low he quickly opened the cupboard door, but there was nothing there. Just a few cleaning supplies.

"Its not there," he told Alannah.

"It has to be. It's always there."

"Unless whoever set the fire took it with them."

~~ce there was no point worrying about it right now, they had to

~, try to gt out, Jake had Alannah remain down on her

hands and knees where the smoke was at its thinnest, while he stood and ran the blankets under cold water.

When he had them as wet as he could get them, he readied himself to make a run for it. With the growing heat and the smothering smoke, the blankets weren't going to stay wet for long, and the wetter they were, the better the chances they wouldn't set alight when they ran through the flames.

"Alannah, I'm going to put one of these blankets over your face, take your hand, and then we're going to make a run for it. I don't want you to stop, not for anything. Okay?"

Jake needed to know she wasn't going to panic and fight against him the second they got closer to the flames because they were only going to have one chance at this.

"O-okay," she agreed, her voice wobbling.

"Trust me, sunshine. I will do everything in my power to get you out of here alive."

"I trust you, grumpy," she said, her voice stronger this time.

Her trust in him when he was directly responsible for them being trapped in a fire meant more to him than he could express, and he didn't fight against the urge to grab her hand and haul her up and into his arms.

Hugging her tight, he turned the faucet off, covered her face with one of the wet blankets, draped another over each of her shoulders, then put the fourth over his own head, making sure he didn't block his eyes so he could see where he was going.

Then he took her hand again and ran, dragging Alannah along with him.

He didn't stop, didn't hesitate.

Not even when they re-entered the playroom and were met once again with the full force of the fire.

In the two minutes or so it had taken for them to get the blankets and wet them, the smoke had thickened, and with orange-red flames giving out the only light it looked and felt like being in Hell.

There was one moment when Alannah tugged on his hand, and he was sure she was going to try to pull herself free, unable to handle getting so close to the flames. He was prepared to throw her over his shoulder if he had to, but thankfully, she didn't try to tug herself out of his grip.

Heat rushed at them, enveloping them as they ran through the flames toward the stairs, but Jake didn't stop.

Couldn't stop.

He had to get Alannah out.

The temperature soared, and the smoke was so thick he could barely breathe.

For a moment, he was sure they weren't going to make it.

That he'd finished off what the fire had started.

But then they were through, on the stairs, and he was pulling Alannah up the stairs along with him, aware from the weakening hold she had on his hand that she was struggling.

"Only a little more," he encouraged her, unsure if she heard him over the roar of the fire.

Finally, he reached the top of the stairs. They'd done it. They were all but free.

At least, that's what he thought.

Until he reached for the door handle and found it wouldn't turn.

Locked.

It was locked, and they were trapped with the fire already barreling its way toward them.

～

October 13<sup>th</sup>
    1:13 P.M.

Why didn't Jake open the door?

With her mind fuzzy and sluggish, Alannah found it difficult to think, and she couldn't figure out why if they were at the top of the stairs, Jake didn't just open the door and let them out.

"I'm sorry, sunshine." He turned to face her, and she didn't like his expression.

Didn't want to understand what it meant even as part of her knew.

"Open the door," she ordered. The smoke was too thick up there at the top of the room, choking out what little oxygen there had been left.

"I'm sorry," Jake said again, and she could see in his eyes that he meant it.

She could see the hopelessness.

The despair.

The guilt.

None of them were what she wanted to see.

Her eyes stung, her throat burned, taking a breath was next to impossible, and her skin was smarting in several places where she was sure the flames had scorched her skin.

The wet blankets that had been covering her shoulders had fallen off somewhere along the way, and the one on her face had tipped back so it was dangling off her head when she'd looked up at Jake.

"Open the door," she insisted.

They had to get out.

Now.

Didn't Jake understand that?

"I can't," he said softly, so softly she could barely hear him over the sound of the fire.

Or maybe it was the sound of her own harsh, panicked breathing that drowned him out.

That couldn't be true.

They couldn't be trapped.

This couldn't be how they died.

Yanking herself free from Jake's grip, Alannah threw herself at the door and hammered on it. "Open the door," she screamed at the top of her lungs as she pounded as hard as she could.

"Stop, honey. You're going to burn up any energy you have left on something that won't help," Jake told her as he grabbed her and pulled her up against his chest, pinning her in place with a strong arm wrapped around her chest.

What did it matter how she used up the last of her energy?

If they were going to die, they were going to die.

"Please," she whimpered as exhaustion hit her all at once, and she sagged in Jake's hold.

His lips touched the top of her head and he sat on the top step, pulling her down with him and holding her cradled on his lap. "I'm sorry, sunshine. So sorry. I never meant to bring this to your doorstep."

"Not your fault," she whispered as she snuggled closer. If she was going to die, she supposed there were worse ways to go than being in the arms of her very best friend in the entire world.

There was nothing left to say. They both knew they weren't going to survive until firefighters found them, so Alannah let her eyes drift closed and tried to block out everything happening around her.

Just as she was starting to drift away, she could have sworn she heard loud voices, then what sounded like something smashing into the door.

Positive she was hallucinating, she tucked herself closer against Jake, wishing it would just happen already and she would hurry up and die. Being trapped like this was like being in a nightmare. Only there would be no waking up. At least not in this world.

"Jake!"

She could have sworn that was Jake's younger brother Jax's voice.

"Get her out of here, hurry," Jake said, and she felt him shifting her.

No.

If she was going to die, she wanted to stay right where she was.

Maybe she mumbled something, but she was getting sleepy, and she didn't want to be disturbed.

Didn't seem to matter what she wanted.

Someone lifted her and the next thing Alannah knew, she was choking on clean, fresh air.

Clean air.

Fresh air.

Not the thick, smoky air of the fire-filled basement.

They were free.

Rescued.

Saved.

Opening her eyes, which she hadn't even realized were closed, Alannah looked for Jake. She knew it wasn't him holding her because the person smelled too clean, and both she and Jake smelled like smoke.

Coughing and spluttering, she looked around as she was carried outside the building and into the street, straight over to an ambulance where paramedics were waiting for her.

When she was set down on a stretcher, she saw it was Jax who had carried her out of the burning building as he crouched down so he was able to look her in the eye.

"You okay?" he asked. One of the medics put an oxygen mask over her mouth and nose, the other picked up her wrist and began to check her vitals.

Unable to speak as she continued to cough, Alannah focused on sucking in deep breaths of the oxygen as she tried to look around him.

She was okay, but where was Jake?

She needed to see him, needed to know that he was alive.

What would she do if he hadn't survived?

The only reason she was there right now was because of him. If he hadn't been with her, if she'd been alone in her office, she would have panicked and never figured out a way to save herself.

Her best friend had quite literally saved her life, and she wouldn't survive knowing he'd given his own in the process.

Grabbing the oxygen mask, she yanked it down as panic grew inside her, taking over everything else. "Jake?" she croaked, looking at Jax and begging him with her eyes to tell her that his brother was okay.

"Is going to be fine," Cade Charleston announced as he stepped into her line of sight.

Not who she wanted to see right now.

She wanted—no needed—to see Jake.

How else could she believe he was okay?

"Where is he?" she begged. If Jake was really okay, why wasn't someone taking her to him? Didn't they know that was what she needed right now? Not paramedics, not oxygen, not her vitals checked, the only thing that was going to help was seeing Jake.

"In an ambulance right beside yours," Cole Charleston said, stepping up beside his older brother.

Since she'd known Jake and Jax since she was four years old, she'd been around when their dad married the Charleston brothers' mom. At the time, she'd been thirteen, the same age as the twins Cooper and Connor, Jax had been a year younger, Jake a year older. Cade had been fifteen, Cole eleven, and the baby of the family, Cassandra, was only five. While it had been a rocky start for the family, after learning their parents appeared to be married in name only, all seven of the siblings had bonded and rallied together.

All of Jake's brothers, biological and step, were like brothers to her, too, and normally she'd feel safe around any one of them.

But not today.

Today she needed only one thing.

And that was Jake.

"I need to see him," she whimpered as she fought through another coughing fit. Her lungs seemed to want to cough their way right out of her body.

"No," Cade said firmly, in what she knew was his don't bother arguing with me voice. "What you need is to sit right there and let the EMTs do their job."

"Please," she whispered as tears blurred her vision. The last thing she wanted was to beg, but she also knew that without seeing Jake for herself, she would never believe he wasn't still down there trapped in those horrible flames.

Cade sighed, but his gaze softened, and he stepped away for a moment. Then a stretcher appeared where he'd just been standing with Jake sitting on it.

Just like that, all her anxiety melted away.

Jake's eyes were open, he was wearing an oxygen mask just like she was, and he appeared to be arguing with the medics trying to treat him.

"Sorry, sunshine. I was trying to tell them I had to see you first," he told her. His voice was rough from the smoke, just like hers, but they were both alive, and that was all that mattered.

But as her fear for Jake began to recede, a different reality was starting to settle in.

That fire wasn't an accident.

Someone must have told the childcare worker to leave with the children because they hadn't been in the basement along with her and Jake. Then that person had barricaded the door to her office, set the basement on fire, and then locked the door at the top of the stairs.

Whoever that person was had wanted her and Jake to die.

Had actively tried to kill them.

Shivering as the full impact of the last several minutes settled down upon her, Alannah shot a grateful smile to Jax when he tucked a blanket around her, and then she let her gaze slowly travel to the six men surrounding her. They were all watching her with a mix of concern, guilt, and regret on their faces.

"I think you better tell me what the heck is going on and why I almost died today."

# CHAPTER *Three*

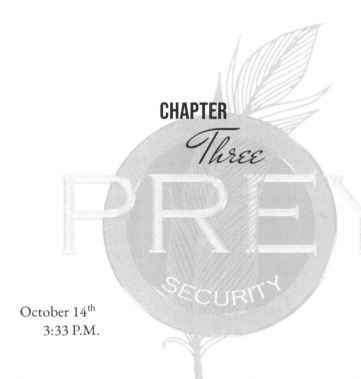

October 14th
3:33 P.M.

"Pretty sure you were supposed to be taking it easy today."

Jake flicked his gaze off the computer screen to see his brother standing beside his couch. Because of the smoke he'd inhaled in the fire the day before, the hospital recommended that he not remain alone overnight. Smoke inhalation could be tricky and appear as though you're okay at first, only to then devolve. While he hadn't thought it was necessary to have a babysitter, his little brother Jax had insisted.

Since he was sure that the fire at Alannah's gym was because of him and the danger haunting his family, it was a logical assumption to make that the final rapist and his stepsister's biological father had moved on to targeting him and the people he loved. That should mean that, for now at least, the heat had been dialed down on Cooper and Willow, Cole and Susanna, Connor and Becca, and Cade, Gabriella, and Essie.

As much as he was glad for his stepbrothers and their girlfriends, he was afraid for Alannah. They'd told her everything, holding nothing back. If the fire was because of him, then she deserved to know why she'd almost died. She'd known the background, of course, lived a lot of it along with him, but she hadn't known what they'd learned the last three months because he'd been trying to keep his distance and not allow her to be dragged into his mess.

Too late for that now.

Alannah was part of this, and he wouldn't let his best friend be hurt again because of him and his family and their quest for answers.

They were so close. They knew three of the four men who had been involved in his stepmom's rape, and as soon as they had the final name, they would be able to prove that his father and stepmom weren't responsible for the assault that took out his dad and stepbrothers' father's team. They would be able to prove that his dad and stepmom weren't traitors and they'd been murdered, not committed suicide.

Jake craved those answers and had dedicated the last almost twenty years of his life to seeking them.

He couldn't give up.

But there was also no way he could allow his personal quest to hurt his best friend.

"You're not supposed to be overdoing things," Jax said again when he gave no response. "Did you even go to bed last night?"

"Grabbed a couple of hours' sleep," he acknowledged. Not that he'd wanted to, but by the time they gave statements and were examined and released from the hospital, then he'd failed to convince Alannah to stay with him or one of his brothers for safety reasons and instead dropped her off at a friend's house, he'd been exhausted. Crashing in his bed as soon as he'd taken a long, hot shower to rid himself of the stench of smoke, he'd lasted only a couple of hours before the need to keep his best friend safe had driven him downstairs to his living room and his laptop.

"You need more. You could have died yesterday."

There was a starkness in his little brother's voice that Jake hadn't heard in a long time. Not since they were kids and Jax used to sneak into his room at night after their mom died because he no longer liked to be alone in the dark.

Back then, it had just been the two of them, clinging to one another because they were the only constant in each other's lives. At just six and four, they were too young to be left alone, but with their dad's career in Delta Force, there were lots of times when he traveled, and how long he would be away changed with every mission. Since no family member wanted to care for them permanently, they were bounced between grandparents and aunts and uncles. The lack of stability had made Jax clingy, and Jake had gotten used to taking care of his little brother.

But that was a long time ago. They were in their thirties now, and they'd long since learned how to survive without parents hovering over them.

For months they'd watched as their stepbrothers were targeted one by one, and while they loved Cade, Cooper, Connor, and Cole as though they were blood, Cassandra too, it didn't change the fact that they were close and for so many years they'd only had each other to rely on.

"Hey, I didn't die. I'm fine. Smoky and sore but perfectly fine. Fine to work. Okay?" he barked.

Not because he wasn't sympathetic to what his brother must have gone through the day before when he heard the news from Cade about the fire, but because gruff was the only way he knew how to handle things, even with his brother. Jax knew he loved him, so Jake didn't need to convince him with a sugary sweet tone.

"I could have lost her yesterday, Jax," he said, allowing a sliver of the emotion boiling inside him to seep into his tone. "She's my best friend. I promised her when she was four that I would never let anyone or anything hurt her ever again. I've failed a lot of times over the last almost thirty years, but never was her life in danger because of it."

"We don't know for certain that the fire was set because of you, because of us and our investigation," Jax reminded him as he took a seat on the other couch and picked up the laptop sitting on the coffee table.

"You don't think it was odd that I've been keeping my distance from Alannah for three months, then I cave and go to spend a couple of hours with her at her gym, and we're locked in a basement and almost burned alive?"

"Of course I do. It's one hell of a coincidence. But until we know more, that's all it is. I'm not saying it isn't because of the people after us, in fact, I think chances are it was, but it would be stupid to cut out any other possibility until we know for sure."

"Who would be after Alannah?" The thought was so preposterous that he actually barked out a laugh at it. Alannah reminded him a lot of the women his brothers had fallen for. She was sweet, kind, and loving, but she also had shields up around her heart that she struggled to lower to let people in, which was why she kept dating the worst guys who were only after her for her looks and her money.

Was it possible ...

No.

It couldn't be one of her exes. Could it?

Honestly, they didn't talk about their love lives much with one another. They were best friends, but they were also family, and he didn't really want to hear about Alannah sleeping with other men. He'd always assumed she felt the same way since she never pushed him about his relationships. Not that there were a lot of them. He was a loner, and he didn't really see that changing.

But Alannah wanted to find love, wanted a partner, a family, someone who would love her unconditionally and see her for her.

Had a relationship spun out of control? Maybe she was just ashamed to tell him. Normally, they only discussed her boyfriends when they became exes and only because she wound up hurt and needed him to cheer her up. Which was ironic since he was the grumpy and she was the sunshine in their friendship.

"You're right," he agreed, shooting Jax a grateful smile. Knowing how close he'd come to losing his best friend had messed with his head and he wasn't thinking clearly, wasn't capable of working through every possibility on his own right now.

"Gang's here," a voice called out as he heard his front door open.

The thunder of footsteps told him his entire family had shown up to have his back, and he couldn't be more grateful for all of them. He'd lost both his parents, but he had a brother, four stepbrothers, a stepsister, four one-day stepsisters-in-law, and an adorable step-niece. His life was full of people who loved and supported him.

"Hi, Uncle Jake," Essie said as she ran into the room like the little tornado of energy that she was.

"Hey, Messy Essie," he returned, making the five-year-old curl up her lip in annoyance at the nickname.

"I'm not messy, Uncle Jake. I *always* puts my toys away when I finish playing with them," she told him, all sassy and indignant. Then her face brightened into a smile. "My mom and dad are having a baby," she announced.

"Essie," Gabriella rebuked gently even as she smiled. Gabriella was no longer Essie's nanny, the little girl had started calling her mom, and he knew she loved hearing the name fall from the lips of the child she loved and had protected at great personal cost when they'd both been abducted last month.

"We're only a few weeks in, and Gabriella has a history of miscarriage," Cade explained, wrapping an arm around his fiancée and pulling her close, placing a hand on her stomach.

"I'm further along than I've ever been before," Gabriella said softly, pain in her pretty green eyes. "We probably shouldn't have told Essie so early, considering there's a good chance the baby won't make it, but we wanted her to be part of this journey if it does."

"The baby is going to come," Essie said firmly, running over to kiss Gabriella's flat stomach. "Cos I'm going to be the best big sister ever."

"You sure are, cuddle bug," Gabriella said as she leaned down to hug the little girl.

Jake's phone rang, and he reached over to snatch it up. When he saw Alannah's name on the screen, something inside him tightened. He was safe, surrounded by family, but Alannah didn't have a family who loved her or cared about her, and even though he'd dropped her off with a friend of hers, and made sure someone was watching the house, he couldn't help but feel a small sliver of fear as he accepted the call.

~

October 14<sup>th</sup>
3:34 P.M.

. . .

Every time Alannah closed her eyes it felt like she was back in the basement at her gym, smoke thick in the air, terrified that she was going to be burned alive.

While she hadn't had a great home life as a child, and she'd struggled to make genuine connections with people even as she grew older because she was so desperate to be loved and belong that sometimes she didn't see people for who they truly were, she'd never been in physical danger like that.

Never wondered if she was going to survive.

Never come close enough to death that she could feel its soft touch as it reached out for her.

To say she was shaken by the ordeal was a massive understatement. It was all she could think about, and the snatched pockets of sleep she'd managed only because she was completely exhausted by the time she crashed had been filled with dreams, reliving the trauma.

Even though she'd been in a house with one of her best friends, the woman's husband, and their four kids, Alannah had never felt so alone.

What she'd needed was Jake, but something had held her back from saying yes when he'd asked her to stay the night at his place. It wasn't because she blamed him for what had almost happened, she didn't. If someone was after his family, then he had no control over that. It wasn't because she didn't want to be around him, in fact, she'd craved nothing more and maybe that was why she'd said no.

She'd needed him, not just wanted him, and for some reason that had felt wrong.

Alannah had chalked it up to the high stakes and overflowing emotion from wondering if she was going to die. She'd also done her best not to think about it.

It wasn't like she didn't have a ton of other stuff to worry about.

Which was why she'd decided she needed this.

It was the only way Alannah could come up with to try to convince her mind and her body that she was no longer trapped. She'd never suffered from claustrophobia before, but she was pretty sure she would going forward. It clung to her skin even though she'd scrubbed and scrubbed in the shower when she got to her friend's house, but that feeling of being trapped remained.

For how long she wasn't sure, but hopefully not forever.

Sliding on her earphones, she set her playlist to her classical music selection, what she listened to when she needed to relax, and set off down the path.

Running had always been her escape.

As a child, she'd been the unwanted sister. As a small infant, her older sister had almost perished to SIDS. Found unbreathing in her crib by their mother, a pediatric neurosurgeon, who had performed CPR and managed to get Amy breathing again. After that, her sister had been the star of the family. The golden child, the one who was fawned over and spoiled to the extreme.

On the other hand, she was the unwanted second child.

Her parents hadn't planned on more kids after almost losing their firstborn, but her mother had accidentally gotten pregnant when birth control failed, so along she came.

Unwanted, and her parents made sure she knew it.

There was no limit on what her parents would spend on hobbies and activities that Amy wanted to try out. Over the years, her sister had tried pretty much everything under the sun, and was praised for giving it a go no matter how good she was or how hard she'd tried.

She didn't get the same treatment.

Told that they weren't wasting money on her, Alannah had gravitated to the one hobby she didn't need anything else for.

Running.

All she needed were a pair of sneakers and some comfortable clothes, and she was good to go. Needing to escape her home where she was constantly being shoved aside, told she wasn't good enough, or smart enough, or pretty enough even though she worked hard in school, got better grades than her sister, treated people better than Amy did, and looked exactly the same as her parents' golden child.

But no one could take running from her. It offered her freedom to let go of everything else, to put her brain in a zone where thinking wasn't necessary, where she could stop feeling for a while and just be.

With the wind in her hair and her feet pounding the paths of the local streets and parks, Alannah had found her happy place. And since her parents were always happy for any excuse to have her out of the house, they never restricted her running time even as they seemed to enjoy taking away other privileges.

Today, though, it wasn't freedom from her unloving parents that she sought but freedom from the mess her entire life had become.

Thankfully, no one other than her and Jake were hurt yesterday. The childcare worker had revealed that a man in a maintenance outfit had requested she leave the space with the children, so no one else had ever been in any danger. Everyone else had filed out when the fire alarms went off.

Only the basement had been damaged by the fire and the resulting efforts of the firefighters to put it out. But since it was the basement, there was the potential for structural problems for the entire building so she couldn't reopen until it had been evaluated.

Then there was insurance to deal with, and the fears that she'd lose members while it was closed, or that people would never come back because they no longer believed she could offer them a safe place to work out.

If she lost her gym ...

No.

She couldn't even allow herself to think that right now. The gym was her baby, her livelihood. She'd put everything she had into it and was so proud of how successful it had become.

What would she do if she lost it?

Forcing all thoughts out of her head, Alannah just ran. She had good speed, but it was her distance and endurance that had won her lots of awards when she was a kid. Now she ran marathons a couple of times a year, but it wasn't about winning, it was just about losing herself in the smooth, steady movements of running.

Alannah was so in the zone that when something bright orange-red appeared in front of her, she startled.

It took a second for it to sink in what she was seeing.

Rubbing at her eyes, positive she had to be hallucinating, when the orange-red didn't disappear but instead started to grow, she knew this was no imaginary fire.

It was real.

Flames sprung to life in front of her, blocking the path she'd been taking through the trees.

Panic fluttered in her chest, and she froze.

How could there be a fire in the park?

How could there be another fire around her in two days?

Were they here now?

The men who were after Jake's family?

She knew they were dangerous, but for some reason, she hadn't grasped fully just how dangerous. She'd thought she'd only been in danger because she was with Jake, never in a million years had she thought they would come after her when she was alone.

Spinning around so fast she stumbled and almost lost her footing, Alannah was about to take off back the way she'd come to backtrack to the parking lot and her car, when more flames sprung to life.

Behind her and in front of her.

Surrounding her.

Trapping her.

She was shaking so badly that she dropped her cell phone when she pulled it out of the pocket of her leggings.

Dropping to her knees, she scooped it back up. Knowing she should call 911 and report the fire, instead it was Jake's name that she brought up on her phone. Jake's number that she dialed. Jake's voice that she desperately needed to hear.

"Sunshine, what's up?"

The sound of Jake's voice had a sob building in her chest. She didn't want to be anywhere near fire ever again, but here it was, once again trapping her. "Jake," she whimpered, it was all she could get out.

"What's wrong?"

His sharp voice ordered her to speak, but she couldn't seem to make her voice work.

The flames were quickly consuming the trees around her. Fall might have started a few weeks ago, and the temperatures were beginning to drop, but it had been a dry summer, and that had continued into fall. It wasn't going to take long for the fire to close in on her.

"Alannah, tell me. Now."

This time the command in his voice spurred her on. "There's a fire."

He cursed. Mumbled something that she didn't think was to her. "Where are you?"

Knowing his voice was coming out harsh because he was afraid for her didn't mean she didn't flinch at the ferocity in his words, and a whimper must have escaped, too, because when he spoke next his tone was gentle.

"Tell me where you are, sunshine, so I can come and get you."

"The park. Running. I was running. The flames are everywhere, Jake. Surrounding me. I ... I don't think I can get through them."

Which meant she'd escaped a fire one day only to be claimed by one the next.

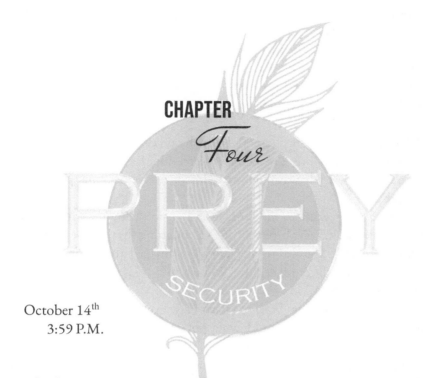

# CHAPTER

## *Four*

October 14th
3:59 P.M.

*The flames are everywhere, Jake. Surrounding me. I ... I don't think I can get through them.*

Alannah's words were playing in a loop in his mind as he jumped out of the car the second it stopped and started sprinting to the location where Alannah was trapped.

"Almost there, sunshine, just hold on a little longer for me," he said into the phone, mustering the most soothing tone he could manage under the circumstances.

Unwilling to leave Alannah alone in case the worst happened, he'd remained on the line with her. After finding out she was running one of her favorite loops at a local park, he and a couple of his brothers jumped into a vehicle and drove to her location. Firefighters were enroute, and Prey had given him Alannah's exact location.

All he had to do was get to her.

In time.

*The flames are everywhere, Jake. Surrounding me. I ... I don't think I can get through them.*

Those words continued to taunt him. She was trapped in a fire for the second time in as many days, only this time, he wasn't there with her. She was all alone, and he was so very aware that the flames could easily claim her before he could get to her.

He could lose her.

"The flames are getting closer," Alannah said on a whimper.

"I know, honey, but I'm almost there. Hold on, Alannah." An order, not a request. He wasn't going to lose her. Not now and certainly not like this.

"I am, I don't want to die, but, Jake, if I do, I don't want you to think it's your fault." She broke off into a coughing fit, the smoke from this fire no doubt aggravating her already damaged throat and lungs from all the smoke she'd inhaled the day before.

Honestly, she shouldn't even be out running.

Doctors had told them both to take it easy. Even though their smoke inhalation was mild, they should avoid physical activity for at least the next couple of days.

What the hell had she been thinking?

Why was she out running instead of safely at her friend's house?

And how could she think he wouldn't blame himself if she died because of him?

"I'm sorry, sunshine," he whispered, nearing her location but still not close enough for his liking.

"Not your fault, grumpy," she said. "Jake, in case I don't ... you don't ... if I—" her words broke off, and he heard a scream fall from her lips. She must have dropped her phone because he heard a thump and then ... nothing.

The call must have disconnected when she dropped the phone because there wasn't a single sound coming through.

"Alannah!" he screamed anyway, insisting she answer him.

Had the flames gotten to her?

Was he too late?

"She's gone," he told Jax and Cole in a panic as he lowered his cell phone from his ear and saw that the call had indeed been disconnected.

Gone could mean only one thing.

That he was too late.

"Hold on, bro, we're almost there," Jax told him as all three of them picked up their pace, and a minute later, the glow of the flames came into view.

They were every bit as bright and ferocious as the ones that haunted what little sleep he'd gotten the night before, and knowing Alannah was trapped between them was a whole different kind of nightmare.

In the distance, sirens began to wail.

Help was coming, but it wasn't going to get there quickly enough.

Somehow, he found extra speed he hadn't known he possessed as he bolted toward them. Fully intending to dart through them and search for his best friend until he found her.

He would have done just that if he hadn't been tackled to the ground just as the heat of the fire began to scorch his skin.

"No, Jake. You can't," Jax said from on top of him.

"Alannah is in there," he roared, fighting to get out of his brother's hold so he could run into those flames and find his best friend.

Trapped alone and terrified in a ring of fire with no way out, and it was all his fault. He should have insisted that she come and stay with him, and if she'd continued to refuse then tell her he'd stay with her at her apartment. If he'd been with her, he never would have let her go out running when she was recovering from smoke inhalation. If she hadn't been out running, she would have been safe from the people targeting him and his family.

"If she's in there, it's probably already too late. I'm sorry," Jax said softly.

Staring at the fire raging before him, Jake knew that his little brother was right. There was no way Alannah could survive. If she'd dropped the phone, it had to be because the flames had gotten close enough to catch her.

That scream ...

It was still echoing inside his head.

Pure, unadulterated terror.

The last thing he'd ever hear from her, and it would stay with him for a lifetime.

As it should.

"Alannah, I'm sorry, sunshine," he yelled into the flames. No doubt Jax was right and she was already gone, but he couldn't stop himself.

Jake didn't cry. Hadn't since he was six years old and realized that no matter how many tears he shed it wasn't going to bring his mom back to life. He hadn't even cried when his dad and stepmom had been killed because, as the second oldest, he'd wanted to be strong for the younger kids. Wanted to be big and tough and stoic like his older stepbrother.

But now ... knowing how horrifying Alannah's final moments would have been, tears blurred his vision.

"I'm so sorry, man," Cole said from beside him.

Jax's weight eased off him, and together, Jax and Cole helped pull him to his feet. He couldn't take his eyes off the fire, knowing that Alannah was somewhere inside the rapidly growing flames had his stomach twisting to the point where he thought he might be sick.

"Come on, Jake, we have to move back, away from the fire," Jax said gently, guiding him further away from the inferno that had stolen his best friend from him.

Those men were going to pay.

When he got the name of the final man involved in the rape and conspiracy, he was personally going to tear him apart limb by limb.

No amount of suffering would be enough to make up for Alannah's final moments, but his rage needed an outlet.

"I'll make sure you get justice, sunshine," he whispered with a determination that sunk down deep into his bones.

He needed something to focus on other than his grief, and revenge was the perfect replacement.

"Jake!"

Head darting up, he whipped around in the direction the voice had come from, and he saw her.

His sunshine.

Dirty, hair a mess, tears streaking her face, but alive and running toward him.

The next thing he knew, she launched herself into his arms.

They closed around her automatically, and he drew her close as she sobbed. There was every chance he would believe he was merely hallucinating, but the smell of smoke had gotten stronger the second he was touching her.

"I thought I was going to die," Alannah wailed, her wet face pressed against his neck.

"You screamed and the phone cut off, I thought ... I thought you were gone. I thought I lost you."

"You didn't lose me, grumpy, I'm here." The arms she had curled around his neck tightened to the point she was almost impeding his ability to breathe, and he didn't care in the least. She was here, alive, and in his arms.

That was all that mattered.

"How did you get out?" he asked, running a hand the length of her spine to calm her, only he was almost as panicked as she was.

"There was a man, another jogger, he came out of nowhere, that's why I screamed. Then he showed me a way out of the flames," Alannah explained.

A jogger who was prepared to walk through an almost impenetrable wall of flames to get to a stranger with no guarantee they could get back out?

His faith in humanity didn't believe that.

Not in the least.

"Where is he, Alannah?" he asked, scanning the area but seeing no one. If some random jogger had saved her life, they wouldn't just disappear, except he, Alannah, Jax, and Cole were the only ones there.

Lifting her head she looked around. "I don't see him," she said, sounding confused. "Where did he go? I have to find him, Jake. I have to thank him. He saved my life."

When she started to struggle to get out of his hold, he tightened his grip on her. Their minds obviously going in the same direction his had, Jax and Cole shifted closer, moving in to flank Alannah on either side.

"I don't think he saved your life to be nice, sunshine."

Brow crinkled, Alannah cocked her head. "What do you mean?"

"I think whoever led you out of the flames is the person who started the fire to begin with."

～

October 14<sup>th</sup>
6:26 P.M.


*I think whoever led you out of the flames is the person who started the fire
to begin with.*

Alannah couldn't stop thinking about Jake's words even hours later
after she'd given her statement to the cops, been checked out by paramedics, packed a bag, came to Jake's house, showered, and eaten.

Well, picked at her food more than eaten it.

Her appetite had disappeared.

Even though she'd showered, standing under the hot spray for a
solid thirty minutes, scrubbing and scrubbing at her skin, and sham-
pooing her hair over and over again, she still smelled like smoke. It
seemed to have permeated deep into her skin and no amount of cleaning
would get rid of it.

The smell made her nauseous, and even though she knew her body
needed the calories and nourishment, she just couldn't settle her
stomach enough to do more than nibble at the food on her plate.

It wasn't just the smell that had her so on edge. Wasn't even the fact
that she had almost died in a fire for the second time in two days. It was
also what some of the cops had implied when they'd been taking her
statement.

They had kept saying how odd it was that she'd been in back-to-
back fires.

Of course, she knew it was odd, but the way they said it made her
feel like they thought *she* was the cause of the fires. Like she'd set them
herself. If it wasn't for Jake being with her in the first fire and
confirming there was no possible way she could have set it, she couldn't
help but feel that instead of sitting in Jake's house right now she'd be
sitting in a police station.

"I didn't set the fire," she blurted out, looking up from her plate to
see all eyes fixed on her.

The way they were watching her made her squirm.

Did Jake's family think she'd set the fire today?

These men were like brothers to her, she loved them more than she loved her own sister. If they thought she was responsible, she wasn't sure where that would leave her. Not just physically, because she wouldn't be able to stay there if they thought she had turned into a pyromaniac, but also emotionally.

Alannah knew she was teetering.

Avoiding rather than dealing.

Sooner or later a crash was coming. Sooner rather than later.

"No one thinks you did," Jake told her, reaching over to give her shoulder a squeeze.

"The cops did. They kept implying I was responsible. That two fires around me in two days could not be a coincidence." It wasn't that she disagreed, it was no coincidence, but they didn't seem to buy that it was because of Jake because he hadn't been there for the second fire.

And she had to admit that was getting to her too.

She was the one who had been targeted both times. If they were really after Jake, surely they would have gone after him and not her.

"*Are* you responsible?" Cole asked her, and her gaze shot to his. His brown eyes were studying her, not unkindly, but certainly not in a he was completely team Alannah kind of way either.

"It's not a coincidence," Jax added. "Two fires around you in two days, no way that happens by chance. And both were deliberately set."

So he'd turned on her too? She'd known Jax since he was three and she was four, nine years longer than she'd known Cole. Surely that would have bought her at least a little bit more loyalty.

Tears stung her eyes, which already felt like they were burning, and she hated that she'd started trembling. Maybe going there was a mistake. If Jake and his family didn't believe in her, she couldn't be there.

Shoving away from the table she would have fled, where she wasn't quite sure, but out of this house, only Jake grabbed her wrist.

His hold on her was gentle but firm, and he tugged her around so she was facing him. "You're misinterpreting what they're saying. No one, and I mean not a single one of us, thinks you started that fire."

"Doesn't sound like it," she whispered, fighting back the tears that wanted to tumble free.

"I didn't mean it how you took it, Alannah," Cole spoke, his voice soothing. "I meant, is there something you're not telling us. Like a bad breakup with a boyfriend who might want to hurt you. A friend you had an argument with. A client at your gym who got angry with you. An employee you had to fire. Anyone who might want to hurt you."

"Hurt me?" That theory had never really occurred to her because Jake had been so adamant from the beginning that he believed the fire at her gym had been set by the people after his family. After hearing the whole story and everything that the Charleston Holloway family had gone through, she'd agreed.

It had seemed so logical that morning, only now, she could see why they were questioning it.

Dropping back down into her chair, Alannah shook her head even as she tried to run through every interaction she'd had with every person in her life over the last several months. "I can't think of anyone who would want to hurt me at all, let alone try to kill me."

"What about your last relationship? How did that end?" Jax asked.

"Not excitingly. We were together for around seven months, and at first, I thought there was a spark, but the more time we spent together, the more I realized he didn't really love me. I don't want to be with someone just because we get along well enough. Call me a romantic, but I want someone who's obsessed, who has to see me and talk to me every day, who can't imagine life without me. And I want to feel the same about them. I want them to be the oxygen my body needs to survive." Alannah blushed, aware she was babbling about things these guys didn't want to hear.

Before she could get too embarrassed, Jake reached out and covered her hand. "You deserve that, Alannah."

"Never be embarrassed about knowing what you want," Cole added. "I wish I had known what I wanted sooner."

"You know now, and Susanna is lucky to have you," she told him.

"I'm the lucky one." The dreamy look on his face when he talked about his girlfriend was exactly what she wanted in a man one day.

Sometimes, it made her feel like she was being needy, but she wanted to matter to someone, wanted to be loved, wanted to be wanted. Growing up with her parents had really messed with her head.

"Truth is, I don't think I matter to anyone enough for them to try to kill me," she said. When Jake growled, she let out a laugh. "I didn't mean that to sound self-pitying, I just meant that I don't think I make that kind of impression on people. The gym is doing well, no issues with employees or clients. I have good friends, no arguments or problems. And the guys I date are nice enough, but none of them are out there pining for me."

"Their loss, sunshine."

Shooting a grateful smile at him, she shifted her hand, which was still under his, and gave his fingers a squeeze. "Thanks, bestie, but I think you might be the only one who feels that way."

Depressing as it was to think about, it was true. None of the guys she'd ever dated had ever been that into her. They'd liked her, maybe thought she was cool, probably thought she was pretty enough, but they didn't love her.

And in the end, that was what she was seeking.

Being loved by someone was nonnegotiable to her, and she wouldn't stop searching for it until she found it.

A giant yawn felt like it split her face into two, and Alannah felt like she was coming close to hitting the wall. Her body was running on fumes, and she needed proper rest with real sleep.

Maybe she could get that with Jake in the next room.

"You're exhausted. Why don't you go up, take a hot shower, and go to bed?" Jake suggested.

"I already took a thirty-minute shower earlier," she reminded him.

"So, take another. You need it, and it will help you relax so you can sleep."

"Yeah, maybe I'll do that." Standing, she rubbed tiredly at her burning eyes. Hopefully, some sleep would help clear them up and they'd feel better in the morning, too. "Night, guys, and thanks for coming to me today when I needed you."

"Don't thank us for that, sunshine. You're family," Jake rebuked her.

"I still appreciate it."

For him, family meant you were always there for one another, for her it meant something completely different. Other than Jake and his brothers, she had no family. Her parents and sister were never going to be interested in her, and she had long since given up trying to earn their love.

At the kitchen door, she paused. "That guy who saved me and then disappeared, I didn't know him. He wasn't someone from my past. If you're right and he's the one who set the fire, he was following me or he knew that was my favorite place to run. Whether he was there because of me or because of Jake, he was there, and now he's out there somewhere."

"We'll find him, Alannah," Jake vowed.

He'd always been her protector, and she'd always believed in him.

Except today.

She went upstairs wondering if anyone could keep her safe.

# CHAPTER Five

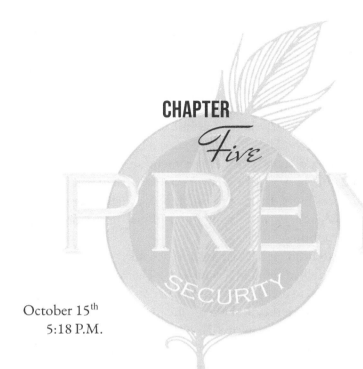

October 15<sup>th</sup>
5:18 P.M.

"You get everything done?" Jake asked as he came up behind where Alannah was sitting at his kitchen table with paper spread all around her.

After a good night's sleep, she'd seemed to be in better spirits, and had woken up ready to tackle the mountain of jobs she needed to get done in order to get her gym open and running again. Seeing lots of encouraging and supportive comments from her customers on social media had lifted her spirits as well, and she'd set about everything she had to do with determination.

Since there was no way in hell he was letting her out of his sight while the final man involved in the conspiracy was still out there somewhere, for the foreseeable future, Jake had already decided he was going to play bodyguard. Having Alannah staying in his house felt strange since they were best friends and she wasn't a date, not that he brought many of them home, but it wasn't strange in a bad way.

Looking up at him over her shoulder, she shot him a weary smile. "I think so. Thanks for your help and for asking Eagle to pull some strings. Only one more inspection needs to be done, and if that goes well, I should be able to open again later in the week."

"That's great." The last thing he wanted was for his problems to affect Alannah's life and livelihood. The gym meant a lot to her, and he knew she'd sunk in most of her inheritance to open it. Her hard work had paid off and she was very successful, but something like this could change that in a split second.

Even though they'd spoken to her last night about whether there could be anyone out there targeting her, he'd never really believed that was a legitimate possibility. It was too much of a coincidence that this had only started when he went to hang out with her in person for the first time in three months.

Seeing the devastation on her face as she'd defended herself, insisting she hadn't set the fire had filled him with rage. The cops that put that thought in her head were lucky he had too much on his plate right now, otherwise, he'd make sure they lost their jobs for treating an innocent victim who'd almost died twice in two days so insensitively.

"Yeah, I'm glad the damage is mostly just downstairs. It will be a while till repairs are sorted out and I can reopen the play area, but I know how lucky I am there wasn't any structural damage that would need to be repaired. That would take months, and I might not be able to survive."

"I'm just glad you weren't hurt." While he would have hated her to lose her livelihood it was still preferable to losing her life.

Twice in just days he could have lost her.

What would life even look like without his best friend?

Not something Jake had any interest in finding out.

"Me too," Alannah agreed as she began to rub at the back of her neck. With the way she'd been hunched over her laptop and phone all day, it was no wonder she had some kinks that needed working out.

"Here. I got it." Nudging her hands out of the way, he moved so he was right behind her and covered her shoulders with his hands. While his fingers worked the tight muscles in her shoulders, his thumbs attended to the ones along the back of her neck.

With a moan, her head tipped forward, and he almost froze.

That sound.

It did ... things to him.

Things down south that he should have no business thinking about when it was his best friend moaning like he'd just given her the best orgasm of her life.

What would Alannah look like in bed? Would her creamy skin pinken? Would her golden-brown eyes light with desire? Would she toss and turn her head on her pillow as he worked her higher and higher until her blonde locks spread out around her face like a halo?

Would her hips come off the bed seeking more as he put his head between her legs and made her come with his mouth?

How tight would she feel as he sunk inside her?

How loud would she scream his name as she came, clamping around him and setting off his own orgasm?

"Jake? Everything okay?"

It wasn't until her pretty golden eyes looked up at him that he realized he'd stopped massaging her shoulders and instead was just standing there with his hands resting on them, staring at her with an intensity he couldn't help but feel was betraying every inappropriate thought he'd just had.

How tacky could he be?

Alannah had just survived two fires. She was scared and vulnerable, staying in his house because her safety was at risk, and there he was, daydreaming about having sex with her. Sex that would without a doubt ruin their friendship.

He wasn't losing his best friend for anything, including sex.

"Uh, yeah," he said, taking a step back so he wasn't tempted to touch her again. "Just thinking we should order something for dinner since we both worked right through lunch."

The look she gave him told him she didn't quite believe him, but thankfully, she didn't push. "Actually, instead of ordering, I'd much rather cook. I could use the distraction for a while, and I've got a craving for homemade lasagna."

"Course you do," he said with a smile and an eyeroll.

Alannah was a great cook, and it was often her go-to when she was stressed. She'd taught him everything she knew about cooking, and as kids they'd spent hours in his house cooking dinners for the three of them. Whoever was babysitting him and Jax was always happy to have one less job to do and her parents didn't care where she was and what she was doing. So, the three of them had banded together, and thanks to her, they'd been able to eat delicious homemade meals rather than frozen junk.

"Unfortunately, I don't think my cupboards are prepared for that."

"Oh." Disappointment lit her face, and she chewed on her bottom lip. Something he'd seen her do hundreds of times before, but never once had he thought about replacing her teeth with his own as he kissed and nipped at those plump lips of hers.

To shove all thoughts of kissing his best friend out of his head, he offered something that wasn't the best plan given their situation. "We can hit up the grocery store down the street. I'm sure they'll have everything you need."

Immediately, her eyes lit up with hope. "Are you sure that's okay to do?"

"We can be quick. Straight there and straight back. You stick close, and if anything feels off we'll leave immediately."

"Done, done, and done. Let me grab my shoes."

While she ran upstairs, he found a pair of sneakers by the door and shoved them on. For some ridiculous reason this almost felt like a date. Taking her to the store, helping her cook dinner, and eating it together while they watched a movie.

*No.*

*No date.*

*Stop it, Jake.*

His reminder to himself did little to help when Alannah came back downstairs looking adorable in a simple pair of black leggings and mint green oversized sweater, with her hair in a messy ponytail.

Together they headed outside, and when a scan of the busy little street he lived on didn't reveal any potential threats, they started walking. As they walked, Jake couldn't quite get out of his mind how Susanna had been attacked after a late night trip to the grocery store. These people were always watching, and once they marked you as a target, they didn't let up.

It was too late to pretend that Alannah wasn't an important part of his life, but maybe he could see if she'd be willing to go with the others to stay with Delta Team until this mess was over. The guys had finally made the decision to send Willow, Susanna, Becca, Essie, and Gabriella away. No one was happy about it, but the Delta Team guys were ... something else entirely, and Cassandra was already staying with them. There was literally no safer place in the world right now, no one even knew where those guys lived. Well, he suspected Eagle did, but no one else, and it wasn't like Prey's CEO and founder was going to tell anyone.

"All right, we'll be quick. Grab what you need and get out," he reminded Alannah as they stepped inside the small store. It was about a fifth the size of a supermarket, but it sold pretty much everything you'd need, just in smaller quantities and with fewer brand choices.

"Agreed." Alannah shivered, betraying her nerves.

Even though he'd love to split up to get this done quicker, it was safer to stick with her. So he followed her down the aisles as she grabbed the ingredients she needed to make her lasagna.

"Oh, I forgot the tomato paste," Alannah announced, quickly spinning around. "It's just down the other end of the aisle."

Before he could stop her, she was hurrying back the way they'd just come.

One second she was there, the next, items from the shelves were crashing down around her as flames leapt to life.

～

October 15th
5:40 P.M.

One second, she was turning to search for the tomato paste on the grocery store shelf, the next, cans were flying off the shelves toward her.

Not just cans and bottles.

Something was on fire.

Alannah felt the searing heat as it brushed against her skin before whatever it was landed on the floor beside her.

People screamed around her, and she could hear footsteps. Most seemed to be moving away from her, but one set drew closer.

Jake.

Somehow, she felt him before she saw him. Before his arms wrapped around her, snatching her off her feet and carrying her away from the small fire already dying out on the linoleum floor.

Three days.

Three fires.

No coincidence.

This one, like the last, seemed to have been aimed solely at her, but she still couldn't figure out a single person who would want her dead or even suffering. She just didn't make that kind of impact on other people. People liked her, seemed to enjoy her company, but they didn't love her. They didn't become obsessed with her to the point of wanting to destroy her.

If this was about Jake and his family, why did these people think she was the best person in his life to target? She could see targeting Cade's daughter, that made sense. Even going after Connor's ex-girlfriend, who he hadn't seen in twelve years, could kind of be explained. But she was just Jake's friend. Best friend, but still. Then again, these men had targeted Susanna, thinking she was Cole's girlfriend when in reality they were just neighbors.

So ... maybe it made sense?

"Are you okay? Are you hurt?" Jake's urgent questions managed to penetrate the thick fog settling over her and because she could hear the thread of worry in his voice, she gave a shake of her head.

Not hurt, just scared.

Terrified really.

When was this going to stop?

Reality was sinking in and Alannah realized the gravity of the situation she found herself in.

It definitely should have sunk in earlier, after all, she could have died twice in the last two days, but somehow it was this fire, by far the smallest of them all, that really drove the point home.

They weren't giving up.

These people who had been targeting Jake's family for months now had set their sights on her, and they didn't seem to want to turn away from their new focus. What would make them give up? When she was dead? The others had all managed to survive their ordeals but that didn't mean she was going to.

"I'm going to need you to answer me with your words, sunshine," Jake told her.

A tap on her cheek had Alannah blinking, and then Jake's face came into view. He must have carried her down the aisle away from the small fire, and then set her down on the floor because he was crouched in front of her. His large body blocked her view of pretty much everything else, and his hand on her knee kept her grounded. The fear in his dark eyes made something flicker to life inside her, but she didn't have the time or energy to figure out what that was all about.

"I'm okay, not hurt," she assured him, even throwing in a weak smile, anything to soothe the lines of worry from his handsome face.

It was only because his hand was still on her knee that she felt the fine tremor ripple through it. Her big, strong protector wasn't just worried, he was terrified. Just as much as she was.

"What was that?" Now that she'd noticed that Jake was trembling, her own body responded by shaking.

Shock.

Settling over her like a heavy blanket.

"Someone threw what looked like a rock or something covered in a towel that had no doubt been soaked in something flammable, then set alight and aimed at you. They had to be right on the other side of the shelves." Frustration was in Jake's voice and she knew it had to be annoying to him that he'd been so close to one of the people after him and yet the man had slipped away yet again.

"The cops are going to blame me." Two fires had been enough for them to think she was somehow involved, add in a third, and she'd be lucky if she didn't wind up spending a night in a cell.

"Not going to happen, sunshine." Jake tugged off his zippered hoodie, then picked up one of her arms, feeding it through the sleeve, repeating the process with her other arm, then zipping her up.

Immediately, Alannah felt like she was cocooned in Jake's arms, with his warmth and scent wrapped all around her. Her shaking eased, and her panic receded to a manageable level.

Jake was here so she was safe.

He wouldn't let anything happen to her.

Despite her fears when she'd gone to bed last night, her subconscious mind had been settled enough knowing Jake was nearby to allow her to get a good night's sleep. This morning she'd been able to tackle everything she needed to get done, and Jake's presence in the house had soothed her.

She just needed to trust that he could do what he knew how to do and keep her safe.

Keep both of them safe.

Because she didn't want to lose him.

Not now and not ever.

With a weary sigh, Alannah rubbed at her temples. "I don't know why they think I'd try to kill myself with a fire. I was trapped both times. If you hadn't been with me at the gym, I wouldn't have gotten out, and in the woods ... if it wasn't for that man, the flames would have gotten me." Glancing around nervously, she reached out and grabbed one of Jake's hands. "Do you think it was him? Here today? Did he leave after he threw that fireball thing at me or is he still here watching us?"

"I don't know. These people have been sending in teams of men after us, so I'm guessing there are probably at least a handful of men targeting you and me now."

An icy cold rush of fear hit her system at Jake's words. It wasn't that it was better or worse if there was one man or half a dozen intent on coming after them, they were in danger either way. It was just that Jake spoke about it with such conviction.

They were in danger, and he'd accepted that.

On the other hand, she was having trouble accepting it.

Had been at least.

"Wh-what are we going to do?" she asked, hating the wobble in her voice. Alannah wanted to be all strong and stoic like Jake was. Or at the very least she wanted to be angry and use that as a shield to hold off her fear. Not angry at Jake but at the people who had raped his stepmom then gone to the extreme to try and keep their crimes a secret. From having their victim's husband and his team ambushed, to having her charged with treason, and then everything they'd done these last few months to try to keep the Charleston Holloway family from learning the truth.

She should be angry, and she was, but it paled in comparison to her fear.

One thing was for certain, she wasn't cut out for this kind of high adrenaline, danger-filled life.

"We're going to do whatever it takes to make sure these men don't get to you again," he answered simply. Although that wasn't much of an answer. And why did it feel like he already had a plan in mind, one he had neglected to share with her?

"What does that mean exactly?"

"It means that we'll talk about it when we get back to my place. I hear sirens so cops have showed up. We're going to have to give statements again, and then I want you checked out by EMTs."

"I didn't get hurt."

"Yeah, sunshine, you did." Lifting a finger, he brushed the calloused pad of a finger across her left cheekbone, and she winced slightly as pain flared in her face. "You have at least one bruise where something hit you when he threw that fireball at you. There are probably more, but adrenaline is masking the pain. You get checked out, not negotiable."

There was the Jake she knew so well, all gruff and commanding. The smile on her lips was genuine this time as she caught his hand and entwined their fingers. She needed him close, and she wasn't going to fight her instincts. "Okay, grumpy, wouldn't want you to get those pants of yours in a knot."

The smile slid off her face as she caught sight of cops coming toward them. This mess wasn't even close to being over. Jake and his family still had no idea who the fourth rapist was which meant there was nothing stopping these men coming after them again and again until they finally got what they wanted.

# CHAPTER *Six*

October 15<sup>th</sup>
8:02 P.M.

"I feel like I've had a permanent headache the last few days," Alannah said with a ragged sigh as Jake unlocked his front door and guided her inside.

She was dead on her feet, that was the problem. What little energy she'd managed to recoup after sleeping fairly well last night had been zapped by an exhausting day of dealing with insurance and contractors, and then this third fire had destroyed what was left.

What she needed was to be somewhere safe.

What *he* needed was for her to be somewhere safe.

Risking losing her wasn't an option, which meant they needed to have some tough conversations. Since she'd been his best friend for so long, she knew Cassandra, had known Becca back when she was with Connor the first time, knew Essie and Gabriella, so going away with them shouldn't be a problem for her.

At least on that front.

But his sunshine was stubborn and determined, and she took her responsibilities seriously. He was worried that even with the danger, she wouldn't walk away from her business.

It wasn't that he didn't get that because he totally did. That gym was her baby, and she'd worked hard to build it up. If she had to close it down for any extended period of time, she might not be able to recover.

There was no way he could force her to make that decision, take her livelihood from her. If she insisted on staying, he would hire as much security as was needed to keep her safe and protected.

Unfortunately, with a firebug on her trail, that would be a whole lot harder to do.

Any building could be set alight, and while so far whoever their pyromaniac stalker was seemed to be making sure no one else was hurt, that didn't mean it would last forever.

"You need a shower and food," he told her, locking up the door behind them and then nudging her toward the stairs. "Go up and take a shower, and I'll order some takeout."

A long sigh rumbled from her lips. "Yeah, guess you're right. Shower, food, and sleep will help." Turning to look up at him over her shoulder, she quirked one side of her mouth up into something that vaguely resembled a smile. "At least the cops no longer seem to think I'm the one starting fires."

"With witnesses to two of the three fires saying you didn't do it, it would be hard for them to insist otherwise. And since in two of the three fires you almost died, I think it would be a stretch to believe you paid someone to set them."

While he knew Alannah was upset about the police hinting at her involvement, in his mind they had way bigger problems than that. Something he suspected she knew, too, but that was an easier problem to focus on when she didn't want to truly consider how much danger she was in.

"Shower," he ordered gently, giving her another nudge toward the stairs. "Sorry you're not getting the lasagna you were craving. I'll order pizza from your favorite place, and they have those brownies that you love, too."

Stopping partway up the stairs, she looked down at him, a genuine smile on her face this time. "Cheesy pizza and gooey brownies. Might not be my homemade lasagna but dee-lish-us."

"Delicious," he mumbled his agreement as she ran up the last of the stairs. Why was he thinking about how delicious it would be to trail his tongue over every inch of Alannah's creamy, soft skin?

Had to be the stress of the last few days and how many times he'd come close to losing her.

Anything else would be totally inappropriate.

Putting in a call for their dinner, he hurried upstairs to his room. While neither of them were smoky this time around, the little firebomb had quickly fizzled out when it had nothing else to catch alight, he still couldn't seem to get the smell of smoke out of his nostrils.

The phantom scent seemed to linger in the air everywhere he went, and he knew it was a psychological response to what had happened and not a physiological one.

Still, when he stripped off and stepped into the shower in his bathroom, letting the hot water pound down on his stiff muscles, he scrubbed every inch of his body as vigorously as he had after the fire at Alannah's gym.

Thoughts of his best friend had another part of his anatomy going stiff. Jake glanced down at his hardening length. Wrong as it was to be lusting after a woman who had been through what Alannah just had, not even counting the fact that she was his friend, he couldn't seem to stop himself.

Images of her naked in the other shower, water running in rivulets along her petal soft skin, her head tilted back to get the full impact of the spray, a loofah running over every inch of her body, filled his head.

Would she think of him when the loofah brushed between her legs?

Jake groaned and leaned forward to rest his forehead against the warming tiles. What the hell was wrong with him? Why was he all of a sudden lusting after Alannah? It was crazy, and stupid, and oh so very wrong.

Yet his hand grasped his length anyway.

Began to stroke it.

Alannah's voice echoed in his ears, calling out his name, begging him for more, pleading with him to make her come so hard she forgot her own name.

His hand moved faster, pumping up and down with an urgency he hadn't felt in a long time.

Pleasure built quickly. With everything he'd had going on with his family these last few months, sex and orgasms hadn't even registered on the periphery of his mind. This orgasm came blasting through him with a rush. Squirting all over the tiles as white dots danced behind his closed lids, Jake was hit with a powerful desire to mark Alannah just like that. Cover her with cum and make her ... his?

That was crazy.

This couldn't happen again.

Ashamed of himself for his inappropriate thoughts about his best friend, Jake quickly shut off the water and stepped out of the shower. Alannah didn't see him like that, and honestly, before the fire he hadn't seen her that way either. He'd never gotten himself off to thoughts of her body writhing beneath him, and he'd never come so hard imagining her orgasm setting off his own.

Just as he was wrapping a towel around his waist, he thought he heard someone knocking on the front door. The pizza couldn't be here already, could it?

Walking into his bedroom, a quick glance at the clock on his night-stand told him he'd been in the shower for almost fifteen minutes. Alannah had him so messed up he couldn't even think straight, and she wasn't even trying to mess with his head. She was just being herself, strong but vulnerable, tough yet fragile, and for some reason these last couple of days, that was hitting him differently.

Heading out into the hall, he almost walked straight into the woman herself.

"Jake, sorry," she blurted out, but all he could do was stare at her.

Like himself, she was wrapped in a towel, only hers was tied around her chest, just above her breasts. It hung to just below her backside, and she was using another towel to dry off her long blonde locks. A few drops of water clung to her delicate shoulders, and he had to clamp his teeth together so he didn't reach out and capture them with the tip of his tongue.

It wasn't until he forced himself to tear his gaze away from her lithe, perfectly toned body and fix it back on her face where it should have been all along that he realized she wasn't looking at his face either.

Nope.

Her gaze was roaming his ripped chest, dipping lower and then latching onto where his length was hidden beneath the towel. Something bright danced in her golden eyes, and a faint blush on her cheeks let him know that she was aroused looking at his body.

Relief washed over him.

At least this craziness was affecting them both.

Another knock on his door had her gaze darting up to meet his, guilt in her eyes now, dampening a little of her desire.

"Umm, someone's at the door," she said somewhat lamely.

"Dinner."

"Right. Dinner. I should ... I should get dressed." She said the words but didn't move, and it almost seemed like she didn't want to. Like cheesy pizza and gooey brownies were no longer on her mind.

"I should get the door."

"Jake, wait."

He froze at her words. Was she going to ask him to make love to her? If she did, would he say yes or no?

"You're only wearing a towel," she reminded him.

Disappointment put a stop to his growing erection. Of course she wasn't going to ask for sex. Only as he turned around to head back into his room to put on a pair of pants, he couldn't miss the hungry look in Alannah's eyes. Or the way she blushed harder when he caught her staring and scurried away to the room she was staying in.

Something was changing between them, and he had no idea if it was what either of them wanted or just a result of the high stakes of the last few days. Or if these changes were going to be a good thing or a complete and utter disaster.

~

October 15th
    9:03 A.M.

.  .  .

"I wish I could walk outside without worrying someone is going to set a fire around me," Alannah said with a shudder as she climbed out of Jake's SUV.

Was this ever going to end?

Was her death the only thing that would stop it?

As much as she was trying to reassure herself with the facts that Cole and Susanna, Connor and Becca, and Cade, Gabriella, and Essie, were all alive and mostly in one piece—although all bearing scars, both physical and mental from their ordeals—it wasn't working.

They'd all survived, but she wasn't stupid enough to believe that was a guarantee that she would too.

Whoever this final man was who was desperate to stop the Charleston Holloway family from finding out his identity wasn't just suddenly going to give up and go away. He couldn't. Not after everything he and the others had invested in keeping their secrets. If the truth came out, he'd be ruined.

This family was the only thing standing between him keeping whatever lifestyle he was accustomed to and winding up in prison for rape, for treason, for so many attempted murders she'd almost lost count.

Which meant he had to keep fighting as hard as he could.

"I'm sorry, Alannah. I truly am. I should have continued keeping my distance from you."

There was so much guilt and pain in Jake's voice that she snapped around to look up at him. Instead of his usual gruff expression, the same raw guilt and pain she'd just heard in his voice was written all over his face.

While she absolutely got why he was blaming himself, that wasn't what she wanted. Not at all. It was not his fault that he'd brought these people to her. She was his best friend and he should be able to come to her with his problems. And he'd stayed away for three long months, leaving her to wonder if she'd done something wrong to cost her his friendship.

She'd much rather this.

*Huh.*

Actually, she really would rather this, even with her life in danger and all the close calls she'd had over the last few days. Because without Jake in her life, she felt so alone. She had other friends, but none could even hold a candle to her best friend. Not because they weren't great people who cared about her and who she had fun with, just because they weren't … Jake.

Stepping up to him, she didn't hesitate, just wrapped her arms around his waist and pressed her cheek to his chest. Right above his heart so she could hear the steady beat of it. Even though she'd been the target of the second two fires didn't mean that he wasn't the real target. She was just something to be used to try to manipulate him. Alannah couldn't imagine how bad that made him feel, but she didn't want him taking on guilt that wasn't his to bear. The people to blame were the ones who had raped his stepmom then gone to the extreme to try to cover it up.

"Don't blame yourself, Jake. I don't," she whispered.

For a long moment, he didn't say anything, and his arms hung limply at his sides. Then, ever so slowly, he lifted them and curled them around her.

Cocooned in his embrace, a small sigh slipped past her lips and she nestled closer. They might be best friends, but they didn't often touch, at least not like this. A quick hug, sure, a high five or fist bump, definitely, but they didn't stand there looking like a pair of lovers entwined in each other's arms.

Lovers.

The word whispered through her mind.

It made her the worst best friend in the world, but last night when she'd been leaving the bathroom wrapped in nothing but a towel, and bumped into Jake wearing nothing but a towel, she'd wanted him.

Unable to tear her gaze away from his ripped body, all she'd been able to think about was how good it would be to touch and kiss every inch of his tanned skin. She'd seen him topless before, they worked out at her gym together a lot, and they hung out at the beach in the summer.

But last night had been different.

She'd felt … things. Things that grew as he held her tenderly.

"You should blame me," he whispered, and she could tell that he meant that one hundred percent.

"It's up to me who I blame or don't blame. And I don't blame you. I blame the people who raped an innocent woman then tried to cover it up. But you wouldn't be my grumpy if you didn't go straight to the negatives," she teased.

"My sunshine." A hand swept down her back, and she felt a kiss to the top of her head before Jake released her and took a step back.

There was something in his voice just then, something she hadn't heard before, only she wasn't sure exactly what it was.

Now wasn't the time to try to figure it out. Or obsess about this sudden shift in her feelings. It felt like things were changing in a way that had already taken off, and there was no stopping it. Alannah just didn't know if the change was going to be a good one or a bad one.

*Please be a good one.*

"Come on, let's go upstairs and pack you some more clothes," Jake said as he headed across the street toward her apartment building.

Hurrying after him, she caught his hand as he headed for the front doors. "Let's go into the parking garage first. I need to grab a few things from my car."

After the fire at the park when she'd gone home with Jake, one of his brothers had driven her car back to her building for her. They'd grabbed the bag from her friend's house and taken it to Jake's, but after the third fire at the grocery store, it was apparent she couldn't stay on her own, and she wasn't bringing trouble to any of her other friends.

So she'd be staying with Jake for the foreseeable future, but that meant she needed more stuff. They were there to pack her a bigger suitcase, but she also needed her other set of headphones. The ones she'd been wearing at the park had been lost in the fire, but she had a second set in her car's glovebox.

With Jake watching their surroundings and her worrying that all of a sudden a fire was going to appear out of nowhere, they headed for the parking garage beneath the building. Her parking space was her favorite thing about the whole building. It sounded silly, but she wasn't that great at parking her car, and her spot was right at the end of the entry path, before it turned the corner, which meant she could drive straight in, then reverse right out without having to be careful about turning without hitting another car.

Sometimes, it was the small things that made you the happiest.

At her car, she pulled out her keys from her purse, unlocked it, and hopped into the passenger seat so she could more easily reach the glovebox.

Jake stayed outside, she assumed because it was easier to keep watch. That was fine, it wasn't going to take her long to retrieve the headphones, and then they could go up to her apartment and pack.

It was underwear—specifically whether she owned any sexy lingerie —that was on her mind as she opened the glovebox. Which meant it took her a moment to realize there was a folded piece of paper lying against the pair of green headphones that were the only thing her ears could tolerate.

While she wasn't a neat freak, she did like to keep things organized and the only things she kept in there were a first aid kit, a spare phone charger, a travel mug she'd use if she stopped off for coffee since she hated those disposable cups they gave out, and the headphones.

Her fingers trembled as they reached out to grab the piece of paper.

No one other than whichever of Jake's brothers had driven her car there had been in her vehicle in months. Why would one of them leave her a note when they had her number? They could just call or text if they had something to say to her.

Knowing it was a bad idea and she wouldn't want to know what the note said didn't seem to stop her unfolding the slip of paper.

Back off or the girl will die.

Her heart about stopped beating in her chest when she read those words.

"Jake!"

At the sound of her panicked voice, he quickly jumped into the driver's seat of her vehicle. "What's wrong?"

Instead of answering, she just shoved the piece of paper at him, no longer wanting to touch it as though that could eradicate the words from her mind.

"What the hell?" he roared. Anger and fear rolled off him, adding to her own, and filling the car.

A flash of something in the rear vision mirror caught her attention. A whimper of terror tumbled from her lips when she realized what it was.

Jake saw it too, she knew he did by the curse that fell from his mouth.

A burning car was barreling down the ramp right toward them.

# CHAPTER

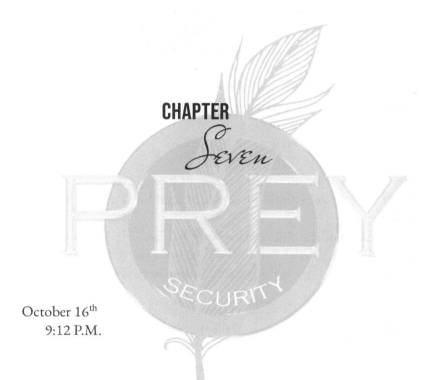

## *Seven*

October 16th
9:12 P.M.

They weren't going to make it out in time.

That fear almost paralyzed him.

A delay of seconds that really could cost them both their lives.

"Jump out," he ordered as he shoved the piece of paper she'd handed him into one of the pockets of his zippered hoodie and threw himself out the open car door.

Thankfully, he hadn't closed it behind him. The car was approaching them quickly and even that delay, especially combined with his moment of panic could have been all it took to steal their chance of survival.

They didn't just have to get out of Alannah's car, they had to get far enough away from it in case the burning car slamming into hers was enough to have hers exploding.

As he rounded the car, he found her scrambling out of the passenger seat, her eyes wide with fear shoved away some of his own terror because he was so damn sick of seeing his best friend afraid for her life.

She didn't deserve this.

All she deserved was everything good the world had to offer. Love, acceptance, safety, and protection. Her life should always be as sweet and sunshiny as she was.

Grabbing her hand, he yanked her away from the vehicle. Jake knew how much she loved this parking space. Alannah was a good driver, but she had a thing about parking. She hated it so much that he'd seen her park a ten-minute walk away from her location just so she could avoid parallel parking.

This spot was a dream for her because of its easy access, but now the ease at which this space could be accessed could wind up costing them their lives.

When Alannah stumbled, Jake didn't hesitate. He bent his knees, used his hold on Alannah's hand to turn her so she was facing him, then his shoulder went into her stomach, lifting her off the ground, all without slowing down.

They were about six spots down from Alannah's when it happened.

Diving behind the nearest car, Jake threw them both to the ground, turning at the last moment so his body took the brunt of the connection with the concrete. Then he turned again so that his body was covering hers.

Pressed tightly against her as he was, chest to chest, he could feel the way her heart hammered wildly. Her fingers curled into his hoodie, clinging to him, and she pressed her face against his neck.

The sound of metal hitting metal filled the air, a horrible screeching sound that he knew would live on forever in his mind, mixed with the small whimper Alannah made.

This was unacceptable.

It had to stop.

Whatever he had to do to get her out of the line of fire, Jake would do.

Nothing was off the table.

There was no way he would be able to handle losing Alannah and knowing that it was because of him and his family's quest. She had to remain in this world. The darkness inside him needed her light. Craved it. It kept him holding on, clinging to control, when the anger inside him wanted to take over.

Thankfully, there was no explosion, and after waiting a solid minute, Jake cautiously lifted himself off Alannah's body enough that he could look through the windows of the car they'd sought protection behind. The car that had rammed into Alannah's was still burning, the front of it a twisted mess of metal as it tangled with the mangled back of Alannah's car.

"Is it safe?" Alannah asked. Her voice strained, but she was doing her best not to fall apart, and he couldn't ask anything more of her. Despite her terror in the face of the nightmare she'd been thrown into completely without warning, she fought to keep control of herself and not let the weight of her fear crush her.

Honestly, he couldn't be prouder of her.

"Yeah, I think we're okay."

"Do you think he's here? The man who loves fire? He has to be, right? Someone had to set that car alight and then push it toward mine."

That was true. The car didn't drive itself and set itself alight. Someone had to do it and given that fire wasn't the usual way of taking out a threat, Jake had to assume that whoever the remaining rapist had hired had a fetish for fire.

But it was unlikely that the firebug had stuck around.

Fire wasn't the usual method used for one reason because it drew so much attention and could so easily get out of control. As soon as that car lit up, it would show up on the security cameras watching the entrance. It had likely already been called in and cops and fire trucks were enroute.

"I think we're safe, I think he's gone," he assured Alannah.

Fear wafted off her, but she reached out and took hold of the hand he held out to her. When he tugged her to her feet, Jake immediately wrapped his arms around her and dragged her into a tight embrace.

Not just because she was afraid and he wanted to soothe her but because he needed to hold her every bit as much as she needed to be held.

Usually, he wasn't a touchy-feely guy. He'd give his brothers a back slap or a fist bump, give Essie hugs when she asked, or piggyback rides, or pick her up and carry her if they were out somewhere and she was tired, but that was about it.

Normally, he was okay with hugs with Alannah. She wasn't like everybody else in his life, she'd always been different, special. Only the last couple of days, that seemed to have amped up several notches, and now it was almost a compulsion to have her close and touch her.

"He must have put the note in my car before following me when I was out jogging," Alannah said, voice muffled since her face was pressed against his chest.

"Probably."

"He knew you'd find it eventually, or that I would and would give it to you."

"Yes."

"Why did he get me out of the fire if he wanted to kill me?" Tilting her head back, she looked up at him with such fear-filled brown eyes, but with so much trust in them as well. Despite him being the reason she was in this mess, she trusted him to keep her alive, to protect her like he always had, and that hit him deep.

It was an exhilarating but terrifying prospect to have someone have so much faith in you.

"I don't know the answer to that question, sunshine. I can guess it's because your death is irrelevant. These people don't care about you. They'll kill you if they have to, but it won't be because that will be enjoyable for them. All this guy wants is to protect himself. He's willing to go to any lengths, and if that includes taking your life I doubt he'll feel any regret, but in the end what he wants most is to force my family to back off."

"Doesn't he realize by now that's not going to happen?"

"You'd think so. But he can't give up. If he backs off and lets us put the final pieces together, he basically forfeits his life. This isn't a choice, he's the last man standing, which means he'll take the fall alone. If he wants to live, he can't give up."

Those words echoed through his mind as he stood there holding his best friend in his arms as he watched the flames dance around her car. A car they'd been sitting in right before the crash.

They could so easily have died today or in any one of the fires other than last night's at the grocery store. These people were watching them and grabbing hold of every opportunity they could to make a move.

He had to get Alannah out of the line of fire.

For now, keeping her in his house, which they had to know was heavily protected and why they weren't targeting them while they were there was working, but it wouldn't last forever. Likely the firebug was already coming up with a plan on how to target the house without getting caught by the men watching over him and Alannah.

Jake knew he was running out of time.

Every day he dragged this out just gave these men another opportunity to try to hurt Alannah, and one of those times she wouldn't be as lucky.

Fate could only be toyed with so many times before she hit back.

There was no way he could allow that to happen when the life of one of the people he cared about the most was hanging in the balance.

It was time to act, to do whatever was necessary to protect the girl he'd once vowed to never let another person hurt. There had been many times he'd failed in that promise over the years as her family continued to cause her pain, but he wasn't going to fail this time.

Alannah wasn't going to pay the ultimate price for his decision to hunt the men who had taken so much from his family.

~

October 16th
    4:39 P.M.

This was so unreal.

How could this be her life?

Alannah could barely comprehend any of it as she allowed Jake to usher her into his house. Half a dozen men watched it, and she had a feeling that as soon as they got inside, Jake was going to tell her that things were about to change.

That made her terrified.

She absolutely got that he wanted to make sure she didn't wind up dead because of the people after his family, but she had no idea of just how he intended to try to make sure that she stayed safe.

The last thing she wanted right now was to be sent away.

Jake and his brothers were the closest thing she had to family. Sure, she had other friends, but now that she knew the extent of the danger, it wasn't like she would go and stay with one of them and risk the people after her setting fire to their homes.

Besides, even if she wasn't afraid of them getting caught in the cross-fire, she didn't want to be around anyone else other than Jake.

*He* made her feel safe.

*He* made her feel protected.

*He* made her feel cared about.

No one else could give her the sense of security she needed so badly since her life had been flipped upside down.

But things were about to change.

Even if she hadn't known Jake most of her life, she would be able to sense the shift in him.

Although he'd comforted her after the fire in the parking garage at her building, by the time cops and firefighters had shown up he was already withdrawing. He'd been almost brisk with her, not rude, but the gruff, edge-of-annoyed way he spoke to other people he was now using on her.

Not something she was used to.

Jake was grumpy, but he was *her* grumpy, and he was always so sweet with her, softer and gentler. She liked that and didn't want it to change. The fact that it *was* changing told her that he was already shifting into Delta Force Jake and that meant he had stopped seeing her as his best friend and started seeing her as a problem that needed to be solved.

Only the last thing she needed was to be treated like a problem that had to be solved rather than a human being, his best friend, who had been through hell, was scared out of her mind, struggling to hold it together, and could do with comfort and reassurance.

Because she couldn't wait a second longer, as soon as Jake finished talking to the man standing on the doorstep and closed and locked the door behind them, she blurted out the words that had been weighing heavily upon her since this last fire.

"Are you sending me away?" Alannah demanded.

There was a brief moment of shock on his face before he schooled his features into one of distance and borderline disinterest.

It was an expression she was used to.

One she'd seen a thousand times growing up.

The same expression her parents always gave her when they were forced to acknowledge that even though they hadn't planned on having her, and even though they hadn't wanted her and never missed an opportunity to make sure she was aware of that, they were legally required by law to provide for her basic needs.

That was how Jake looked at her now.

Like she was an unwanted responsibility.

Even though she knew he was doing it to protect his feelings it still hurt. For once she wanted someone to put her feelings above their own. She got that he felt guilty, but he didn't have to take that out on her. She was his best friend, and she didn't blame him. Together they could work out a plan that meant she was safe so he could focus on getting the answers she was well aware he and his family needed.

"Don't do that to me, Jake. Don't make me feel like a burden, you know how much I hate that."

There was a flare of guilt in his dark eyes, but he shut it down quickly. "I brought this mess to your doorstep, made my problems your problems, I absolutely will do whatever it takes to make sure you don't wind up paying the ultimate price for my mistakes."

There was something in his tone she didn't like in the least. "What does that mean exactly?"

"It means I need you safe."

Like that answer was going to pacify her.

Safe how?

Like hiring her a bodyguard or like locking her away somewhere?

Neither were particularly appealing options, but she would for sure go for the former rather than the latter.

"Explain," she ordered. If she didn't know where his head was at and what he had planned, she couldn't counter any outrageous ideas. It wasn't like she was intending to plant herself in the middle of a park again and wait for this pyromaniac to come for her, but she also wanted to be reasonable. This might be Jake's area of expertise and not hers, but she wasn't some stranger. She was his best friend, and she didn't want that to get forgotten as he scrambled to put together what he thought was the best plan.

"You know Cassandra went to stay with Delta Team after we found out she was the product of our mom's rape. That was the safest place for her, and she's the only living proof of what happened. We couldn't let those men get to her. After what happened to Essie and Gabriella, we thought it would be best for all the girls to go and stay there. Then these last few days with fire after fire aimed at you, the guys and I talked and all of us are going to go there."

A part of her actually liked that plan because it meant Jake was treating her like family and that soothed the torn edges of her heart that her parents' neglect had caused.

But another part of her couldn't agree to that.

Playing it safe was sensible, but she couldn't be so far away from her business right now. She had to stay alive, but she also had to have a way to pay her bills when this was all over. And the gym was her livelihood as well as her passion.

"Where do they live?" she asked, willing to have a reasonable discussion on the topic. If they were close by, maybe she could make that work.

"Nobody knows. Well, I'm sure Eagle does but no one else. Those guys ... they're not like everybody else."

"What does that mean exactly?"

"It means they have secrets. Big ones. But they're good men, and they've been taking good care of Cassandra. They'll take care of you guys as well."

"I can't just disappear, Jake. I'm already losing money every day that my business is closed. I can go away for a bit, but I have to be close by for me to come back for meetings and such."

"You can do meetings over the phone."

"For most things, sure. But not for everything, and definitely not when I reopen if I want people to trust me enough not to take their business elsewhere."

"You care more about your business than your life?" he snapped.

"Of course not," she said soothingly, refusing to lose her cool and be drawn into an argument. "But I also have to be practical. Once my gym is open, if I want to minimize damage and get things going again, I have to be there."

"Alannah, this isn't up for discussion. In the morning, we're all leaving and you're coming with us."

"What does that mean, not up for discussion? What are you going to do if I refuse?"

"Whatever I have to."

"And that means ...?"

"It means I'll drug you and tie you up if I have to in order to get you on that plane."

Alannah gasped. "And when we get there? How would you make sure I didn't leave? Would you keep me locked up like a prisoner?" He wouldn't really do that. Would he? Yet the answer was written clearly on his face.

He would.

He'd do anything it took, just like he said he would.

"Jake, right now, I'm the one being targeted. I don't think I should be anywhere near the others."

"And these people could just as easily switch back to one of the others. You're coming, Alannah. It's not a discussion. I'm telling you what's going to happen. You can either come along nicely without causing trouble, or we can do it the hard way. Your choice."

"Why are you being so unreasonable?" Seeing Jake like this was unnerving. This wasn't the sweet to her best friend who was grumpy to everyone else she knew and loved. This man was ... scary. Intimidating. Would be terrifying if she didn't know he was doing this out of fear and not to hurt her.

"Because I promised to protect you," he roared, like the words he'd spoken as a five-year-old were a binding-for-life vow.

"And you've always done your best to do that," she reminded him, reaching out to rest a hand on his forearm.

"I've failed. So many times."

"You haven't."

"Have so. How many times have you cried over your parents over the years?"

"Oh, Jake." Stepping closer, she wrapped her arms around his waist and pressed herself against his large body. She could feel ripples of fear trembling in his chest and held on tighter. They were both afraid, and arguing wasn't going to make things better or make them safer. "What about a compromise?"

"A compromise?"

"I agree that I'm not safe, and I don't want to die in a fire. But I have to consider my future because I don't intend to die. I need my gym, and I have to be somewhat close to it."

"Doesn't sound like a compromise is coming anytime soon, sunshine."

She smiled at his surly tone. "I was getting to that. What if I took out my boat? That way these men wouldn't know where I was, so they couldn't get to me, but I could still be close enough if I had to come back. If you give me the names of some people you trust, if I have to come back, I can call them to come and protect me while I attend to the gym."

A large hand palmed the back of her head, guiding it backward until she was looking up at him. "You're crazy, sunshine, if you think it will be anybody but me protecting you."

"But you'll be with your family, staying with Delta Team," she reminded him.

One of his fingers tapped the end of her nose. "You're cute when you're confused. If you're dead set on going away on your boat, I'll go with you."

Her heart warmed at how seriously he made his declaration. "But your family, Jake. They need you."

"And I promised to protect *you*. The others will be safe enough without me. There is no way I'd let you go off on your own, sunshine, you should know that."

There was warmth in his dark eyes that she hadn't seen before, and as they stared at one another, it was like a string materialized out of nowhere, drawing them together.

Maybe she should have fought it, but she didn't.

Her head tilted back further, and she lifted onto her tiptoes, her lips already tingling in anticipation as Jake's head dipped.

Somehow, this was wrong and yet right.

Because one thing Alannah was sure of was that she wanted this kiss and the consequences of what could happen could just be damned.

# CHAPTER
## *Eight*

October 16th
4:57 P.M.

Was he really going to do this?

Was he really going to kiss his best friend?

Was he really going to risk losing her by messing up their friendship with a kiss?

For some reason, none of that mattered as Jake leaned down. It was as though an invisible cord was pulling him toward Alannah, and he seemed powerless to do a single thing about it.

Like two magnets drawing closer, his lips hovered mere millimeters from hers, from what he somehow knew would be the sweetest kiss of his life, when his front door suddenly banged open.

As though they were teenagers caught making out by their parents, they sprung backward, and he saw Alannah's cheeks turn bright pink.

"Umm, are we interrupting?" Jax asked, his gaze darting between them.

There was no way his family hadn't seen what was about to happen, and for some reason, that set him on edge. That little bit of peace he'd finally found when Alannah had agreed to go away on her boat for a while vanished as though it had never existed.

"No, not interrupting anything," he answered, his tone firm, brokering no argument, but he couldn't help noticing that Alannah flinched at it and took a small step away from him.

Clenching his hands into fists at his sides was the only way to stop himself from reaching out for her. There was a time when he wouldn't hesitate to reach out and give his best friend whatever comfort she needed. They'd been friends for thirty years, there had been plenty of times he'd held her when she cried about some new way her family managed to show her just how little she meant to them.

But something had changed, shifted slightly, and he felt like he was standing in a huge hole filled with quicksand, one wrong move and he'd sink. The rules felt different now, almost kissing her wasn't best friend appropriate, and he wasn't sure how to proceed.

"It looked like you and Alannah were going to kiss," Essie very unhelpfully pointed out.

"Shh, cuddle bug," Gabriella shushed the child as everyone piled into his front hall.

Glad to have a reason to move instead of standing there and doing something stupid like taking back his answer and offering a more truthful one, instead, Jake led everyone through to the kitchen.

"But that's what it did look like, Mommy," Essie continued, the slightest hint of a whine to her tone. "You and Daddy kiss all the time."

"Not *all* the time," Cade protested, looking slightly embarrassed, although there was no reason for him to. Still, Jake got it. They were the two who had the most trouble showing their emotions, they were both stoic, gruff, grumpy, and filled with anger.

Except Cade had now found a balm to his anger since admitting to himself, Gabriella, and the rest of them that he had feelings for the former nanny.

A surge of jealousy hit him hard and fast, coming out of nowhere and catching him by surprise.

"Pretty much all the time," Gabriella teased, not put off by Cade's gruffness in the least, just like Alannah was never put off by his.

Cade rolled his eyes, although he leaned down to brush a kiss to Gabriella's lips when she tilted her face up toward his.

"See, Daddy, alls the times," Essie said excitedly, bouncing up and down in her boundless energy way. "And Uncle Cooper and Willow kiss lots, and Uncle Cole and Susanna, and Uncle Connor and Becca. If you and Alannah are going to do lots of kissing, Uncle Jake, then that means you have to get married sos I can be the flower girl."

"Married?" he repeated, his voice giving away his shock.

"Uh, I don't think they're going to get married, Essie," Gabriella said, quickly ushering the girl up to the table and rifling through his pantry to find her something to eat, no doubt to keep her occupied.

"But they were going to kiss, I saws it," Essie protested. "Only peoples going to gets married do kissing."

"Uncle Jake and Alannah are just friends," Cade told his daughter, although the look in his eyes said he didn't quite believe what he was saying.

"So friends can kiss too, like you and Mommy do?"

"No," Cade quickly answered his daughter. "I don't want you trying to kiss your friends like that. It's only for grownups, and I don't want you kissing anyone until you're married."

"Yeah, that'll work," Gabriella said with a snort, then handed Essie a couple of Oreos.

"Then only peoples getting married *do* kiss," Essie said, looking confused. "Then I can bes the flower girl at their wedding."

"You know what, Essie girl, you absolutely can be the flower girl at my wedding when I get married, it just won't be Jake as the groom," Alannah told the little girl, walking over to give her a hug.

That little spark of jealousy he'd felt when he watched how easily his brothers interacted with the women they loved turned into a full-on raging inferno at the thought of Alannah falling in love and marrying another man.

He'd seen her date before, and now that he thought about it, he'd always felt a little unsettled by the idea of her with another man. But he was her best friend, they weren't lovers and were never going to be.

Watching her fall in love and get married one day, find the love she'd longed for all her life was something he was going to have to accept.

"Yay!" Essie cheered. "That means I gets to be a flower girl in one," she held up a finger as she pointed to Gabriella and her father. "Two." She held up another as she pointed to Cooper and Willow. "Three. Four. Five." She added another finger each time she pointed to a different couple, finishing on Alannah. "Five. I gets to be a flower girl five times."

"Very exciting, Essie," Alannah said, her gaze darting over to him and then skittering away.

"Okay, enough talk about weddings," Gabriella said, and he couldn't be more grateful to her because he wasn't sure he could handle any more of this conversation without doing something stupid.

"Right," Cole agreed. "Did you talk to Alannah about our plan?"

"Yes," Jake answered, suddenly not sure he liked this topic any better than the last one. How was he going to survive out on a boat alone with Alannah and resist the pull that had been drawing them together in his front hall just moments ago? A pull he still felt lingering in the air.

"And?" Cooper prompted.

"And I said I can't go away with you all," Alannah answered.

"Then are we ...?" Connor asked, not needing to finish the sentence because they all knew how it ended. Even Alannah, since he'd been honest and told her that her safety was his number one concern and he'd do whatever it took to ensure it.

"No, you're not drugging me and restraining me and then kidnapping me," Alannah told him.

"Connor." Becca swatted at her boyfriend's shoulder. "You were going to do that?"

"She's part of this family, Becca. She has to be safe," Connor replied.

"Well, it's not necessary," Alannah assured him. "I'm not stupid. I don't want to die. But I can't leave my business right now and not know that I can come back and start it up again as soon as I'm cleared to use the building. So we came up with a compromise."

"A compromise?" Cooper asked.

"Yes. I'm going to take my boat out," Alannah explained. "That way, I'm out of the line of fire, but I can come back if I need to. I offered to hire bodyguards when I come back but Jake ..." she trailed off and looked to him like she wasn't positive he wouldn't have changed his mind.

How could she not know that the vow he'd made to her almost thirty years ago was one he took seriously and intended to keep?

"I told Alannah I'd go with her rather than with you guys," he finished her sentence for her.

When she gasped and looked over at him, seemingly surprised he'd admitted it and still wanted to go with her, he held her gaze. Allowing how serious he was about his vow to shine through so she would know this was what he wanted.

"I'd prefer if we were all together, but I understand," Cade said.

"Course we understand," Cole added.

"She needs to keep her business running and can't do that from anywhere like the rest of us," Willow added. "I can work on a story from anywhere, especially in the preliminary stages. And Susanna is joining Prey anyway, and Becca can still run her charity, and Gabriella hasn't decided what her new job is going to be, so we can all take this time away. You can't and we get that."

"Thank you for understanding," Alannah told Willow, her gaze then including everyone. "I appreciate you all for treating me like family even though I'm not."

"You are," Susanna said before anyone else could get a word in. "Trust me."

Susanna was quiet, shy, but she was the kind of person you did find yourself trusting when she spoke, and Alannah nodded, although there was a tiny flicker of doubt in her golden eyes.

"I'm hungry, Daddy," Essie spoke up, finishing off her cookies.

"Right, dinner," Cade said, heading for the grocery bags that had been stacked on the kitchen counter.

"Guys cooking tonight," Jax announced.

From the look on his brother's face, an expression that was echoed on the faces of all four of his stepbrothers, Jake knew he was about to be given the third degree.

The problem was, he didn't know what he was going to tell him. Alannah was his best friend, that couldn't change. He didn't know if he wanted it to change, or if she did, but he did know that if they tried to change their relationship and it didn't work out, he'd lose his favorite person in the world.

∼

October 17<sup>th</sup>
   8:52 A.M.

Finally.

A sense of freedom, of peace, of security settled over her as they stepped onto her boat.

Alannah took the first deep breath she'd enjoyed in days. There was no smoke in the air, no fear that suddenly someone was going to jump out and start a fire. There would be no burning cars rushing toward them, no fireballs thrown at her as she walked in a grocery store.

It felt amazing.

She was so glad she'd come up with this idea. Not only did it solve the problem of keeping her safe, but it was also going to give her the space and time she needed to start healing from the ordeal the last few days had been.

Definitely helped that she wasn't alone.

While she would have absolutely understood if Jake needed to be with his family right now, it wasn't something she would ever have held against him, she was glad that he'd decided to come with her instead.

And maybe there was a teeny tiny piece of her that wished it wasn't just because of a promise he'd made to her when he was five years old.

That made her feel a little bit like a responsibility he'd rather not have, and yet at the same time, she knew that was her own insecurities talking. The emotion and intensity in his voice when he'd told her that he was a failure and he hadn't protected her like he wanted to told her that he wasn't here out of obligation.

Her head knew that, but her heart wanted ... more.

Which was stupid.

Jake had been clear yesterday in what he wanted, and she couldn't even argue with him. It wasn't like she expected him to suddenly fall in love and want to marry her.

One day she'd find the kind of love she saw between his brothers and the women who had captured their hearts.

"Why don't you go and put our things away and I'll get us going," Jake suggested as he carried the last of the bags of groceries down into the little galley kitchen below deck.

"Umm, you aren't much of a sailor," she said a little hesitantly. It wasn't like she was going to be winning races any time soon, but her parents had a boat when she was growing up, and virtually the only happy memories she had of her childhood was the time spent on it.

It wasn't that they'd shown her any love and attention, it was the same as it was at home, but out there with the fresh sea air and the warmth of the sun on her skin, she'd found a peace that remained elusive at home. She'd find a little corner of the deck to make her own and watch for dolphins or whales, she'd read, she'd watch the sunlight glimmer like diamonds on the water, and just enjoy being miles away from anywhere.

"I think I can manage getting us out of the marina," he told her in that macho way that said his boy brain had already decided it was his job to drive.

Arguing seemed pointless, and she didn't want to ruin this tranquil feeling she had, so Alannah merely shrugged and headed down. Her yacht wasn't huge, but it was cute and cozy. She'd bought it as a treat when her gym started making money, and she loved it. There were two reasonably sized bedrooms, then the galley kitchen that opened out onto the small living room space. Both bedrooms had their own tiny bathrooms, and although the entire space was small, it was cute, and it was all hers.

After about thirty minutes she had her clothes unpacked in her room, and Jake's suitcase sitting on his bed in his room. The groceries were all packed away, and she paused in the kitchen to make them both a snack, then took it back up to the deck.

As soon as she stepped out into the fresh air, she felt another piece of the stress she'd been carrying around these last few days melt away.

They were no longer in the marina, and while she could still see land when she looked behind her, out in front of her there was nothing but sparkling blue water.

Perfect.

Exactly what she needed.

"I see you got us out of the marina without crashing into anything," she teased Jake who had almost crashed the yacht the last time he'd gone out on the water with her. He'd decided he didn't need to listen to her instructions and could handle it himself, which turned out not to be true.

He grumbled, mumbling something under his breath, with both his eyebrows drawn down into a frown, but there was a sparkle in his eyes. He knew she was teasing, and he was playing along. There might be a little awkwardness between them after the almost-kiss the previous afternoon, but it hadn't ruined anything.

As disappointed as she'd been not to kiss Jake, she had to agree it was for the best that they'd been interrupted.

After all, she didn't want to lose this.

This easiness that had always been between them. The next however long they were going to spend at sea would eradicate the awkwardness and then things could go back to the way they'd always been.

Brushing away the little twinge in her heart, Alannah carried the bowl of chips and two glasses of soda over to the little table that sat undercover. "I brought snacks if you're hungry," she said as she laid them out.

"Corn chips?" he asked hopefully, eyeing the bowl.

"Course. I know your favorite snack," she reminded him with a laugh.

"And it's Coke, not Pepsi, since I know that's also your favorite."

"Perfect."

There was something in his voice that made her shiver as though there was another meaning to his words even though she knew there wasn't.

It wasn't like her feelings for him had changed, so how could she expect his for her to have changed?

Although part of her believed that, a voice whispered at the back of her mind that it was a lie. Her feelings *had* changed, she just wasn't sure to what. Alannah had no idea what she wanted right now, and she had to put down all this uncertainty, confusion, and swirling craziness inside her as a result of almost dying several times over.

Since they were almost a month into fall, the weather had cooled dramatically, but it was a sunny day, and even with the sea breeze she wanted to feel that sunshine on her skin.

Slipping off the T-shirt and jeans she'd put on that morning, leaving her in a bright red bikini, she stepped out into the sunlight. Then she chose a spot right in the middle of the deck and lay down, stretching out and closing her eyes.

A small moan of delight fell from her lips as the sun's rays hit every inch of her skin. It had been far too long since she'd been out on the boat. The summer had flown by, and she'd been preoccupied with Jake's sudden disappearance from her life.

If she'd known what had been going on for him and his family, she would have made sure to do anything she could to help. Even though she got why he'd kept her out of it all, a decision she couldn't argue with given how she'd been targeted as soon as he made contact with her, it still hurt a little.

Did she want more than Jake was capable of giving her?

Truth was, she didn't know what she wanted or even what she needed.

All she knew was that something kept pulling her toward Jake, and the more she tried to ignore it, pretend it didn't exist, or fight against it, the stronger the pull became.

"You shouldn't be getting all the fun," Jake's voice rumbled suddenly right beside her.

Blinking up at him, Alannah found the boat was no longer moving, and Jake had stripped off his T-shirt, leaving him in just a pair of shorts that hung low on his hips.

Try as she did, she couldn't seem to stop her hungry gaze from roaming all over his tanned skin and that delectable six-pack. She knew she had a decent body, she certainly spent enough time working on it in her gym, but Jake was something else.

With the sunlight streaming down on him, the breeze ruffling his brown locks, and his perfectly cut and muscled body, he looked more like a Greek God than anything else, and she found she was almost drooling over him.

*Don't look lower.*

The whispered order did nothing to stop her gaze from dropping to the waistline of his shorts and the v that couldn't help but guide her eyes right to the bulge at the front of his shorts.

What would it be like to make love to Jake?

Would it be better than all her previous sexual encounters?

As embarrassing as it was to admit as a thirty-two-year-old woman who'd had her share of partners, Alannah had never had an orgasm in her life.

Not even when she'd tried touching herself.

Would that be different with Jake?

Realizing her thoughts were straying into dangerous territory, she cut them off with a ruthlessness that Jake would be proud of. He was always telling her she was too kind, too trusting, too sweet, and it was why she kept picking the wrong men.

Jake would be a wrong pick, too.

Because he wasn't in love with her, and he didn't see her as anything other than a friend. Something she had a feeling she was going to have to keep reminding herself of while they were stuck alone together on her boat.

The last thing she wanted to do was make a fool out of herself.

# CHAPTER
## *Nine*

October 17<sup>th</sup>
6:36 P.M.

"The colors are spectacular, aren't they?" Alannah asked in a dreamy voice as she sat beside him on the deck of her boat.

There was no denying that the colors of the sun setting into the darkening blue of the water were beautiful, but it wasn't what kept capturing his attention.

What kept capturing Jake's attention was the stunning woman snuggled beside him.

Although they'd sunbathed earlier, soaking up the warmth of the sun's rays as they lay stretched out on the smooth wooden deck, as the day wore on and afternoon began to turn to evening, the temperature had started to drop. Jake had held on as long as possible, wanting to keep Alannah right where she was because he couldn't get enough of the sight of her in that sexy red bikini, but eventually, they'd both gotten too cold.

Since she'd made snacks and lunch, he volunteered for cooking dinner duty and brought her up a sweater before heading into the little galley kitchen. His cooking skills were nowhere near as good as hers, but he wasn't helpless in the kitchen, and he whipped them up a decent meal of cheesy pasta and steamed vegetables on the side.

They'd eaten side by side up on the deck because Alannah loved being out there with the wind ruffling the strands of hair that kept falling loose from her ponytail, and the wide expanse of ocean spread out around them. He was a sucker for anything that made her happy, especially given she was only out there hiding from people who wanted to hurt her because of him, so it was no hardship to settle down up there for the evening.

When the temperature dropped more, Alannah produced a soft fleece blanket and asked him to move to sit beside her so she could tuck them both in.

Apparently, he was a masochist because he agreed even though it was torture to have her toned body pressed against his side.

But it made her happy, so that was where they were sitting, watching the sun sink lower into the horizon, looking like a huge golden ball was slowly being consumed by the ocean. The colors were beautiful, the sky painted a mixture of golds, reds, pinks, and oranges, and the sunset brought out the golden highlights of Alannah's hair as well as making her golden-brown eyes look like two orbs of pure gold, but again it was the woman beside him that stole the show, not nature.

"Jake?"

"Hmm?"

"I said, aren't the colors spectacular?"

"They're very pretty," he agreed, although he'd spent far more time trying to sneak surreptitious glances Alannah's way.

"Is there anything better than watching the sunset alone out on the ocean?" There was such wonder on her face as she couldn't take her eyes off the sunset, and the peacefulness in her tone soothed his guilt and frustration from the last few days that he'd brought her into this mess and didn't know how to get her out of it.

When watching the sunset out on the ocean was sitting with his best friend at his side instead of alone, then he could absolutely agree with her assessment.

"Well, I guess there is something better, or at least the same. The sunrise." Her accompanying giggle did something to him, loosened something inside him, softened the edges of his hard heart.

Hardening his heart as a child hadn't been a choice, it was born out of necessity, a will to survive. Losing his mom at six years old had been rough. Learning his dad wasn't going to leave the military so he could be home more to raise him and Jax had been harder. Then knowing how unwanted he was by relatives, what a burden they considered him and his brother, was the hardest of all.

Family was supposed to be there for you no matter what, support you, love you, and care for you. Instead, his family hadn't wanted to step up after his mom's death, and to make it worse, they hadn't cared about letting the two small motherless boys know it.

While it had been as much a shock to him and Jax as it had been to the Charleston brothers when their parents married, to them it wasn't a bad one. He'd kind of liked the idea of having a new mom even though he was fourteen and beginning to think of himself as a man.

The hatred Cade, Cooper, Connor, and Cole had spewed at him and Jax those six months had been just another blow. Even as a teenager, he'd understood it wasn't them specifically. They were grieving, and now their mom had remarried and added a stepfather and two step-brothers to their family without giving them time to breathe and process their loss.

After their parents were arrested and they found the sofa bed in the master bedroom they'd all understood, young as they were, that the marriage was a sham.

Nothing could have prepared them for what they'd learned over the last several months, though, and he was glad that in the aftermath of their parents' deaths, they'd pulled together and not apart.

He needed his family.

They grounded him, gave him a purpose and a place to belong, and they made him feel loved and wanted.

But they didn't soften the heart he'd long ago learned to harden against the harshness of the world.

Alannah did, though.

She was all softness and light, and even though he was always telling her not to be so trusting because he didn't like seeing her get hurt when people took advantage of her, he didn't really want her to change.

He needed his sunshine, his world needed her light.

"We can watch the sunrise and the sunset every day," he assured her. He was used to getting up early so it would be no hardship to make sure he was up before dawn and had breakfast ready to go so they could sit up there and eat and watch the sunrise.

The smile she gifted him was everything. It was like pouring water into the mouth of a dehydrated person. It didn't just make him feel better, it revitalized the parts of him that had been dying and brought them back to life.

Which was exactly what it felt like Alannah was doing.

While he knew lots of people had a worse life than he'd had, with a tougher childhood, more trauma, and less of a support system, his life had been hard, and because of that he'd become hard.

When he was around Alannah he wanted to change.

One thing he knew about his best friend was that she wasn't looking for a man who was hard, gruff, and struggled to trust and let people in. She wanted, perhaps even needed, softness to echo her own.

That was something he could never give her.

As her best friend, it had always been his job to protect her, something he wished he'd done a better job at. She never seemed to mind his harsh edges, always laughing and affectionately calling him grumpy, but deep down, she had to know that he could never offer her anything more.

Was that enough?

It wasn't something he could put a finger on exactly, but things between him and Alannah were changing. As much as he didn't want them to, he couldn't deny it. Jake was happy with things remaining as they'd always been, the last thing he wanted was to do anything that would jeopardize keeping his sunshine in his life.

What Alannah needed was never going to be something he could give her, and above all else, he wanted her to be happy.

Happiness wasn't something he necessarily saw as part of his future.

Not that he was unhappy now, it was just that he had too much going on to think much about it. For so long, he and the rest of his family had been entirely focused on answers. Now those answers were almost within their grasp, and he didn't know what his future looked like when he wasn't spending every spare second looking for the truth about what happened to his dad and stepmom.

"Jake?"

"Yeah, sunshine?"

"You look like you're thinking really hard. Is something wrong?"

That right there was exactly why he cared about this woman so much. She could read him like a book, and she cared. Even when she was scared and being forced to run for her life because of him and his family's quest for answers, she still cared about what was going on with him and would try to make it better if she could.

"I'm okay, sunshine."

"Is there anything I can do to make you feel better?" she asked, obviously seeing right through his lie.

"You're already doing it."

At his words, she gifted him one of those beautiful bright smiles, and when she snuggled closer and rested her head on his shoulder, his heart swelled until it felt too big for his chest.

What was she doing to him?

Why were things changing?

And how did he stop it before he ruined things and lost the best thing he had in his life?

～

October 18th
2:24 A.M.

"Mmm," Alannah gave a content sigh as she rolled over in bed.

Half asleep, she almost expected to find Jake there just as he'd been in her dreams.

In her dreams, he hadn't just been lying in the bed beside her, he'd been kissing her, his large hands roaming her body, teasing her nipples and making them pebble at his ministrations. Those hands of his had been dipping lower, trailing along her stomach. Her body felt like it had been set alight, the good kind, the kind where every touch felt exemplified, every nerve ending extra sensitive.

She'd been so ready for more that when she rolled over, she absolutely expected Jake to be there.

*Wanted* him to be there.

Which was crazy and mixed up, and she didn't even know how to process it. All she knew was that when her hands found the cold sheets beside her, and she blinked open sleepy eyes to find the bed empty, she was disappointed.

With a sigh, she sat up and shoved off the covers. There was no point in just lying there, she'd woken herself up enough that she wasn't going to drift back off to sleep.

May as well go up on deck and check that everything was going smoothly. They'd set down their anchor at dinner time last night, and she hadn't intended to move again until after breakfast. They were on no schedule, had no plans of where they were going, and no set time they had to be back.

There were a lot of little islands dotted off the coast and she thought they might slowly make their way around them, spend the odd day on shore before setting off somewhere else. It was safer to keep on the move most of the time just in case anyone was looking for her.

Not that she thought they would be.

Well, not out there at least.

Climbing out of bed, she didn't bother to put on any shoes as she padded quietly through the living room, careful not to make a sound and disturb Jake.

Something was going on with him, he'd seemed ... different, last night.

Not necessarily in a bad way. After knowing Jake for so long, growing up together, she knew him better than most people did. Maybe even better than Jax and his stepbrothers. She knew him in a different way, and she knew he had a lot of unresolved feelings leftover from his childhood and no outlet for them. Both his parents were gone, so it wasn't like he could yell at them for dying and leaving him, and the rest of his family he'd gone no contact with after his dad's death.

He and Jax had stayed with the Charleston kids' grandparents, and she knew it had hurt Jake further that his biological family hadn't had a problem with allowing people they didn't know to take over raising their relatives. Even though staying with his stepbrothers was what he'd wanted, it still hurt when family didn't fight for you.

She knew from firsthand experience.

Right now, Jake had something on his mind, something that was worrying him, and she hoped that soon he'd feel comfortable talking to her about it.

Making her way up the steps, she drank in a deep breath of the clean, fresh air and tipped her head up to take in the stars.

There was something different about the stars out there. It wasn't like at home when you looked up to see a few stars dotted about, there was too much light pollution to see them in all their glorious majesty.

But out there ...

It was breathtaking.

The sky was literally filled to the brim with twinkling little lights. They looked so bright and happy, and they immediately put her at ease.

As much as she adored watching sunrises and sunsets on the water, there was something equally as magical about the night sky.

Feeling like the whole world was finally smiling down on her for once, she was halfway to the cockpit when the boat suddenly gave a violent shudder.

It was so strong, in fact, that it knocked her down to her knees.

What the heck was that?

Scrambling back to her feet, Alannah hurried over to the edge of the boat to look out across the ocean, wondering if it had perhaps been a freak wave.

It hadn't felt like one, though.

And when she looked over the sea, she saw it was almost completely calm.

If it hadn't been a wave knocking the yacht about then what was it? It had felt like it was the boat itself shuddering, independently of the water in which it sat.

But what would make the boat shake like that?

She was almost wondering if she'd imagined the whole thing, that seemed a more logical conclusion than anything else her imagination could conjure up, when the boat suddenly shook again, this time almost sending her flying over the railing and into the water.

Something was wrong.

She had no idea what, but it didn't take a genius to figure out that the boat had a problem. One she wasn't sure she would know how to fix. Just because she knew how to drive her boat didn't mean that she knew anything about the mechanics of how it worked.

Still, she had to do something.

As she was running toward the cockpit, she heard Jake shout her name.

"Over here," she called back as she began checking over the controls.

"What the hell was that?" Jake asked as he ran up behind her.

"No idea."

"Are you okay? Did it wake you?"

"I was already out here. Woke up, couldn't go back to sleep, and thought I'd come and look at the stars. It knocked me to my knees as I got to the deck. Are you okay?" Alannah paused to give him a quick once-over. He looked all right. Actually, he looked more than all right. With his hair sleep mussed and wearing nothing but a pair of sweatpants hanging low on his hips, he looked delicious. Like a tasty treat she wanted to devour.

*Focus, Alannah.*

"Fine. We need to figure that out, though."

"We should put on life vests," she added, already moving to grab them from the small cupboard beneath the controls. Since both she and Jake could swim, and they were planning to be out on the ocean for a while, it wasn't like they were going to wear a life vest permanently. But with the boat acting up it was better to be prepared for the worst rather than get caught out.

Right as she was reaching for the bright yellow vests, she noticed it.

A slip of paper eerily reminiscent of the one she'd found in the glove compartment of her car right before a burning vehicle came barreling toward them.

"J-Jake," she stammered, unable to reach out and pick it up.

She hadn't put it there.

That she was certain of.

Why would she write herself a note and hide it with the life vests that she'd never used?

"What?"

"L-look?"

Following her trembling hand, she knew the second he saw what she was pointing at because his entire body stiffened.

"I think ..." Alannah trailed off unable to say it out loud.

Because saying it out loud was acknowledging it.

And acknowledging it was admitting that someone else had been on her boat without her permission.

Not just someone but the people who were out to hurt her to try to convince Jake to back off and stop looking into what happened to his dad and stepmom.

If she accepted all of that, she also had to accept that whatever was wrong with the boat wasn't an accident, and it wasn't a malfunction.

Someone had guessed she might come to the boat so they'd sabotaged it.

Jake picked up the piece of paper, opened it, and read it. If it was possible his body went even stiffer at whatever it was that he read.

Even though she didn't want to know, Alannah couldn't seem to stop herself from asking, "Wh-what does it say?"

"Nothing," he muttered, shoving the paper into his pocket.

That lie was as obvious as the fact that they were out on the ocean on a boat that was no longer safe.

As if to prove her point, the boat suddenly shuddered again sending her flying sideways. Jake's hands snapped around her biceps before she could hit the deck, dragging her up against his bigger, stronger body.

"What does it say, Jake?" she asked again. It was bad, she knew that already, but she had to know how bad. Had to know if the boat was about to catch fire. They were surrounded by water, so they could avoid the fire, but it would only end with them trapped in the water because there was no land nearby.

Could they make it back to the marina?

Or the closest island?

"It says your friend should have listened, now you have to pay the price." Jake growled, and she knew he wasn't angry with her, just the situation, and maybe himself as well.

"P-pay the price?" she repeated, voice wobbling. "That means they knew I'd come here, they wanted me to find the note, to know that I was going to die because of you." Digging her fingers into his forearms as she clung to him, she couldn't stop a couple of tears from tumbling free as reality sank in. "That means we're both going to die."

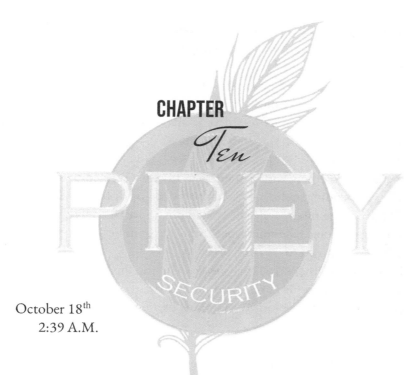

# CHAPTER

*Ten*

October 18th
2:39 A.M.

"We are not going to die," Jake growled into the night.

That was almost definitely a lie. If the boat had been sabotaged and they couldn't make it to land then the chances of them surviving were slim, but Alannah was in his arms, trembling and crying, and he had to do something to calm her down.

He should have had the boat checked out more thoroughly. When they arrived, he'd done a quick sweep and not come up with anything. Since he hadn't really expected the men to have done a deep enough dive into Alannah's life that they would know about the boat, let alone that they would think she might go to it, he hadn't thought he needed to do anything other than a cursory sweep.

Stupid.

It was his job to think up every possible scenario and play them all through.

Because of his mistakes, Alannah really was going to wind up paying the ultimate price.

From the note, it seemed they thought that Alannah would wind up on the boat alone and not with him, because unlike the last note that they'd left in her car, this one was speaking to her and not to him.

But he *was* there.

Which meant maybe they still stood a chance.

At least he hoped they did.

"Alannah, listen to me." Hardening his voice, pretending that it wasn't his best friend shivering in fear in his arms, he spoke to her like he would anyone else.

The lack of softness and gentleness in his tone seemed to snap her out of her impending meltdown, and she looked up at him. Even in the thin light from the moon and stars spread out above them like a canopy of twinkling diamonds, he could see the raw terror in her eyes.

This was supposed to be a safe place.

She'd gone out there thinking she was eliminating herself as bait to control him and thus his family, and instead she found she was still in the same position she'd been in the previous morning before they set sail.

A worse position in fact.

Because on the ocean they didn't have many options.

"I need you to hold it together," he said, keeping his tone brisk when all he wanted to do was hold her tight and apologize to her, begging for forgiveness for getting her into this mess.

It was too late to wish he'd maintained his distance, that he hadn't given in to the urge to spend a little time with the best friend who kept him grounded. What was done was done. There was no going back and redoing it, all he could do was deal with the problems set out before him.

"I want you to go and put on warmer clothes, then your life jacket. I'm going to see if I can take a look and figure out what exactly they did to the boat."

Giving a jerky nod, she went to move out of his arms then hesitated. "I'm scared, grumpy."

"Me too, sunshine." Admitting his fear wasn't something he would normally do. Not even with his brothers. He'd been scared in his career in Delta Force and in his career with Prey as part of Charlie

Team. He'd also been scared of losing his brothers while each one of them fought for their lives and the women who had claimed their hearts.

But this level of fear was something else.

It was akin to what he'd felt when they were trapped in the basement of Alannah's gym, and again when he thought he'd lost her in the fire at the park.

This fear was about losing Alannah not losing his own life.

Without her he ...

Couldn't even allow himself to go down that path for fear he might not be able to come back.

Another nod and she was off, hurrying back below deck. If they had to jump, dressed in nothing but the tiny sleep shorts and tank top she was wearing, she wasn't going to last long in the cold water. Too bad they didn't have proper wetsuits on board, those would help keep them warm in the water and not impede their ability to swim.

With no time to worry about that right now, Jake turned his attention to the boat. If he could find out what they'd done then maybe there was a way to fix it or at least minimize damage.

First things first.

What he should have done before allowing Alannah's panic and his own to take hold was get out a distress signal. He could use the radio to let the coast guard know they needed help, then he'd use the satellite phone to call his brothers.

As he was reaching for the radio, the yacht gave another violent shudder.

Whatever was wrong was getting worse. This time the shudder was enough to send him to his knees, his hip crashing painfully into the side of the controls as he went down.

The pain registered only briefly as he snatched up the radio and shoved back to his feet.

Silence met him as he flicked the switch.

Nothing to indicate it was working.

Damn.

Had whatever these people done to the boat taken out the radio system so they wouldn't be able to call for help?

"Jake?" Alannah's scared voice called out to him as her head appeared at the top of the stairs. "Are you okay?"

"Fine. You?"

"Yeah, okay." There was a slight wobble to her voice, and he wasn't sure if it was because she was just afraid or if she'd hurt herself when the boat shuddered. There was no time to grill her about it.

"Radio is out."

"Then we can't ... can't call for help." She appeared before him, dressed in a pair of leggings that would be easy for her to swim in if they had to bail, and a long-sleeved T-shirt that was also not bulky so wouldn't impede her ability to swim. She'd put her hair in a ponytail and slipped her feet into a pair of sneakers. Those would weigh her feet down, but if need be, she could always kick them off if they had to abandon the boat.

"We still have the satellite phone. Can you go grab it while I see what I can do here."

"Here." She shoved one of his long-sleeved T-shirts at him, then hurried back down below deck while he leaned over to assess the controls and see what he could do to keep them afloat and safe until they could get help.

Nothing.

As he looked at the control, he realized that was the answer.

There was nothing he could do to fix this.

Not a single thing.

Because the control panel was dead.

Whatever they'd done to sabotage the boat had taken out all power to the controls.

There was no way to fix that, especially since the boat seemed to be experiencing some kind of problem.

"Yes, he's right here, I'll hand you over," Alannah was saying into the satellite phone as she came back up onto the deck.

Thank goodness.

At least they had alerted his brothers that something was going on.

A tiny flicker of light caught his attention right at the back of the controls almost hidden where the panel met the floor.

"One sec," he told Alannah when she held the phone out to him and crouched down.

That's when he saw it.

Tucked away out of sight unless you were looking directly for it. The only reason he could see it now was because it was night and dark out, meaning the tiny little light was just visible.

The little light was attached to a bomb that was promptly ticking down the seconds until their demise. Whatever the saboteur had done to mess with the yacht's computer system was obviously set to have a delayed response so they would be out alone in the middle of the ocean with no way to stop whatever was going to happen.

Sensing his fear, Alannah leaned over to see what he was looking at. "What's wrong? Did you find something. Yeah, I think he found something," she said into the phone.

Another violent shudder sent him crashing sideways.

Alannah screamed as she was also thrown about.

"Jake, the phone!" she yelled as she must have lost her grip on it.

That was the least of their concerns.

"Forget the phone." Pushing back onto his feet, he reached over and grabbed her hand. She still had the life jackets in her arms, and he took one and quickly put it on her. Then he took the other and slipped it on.

"You're scaring me, grumpy."

"We have to go," he told her. As soon as they were both in the life jackets, he towed her down to the far end of the boat.

"Go? We can't go. We're in the middle of the ocean." Alannah pulled back against his hold on her, but he tightened his grip.

"There's a bomb, Alannah. The entire computer system is down, and we have about sixty seconds to get as far away from this yacht as we can if we don't want to die."

"A b-bomb?"

"If you hadn't woken up and come out here when you did, we wouldn't have known."

The shuddering would have woken them both, but the fact that she was already up and about had saved them the seconds they needed. Those sixty seconds would otherwise have been him going into her room to check on her.

It gave them a chance, but that was all.

No guarantee.

"Jump, Alannah," he ordered.

When she gave a shaky nod, her eyes full of fear but also trust, together they leaped off the boat and into the freezing water.

~

October 18$^{th}$

2:47 A.M.

No sooner was she encased in freezing water than the deafening sound of an explosion rocked through the otherwise quiet night.

Even though Jake had been holding her hand when they jumped off the boat—luckily since she wasn't sure she would have had the guts to do it alone—when the boat blew up, it tore her out of his grasp.

Alannah had been out on the ocean in rough seas before, knew how dangerous the water could be, how deadly, and she respected it as such.

But this was nothing like anything she'd experienced.

It was like in the Disney movie Moana, where the water was alive and it picked up things and people and moved them, putting them where it wanted them. That was exactly what this felt like. The water grabbed hold of her and threw her about, tossing her around like she was nothing.

With the dark of night and the ocean all around her, it was hard to figure out which way was up.

The water wasn't the only danger as she kicked and used her arms to try to find a way out and back to the surface, burning bits of debris from the boat were everywhere. They plowed through the water, and something slammed into her, knocking her about more and causing her to become even more disoriented.

Which way *was* up?

If she swam too far in the wrong direction, she'd get lost and drown in the depths of the ocean.

Unprepared as she'd been for the explosion to come when they were still so close to the boat, Alannah hadn't taken a deep breath of air before she was shoved down deep below the surface, and already her lungs were screaming at her for air.

For oxygen.

For life.

Only she didn't have any to give them.

Desperately she swam, trying to find something to guide her. Then she saw it. Fire. It had to be whatever was left of the boat that hadn't been torn to shreds and littered throughout the ocean.

That was where the surface had to be.

Focusing all her energy on swimming toward the fire, which in some ways seemed counterproductive considering someone was trying to kill her with fire, Alannah gave it everything she had.

If she couldn't get up there in time ...

Then whoever this final man was involved in the plot to cover up their crimes would get what he wanted.

She'd be dead.

Jake could be, too.

An arrow of pain shot straight through her heart at the thought of the explosion killing Jake. What would she do without him? Not just right now, alone out there in the middle of the ocean, at night, with no boat and nothing solid to hold onto, but for the rest of her life. She needed Jake. Needed his steady, protective, no nonsense, tell it like it is presence in her life.

*Needed* him.

Not a want, definitely a need.

With lungs feeling like they were about to burst, right when Alannah thought she wasn't going to be able to hold her breath for a second longer and would be forced to take in a lungful of sea water, her head breached the surface.

Fresh air finally available, she dragged in a deep breath, then another and another, until her brain began to process the fact that it was no longer starving for oxygen.

She'd come up about ten yards or so away from the remainder of the yacht. Close enough that she could still feel the heat, but not close enough that she was in danger. Smaller pieces of debris floated around, but as she treaded water, she scanned the ocean searching for something else.

Someone else.

For Jake.

Had he been injured in the explosion? Was she already too late? It didn't take long to drown, especially if you'd been knocked unconscious and could do nothing to save yourself.

Tears burned her eyes, and a sob worked its way up through her chest. When it left her lips, she was struck by what a pitiful, painful, soul-crushing sound it was.

But that's what it felt like not knowing if Jake was dead or alive.

It felt like someone had grabbed hold of her soul and was trying to physically rip it out of her body.

"Alannah?"

Lost to her terror as she was, it took her a second to realize that the sound wasn't the ocean, wasn't the crackling fire, and hadn't come from herself.

Someone had called her name.

Relief hit her so hard it stole her breath and almost her ability to keep her head above the water.

As it closed around her again, she quickly snapped to her senses. "Jake!"

There was a beat of silence. "Alannah?"

"I'm here. Over here." She waved her arms about even though she knew the chances of him spotting her had to be slim. It was dark, and the fire seemed to dominate the landscape, making it hard to see anything else.

"Call out again, sunshine. I'll find you."

"Here, I'm here." As she yelled, she continued to wave her arms around thinking it couldn't hurt even if it didn't help much.

Then finally she saw him.

Jake.

Her fierce, grumpy protector.

Swimming with smooth, determined strokes through the water heading right toward her.

The relief of seeing him, knowing he'd survived, that he hadn't left her, almost sapped the last of her energy. She'd already been running low given the trauma of the last week, but the explosion, believing they were going to die, and then the fear of losing Jake had stolen most of what she had left.

Not a good thing.

They might both be alive, but they weren't out of danger.

To survive, she was going to need every drop of stamina she had left.

"You're alive," she said on a sob when he stopped beside her. Not content to allow her eyes to be the only thing to convince her, she reached out and grabbed hold of him, running her hands all over his face and shoulders, needing to feel him beneath her fingertips to believe she hadn't lost him.

"I'm alive. Damn, Alannah, I thought … I couldn't find you and you weren't answering."

The fear in his tone echoed what she felt inside and she curled her fingers into his life jacket, clinging to him, unwilling to let anything separate them.

"I went under," she explained.

"You went under? Your life jacket should have kept you afloat."

That was something that hadn't even occurred to her, although he was right. Even tossed about as she was when the boat exploded, she shouldn't have been knocked down so deep into the ocean.

"Something hit me, maybe …" Running her hands over the life jacket, she found it had been torn to shreds, no longer anything that was going to be useful in keeping her alive. "It's ruined, Jake. All torn up."

Jake muttered a curse. His hands grabbed her life jacket, removing the useless material from her body, then he was taking off his own life jacket and trying to put it on her.

No.

She couldn't let him do that.

"You need it," she protested, attempting to stop him.

"You need it," he shot back.

"It's yours, keep it."

"No way in hell am I wearing this while you have nothing."

That was a tone she recognized all too well. It was Jake's don't bother arguing with me, I've already made up my mind and it won't be changed, voice.

Allowing him to slip on the life jacket, as soon as it was snapped into place, Alannah realized how much it helped keep her afloat. It wasn't necessarily going to save her life, but it took some of the pressure off, allowing her to keep a little of her energy rather than expending it all on just trying to keep her head above water.

But now Jake didn't have anything to help him.

He was big and strong and highly trained, but he was still human.

"We take it in turns to wear it," she said, making her tone imitate the one Jake had just used. As far as she was concerned, that wasn't up for debate.

"We'll see," Jake said, and she knew he wouldn't make it easy for her. But they were a team, and they were in this together. They needed to work as one if they wanted to try to make it out of this ocean alive.

A distracted note to his voice set her on edge, and she noticed that he wasn't looking at her. Instead, his gaze was focused on the sky above them.

With dread pooling in her stomach, Alannah tipped her head back to follow his gaze.

Immediately, she saw what had captured his attention and what had tension rolling off him in waves she could feel.

The sky was no longer a clear black canvas dotted with millions of twinkling stars.

Now it was a mass of dark black clouds.

Storm clouds.

Because life couldn't give them a break. Not even a teeny, tiny, little one.

Trapped in the ocean, with nothing to keep them secure, and only one life jacket between them, there was no way they could survive the raw power of a storm.

"A storm," she said, surprised when her voice came out even, not betraying the raging terror inside her. Already feeling the change in the air, the storm would be there any moment. "We're going to die, and I'm never going to get to experience an orgasm and what all the fuss is about."

# CHAPTER
## *Eleven*

October 18<sup>th</sup>
  2:53 A.M.

Alannah's totally unexpected words shocked him out of his fear for a moment.

Turning his attention from the sky to the woman beside him, Jake found she was still staring at the gathering clouds above.

Had he really heard her say what he thought he heard her say?

Surely, he must have misheard.

*Surely*.

Because there was no way what she'd said could possibly be true. While he'd never particularly liked thinking about it, even less in this moment, Alannah was a woman in her early thirties who'd had a few serious relationships.

Serious relationships meant sex, so no way could she really never have had an orgasm.

Unless ...

They might be best friends, but they didn't discuss their sex lives with one another. Was it possible that Alannah was a virgin and he'd just never realized it?

"What the hell, Alannah?"

Tilting her head back down so she was looking at him, she blinked her eyes slowly as though only just realizing what she'd blurted out in her fear.

"Umm ..." she dragged the word out and didn't add anything to it.

"Are you a virgin?" Jake was totally aware that not only was his question completely inappropriate, but now was not the time to be having this conversation. A storm was coming, the wind was picking up, the waves getting bigger, they had to get moving while they still could, and yet ...

He couldn't seem to let it go.

"Jake ..." There was a clear warning in her tone. She wanted him to drop it, and he should, he just couldn't.

"Are you?" he barked, not quite sure why it mattered so much.

"No," she muttered, averting her gaze by turning her head away from him.

Nuh-uh.

No way was she hiding from him.

He was her best friend, he was supposed to be the one person she could confide in without fear of judgment.

Something he'd obviously failed at conveying.

Just because he could be gruff, didn't engage in conversation that he didn't personally deem necessary, could come across as being aloof and uncaring, didn't mean that any of those things applied to Alannah. He thought she knew that, but maybe she didn't.

"If you're not a virgin, then what did you mean?"

The wind continued to pick up, and with the way it whipped up the waves, sending them crashing across the surface of the ocean, it was getting harder to hear.

Although he suspected why he didn't catch Alannah's response was more because she muttered it under her breath than because the weather was making it too difficult to hear her words.

"Look, can we just forget I blurted that out in a panic?"

Despite the pleading note to her voice, he shook his head. "No."

"But, Jake—"

"I said no, Alannah. Now tell me. How is it possible that a woman as drop-dead gorgeous as you, who has been in several serious relationships, who isn't a virgin, is worried about dying without ever having an orgasm and not getting what the fuss is about? Tell me. I want to understand," he added, gentling his voice on those last words.

"It's embarrassing, okay?"

"Sunshine, this is me. Your best friend. There isn't anything you can't tell me."

When she scoffed, he realized how stupid those words sounded when he said them aloud. While he absolutely one hundred percent meant them, he'd never encouraged Alannah to treat him as her safe place, even as he vowed to be her protector. Since he was a guy and she was a girl, he'd always assumed she took her talking needs to her other girl friends.

Now as he managed to catch how miserable she looked even in the darkness, he realized that had been a mistake.

Being betrayed by her own family in such a horrible way meant she had trust issues. He knew that, understood it. But since she had lots of friends and was always in some relationship or another, he usually worried more about her getting taken advantage of than her emotional needs.

Mistake.

Big one if the way she inched away from him, putting what distance she could between them was any indication.

"Talk to me, please?"

"I've just never orgasmed, okay? It's no big deal, I shouldn't have said it. I don't even know why I did, it just came out. We have bigger problems than the fact that there's something wrong with me and I'm terrible at sex."

A growl rumbled through his chest before he even realized it. "If you didn't come during sex, that's your partner's fault, not yours."

The small smile she gifted him was full of pain and not her usual sunshine. "I'd believe that, but I can't come on my own either. Trust me,

I've spent a small fortune on enough toys to know that it's not the toys, and it's not my partners' fault, it's all mine. I guess I'm just defective." She gave a humorless laugh that broke his heart, and he was filled with a determination to fix this for her somehow.

"I doubt you're defective. You just have to learn your body, what it likes and what makes it hum with desire and need."

"Hum with desire and need?" Alannah gave another laugh, this one a little more genuine. "Who are you and what did you do with my grumpy best friend?"

Just because he wasn't even close to being the most demonstrative guy around, he always made sure to attend to the needs of any lover he had. Long term relationships had never been his thing, but if he was going to sleep with a woman, he was damn sure going to ensure it was good for her, that she didn't walk away thinking something was wrong with her like Alannah's partners had done to her.

Before he could say anything more, there was a huge crash of thunder, and like someone had turned on the faucet, rain suddenly pounded down around them.

Following the roar of thunder, a crack of lightning lit up the night sky.

This was not good at all.

If a spark of lightning hit the water close to them, they'd be dead.

Electrocuted.

As if they needed another problem right now.

The temperature was dropping, they weren't dressed to be out in the water, and they had only one working life jacket. Between the wind, the rain, and the growing waves, swimming was going to be difficult, and keeping close to each other next to impossible.

Losing Alannah to the ocean was not an option.

But how was he going to ensure they didn't float away from one another?

He had no rope, nothing to tie them together, they could hold onto each other, but they weren't going to be any match for the storm, and the ocean could quite easily rip them apart.

They'd been tossed around too many times after they jumped and got caught in the explosion, then he'd been too focused on finding

Alannah rather than trying to keep a direction in his head. There were no prompts in the sky since the stars were covered by thick clouds, so he had no idea which way to swim to get them to the closest piece of land.

Failure wasn't an option.

Not when he had Alannah with him.

Twenty-eight years ago, he'd made her a promise, he'd vowed to protect her, and while it was quite obvious he'd failed several times over the years, this couldn't be one of those times. Now her life was at stake, he was responsible for her, he'd agreed with the yacht plan rather than going with the rest of his family to Delta Team, and he was the one who hadn't done a detailed enough sweep of the boat.

Alannah was in danger because of him.

So he had to fix this.

He had to figure out a plan.

"I'm scared, Jake," Alannah's voice somehow managed to rise above the storm raging around him, even though he knew she hadn't spoken particularly loudly, certainly hadn't been screaming to be heard.

But he heard her.

Saw her.

Knew her.

Better than anyone else did.

Wrapping an arm around her, he pulled her close, needing one moment to just hold her, flood his senses with her feel and her smell, then he could compartmentalize and do what he had to do to get them out of there alive.

"I'm scared too, sunshine," he admitted, allowing himself one second of weakness and vulnerability. "But I promise you this, Alannah. I will get you through this, I swear it."

There was sadness in her eyes that he caught only because of a well-timed flash of lightning. "Us, grumpy. We have to get both of us through this."

That was the plan, but in the end, if only one of them could survive it wasn't going to be him. It was going to be his sunshine.

～

October 18<sup>th</sup>
   5:50 A.M.


Swim.
   Swim.
   Swim.
   Don't stop.
   Don't give up.
   Swim.
   Swim.
   Swim.
   Don't stop.
   Don't give up.
   The words played on a constant loop in Alannah's mind.

Alannah had zero idea how long it had been since she and Jake found the bomb and jumped off her yacht, but she knew it felt like a lifetime. It could have been minutes that had passed, it could have been hours.

Time had no meaning when it was dark, the rain pounded down around you, the waves did their very best to grab you and shove you under, and your entire body was working against you.

Exhausted didn't even begin to describe how she felt. She'd thought she knew what it felt like to have no energy, that's how she'd felt in those days following the first fire. Empty, drained, barely able to function.

But this was different.

This was all-consuming.

This was barely functioning.

This was wondering how you were could possibly keep going.

It shouldn't be possible. Her limbs felt like lead, she was so cold she shook uncontrollably as she swam, and pain painted her entire being.

Whether or not she had any actual injuries, Alannah wasn't really sure, but she knew she hurt, knew she couldn't keep going like this indefinitely.

Then again, what choice did she have?

It was keep swimming or die.

Which was why the mantra continued in a loop.

Swim.

Swim.

Swim.

Don't stop.

Don't give up.

Swim.

Swim.

Swim.

Don't stop.

Don't give up.

She didn't want to give up, didn't want to die out there, didn't want to leave Jake all alone to face the horrors of being lost at sea in a storm.

But it was getting harder and harder to force herself to move.

It felt impossible.

How could her body feel so heavy? Her feet were barely kicking anymore, and her arms weren't really doing much of anything to propel her through the cold, rough water. It was likely only Jake's hold on her that kept her moving forward.

If he let go ...

She couldn't help but feel like she would just float away and disappear.

There had been a lot of times as a kid that she wished she could just stop existing. Not in a she wanted to end her own life kind of way, just in a she didn't matter to anyone way, and she was tired of trying to earn love and affection that would never be given.

Jake had kept her alive back then.

And Jake was keeping her alive now.

His steady presence was the only thing that kept her going.

Everything else had receded into a haze. There was no fear anymore, she didn't have the energy for it. There wasn't sadness for what felt like her impending death. There was nothing. Just the knowledge that she had to keep moving.

A huge wave crashed into her, and for a second, she went under.

No match for the fierce ocean, she struggled and spluttered, tried not to inhale the salty water that was a threat in more ways than one. It wasn't just that the sea could drown her and Jake if it so chose, but if they drank too much of the salty water, it would poison their bodies.

Jake's hand kept her from being swept away.

Until it didn't.

The second his hold on her slipped as the waves tossed him about as well, she was gone.

Dragged away into the darkness.

Serious about her intention to share the life jacket, Jake was the one wearing it. Now without his steadying hold keeping her afloat, she started sinking quickly.

Even though she didn't want to die, didn't want to give up and let the ocean claim her, Alannah didn't have enough left in her to fight against the inevitable.

Bit by bit, the water dragged her down.

It was actually warmer down under the surface away from the pounding rain and relentless wind. A little gentler as well since there were no waves crashing on her.

The warmth made her sleepy.

It couldn't hurt to close her eyes just for a moment, could it?

That would be so nice.

So peaceful.

Just one moment of rest.

Then she'd start swimming again.

She deserved it after hours of fighting her way through the impenetrable sea.

Her eyes fluttered closed.

One second just to …

The sting of rain hitting her skin had her jerking upright, and she found herself back above the surface, Jake's hand clutching her sodden long-sleeve T-shirt. Fisted in the material with a tightness she felt even though he was holding the clothes and not her body.

When she blinked and looked at him, she could see raw fear on his face.

Had she done that?

She hadn't wanted to scare him, she'd just needed one second to rest.

"S-sor-ry," she stammered, her teeth chattering wildly. Now that she had her head above the water again, any warmth she'd felt had evaporated and she was back to freezing cold, her entire body shaking with the force of it. At least it was shivering, her body hadn't completely given in to hypothermia yet, but it would.

That was inevitable.

As inevitable as both their deaths if they didn't find land soon.

Jake couldn't be any warmer than she was, and he had to be every bit as exhausted. He was highly trained, and she knew he worked out every day, brutal workouts, totally incomparable to what she did at the gym. But sooner or later he would wear out too.

"Thought I lost you when the waves ripped you out of my hand," Jake said. His voice was still strong above the roar of the storm.

Or ...

Maybe the storm was dying down.

The wind wasn't whipping into her as strongly as it had been before she went under, and the rain was easing off, more drizzling now than pounding down like a million little stones against her unprotected body. There was a faint light to the sky rather than the oppressive darkness, and the waves weren't quite as strong.

Was it possible that the worst of the storm had passed them by?

"Here, you need this more than I do. I'm not taking another turn, so don't bother asking because I won't humor you again," Jake snapped as he shrugged out of the life jacket and slipped it over her arms, doing up the straps to secure it to her chest.

While his tone was harsh, she knew it wasn't because he was angry with her, it was just because he was afraid. The storm might be dying down, but they were still exhausted and cold. They had to find land soon or it was going to be too late.

"I think we're finally through the worst of it," Jake said, echoing her thoughts.

What he didn't say also echoed everything she'd just been thinking. This was a reprieve, it wasn't a solution.

"Sorry, sunshine, but we're going to have to keep moving. I know you're exhausted, but the longer we stay still, the more we give hypothermia a chance to settle in."

Even though swimming was the last thing she wanted to do,

Alannah knew that staying still was just signing her death warrant. Jake's too. Because there was no way he was going to leave her alone. If she was too exhausted to move, he'd stay right by her side even if it cost him his life. Or he'd pull her along with him and deplete his own supplies of energy in the process.

Above them, the sky continued to lighten, and as she went to tell Jake that she could keep swimming for as long as she needed to, even if that was pretty much a lie, she saw it.

The impossible.

It had to be a mirage.

Yet the longer she looked, the more it formed rather than shimmering away into nothing.

"Jake, look," she said, pointing behind him.

She knew the second he registered what she had seen because some of the tension left his body. If Jake saw it too, it had to be real.

"That's ... land. Right?" she asked, just in case this was in fact some sort of shared hallucination, the cold and exhaustion finally getting to them.

"It's land, sunshine," Jake confirmed, excitement in his voice.

It was still a distance away, and honestly, she wasn't sure she had the energy to make it, but the fading storm and the hope that ignited inside her rejuvenated her.

They could do this.

They had to do this.

With Jake keeping a hold on her like he had the entire time they'd been out there they both began to swim again.

It didn't take long for the rush of energy hope had given her to fade, and she was right back to struggling.

But she wasn't giving up.

Wasn't going to die within sight of land.

So she swam.

They swam.

Side by side.

Bit by bit the land grew bigger and bigger.

Closer and closer.

Then right as they approached the last hundred or so yards, she saw them.

Rocks.

Lots and lots of rocks lining the shore.

How on earth were they supposed to get past them without being broken into pieces?

Safety was so close and yet so far away.

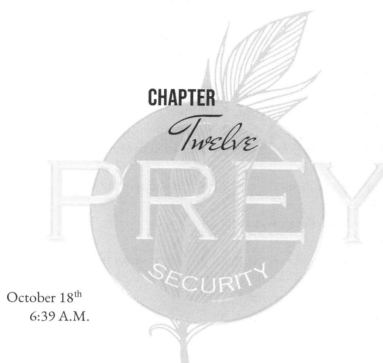

# CHAPTER
*Twelve*

October 18th
    6:39 A.M.

Safety.

*If* they could get past the rocks.

Something Jake wasn't altogether sure that they could.

They were going to try, though.

He'd rather try and die in the process than just float around in the water waiting for the inevitable.

The truth was, Alannah wasn't going to last much longer. She was too cold, too exhausted, and he was worried that she had injuries he wasn't aware of. Already he'd almost lost her once when the wave tore her right out of his grasp. She'd been a mere handful of yards away when he'd watched her go under.

And not come back up.

Luckily, he'd found her, but it had solidified in his mind how quickly he was running out of time. The sense of impotence was crushing him. He was Alannah's protector, he should be doing something, anything, to get her someplace safe, and he was failing.

Thanks to the easing of the storm, they'd been able to spot land, and now it was less than one hundred yards away.

Once they reached it, they would hopefully find people, shelter, a hospital, food and water, dry clothes, and warm blankets.

Sounded like heaven.

"J-Jake, I d-don't th-think I c-can m-make it," Alannah said, her teeth chattering so badly he could hardly make out her words.

"You can." He ensured the words came out strong and sure. Alannah was floundering, and she needed to know he had things under control.

If that was a lie, he didn't care so long as she believed it.

No failure here.

Getting Alannah safe was all he cared about.

"I'll t-try."

"You'll do it," he corrected, anything less was unacceptable.

"M-Maybe you sh-should g-go a-alone. I d-don't w-want you to g-get h-hurt be-because of m-me."

"Absolutely not."

"Y-You c-could come b-back for m-me."

"No. I said no, Alannah," he added when she opened her mouth to argue some more. There was no way he was leaving her alone in the ocean while he got himself past the rocks. There was not a doubt in his mind that when he found help and came back for her, he wouldn't find her.

She was teetering on the edge, and he was pretty sure it was only his presence and her fear of anything happening to him because of her that was keeping her going.

"Come on, we'll do this together."

Maintaining his hold on her because he knew she didn't have the energy to swim on her own and he didn't want to lose her to the ocean, Jake swam them both closer to the shore.

Ironically, it was only because the storm had died down that he thought they stood a good chance of getting past the rocks. If they'd stumbled upon the shore at the peak of the storm, he was pretty sure that any attempts at getting to the sand on the other side would have resulted in nothing other than their bodies being dashed to pieces as the harsh waves rammed them into the unforgiving rock.

Timing was everything.

As he swam closer, he catalogued every rock formation, every small gap around them.

Then he spotted it.

A little to their right, the rocks ended, opening into a little cove, maybe fifty feet wide, before the rocks began again as they circled the rest of the sand within sight.

That was where they'd aim.

Too weak now to do much but give a few feeble kicks, Alannah allowed him to pull her along with him, and her acquiescence was beginning to scare him. Of course, he was glad she wasn't fighting him, but the fact that she had so little energy left to swim told him that he wasn't just running out of time, he was basically out of it.

Thankfully, the sky was lightening, and with the storm dying down and thus the waves no longer as fierce as they'd been earlier, he was able to steer them with relative ease toward where he wanted them to go.

Right as he was rounding the edges of the rocks, a wave slammed into him.

For one horrifying second, Jake was positive that he'd just killed them both.

One strike against the rocks would be all it took to break at least a couple of their bones. Weak as she was, Alannah wouldn't be able to survive, and even though he was doing a lot better than she was, he was running dangerously low on energy as well.

A hit could take them both out.

Permanently.

It had been a long time since he'd gone to the beach, but when he was a kid, he and Jax would spend most of their summer playing in the sand and swimming in the ocean. They'd both gotten pretty good at body surfing. Learning how to read the waves and where to place themselves in their path so they could ride them all the way to the shore.

That was exactly what he did now.

Pivoting so that the wave worked for him rather than against him, he managed to get them both planted right in the perfect position.

As the wave surged again, it took them around the rocks and rushed them right toward the safety of the sandy beach before them.

The next thing Jake knew, he could feel the sand beneath his body.

Relief hit him so hard it almost stole all the air from his lungs.

They'd done it.

They were on the shore.

They were safe.

Knowing that they might have hit land but still weren't completely out of danger, Jake quickly scooped Alannah into his arms and ran with her out of the water.

Lining the sand, which stretched about fifteen yards or so from the water's edge, were trees. Lots of trees. He didn't see any sort of road that indicated a quick and simple way off the beach, and he didn't want to search for one until he made sure Alannah wasn't going to go and die on him.

When he laid her down on the sand right at the beginning of the trees, which stretched out as deep as he could see, Alannah stirred.

Her hands reached up to grip his soaked long-sleeved T-shirt. "G-grumpy, am I h-hallucinating, or are w-we out o-of th-the w-water?"

"Not hallucinating, sunshine," he assured her.

One of those bright, beautiful smiles that he loved lit up her face. "We m-made it. Y-you m-made it," she corrected. "You s-saved m-my l-life. A-again. Th-thank you."

"Did you just thank me for saving you like there was any doubt I would?" he groused as he scanned the area looking for some sticks.

Since her clothes were sodden, keeping them on wouldn't allow Alannah to raise her body temperature. Given the chill in the air, taking them off likely wasn't going to help much either.

At least without a fire.

They literally had nothing on them but the clothes on their backs, but luckily, he knew how to make a fire with nothing but what nature provided.

It took him no more than a couple of minutes to clear a suitable space, pile up a few small twigs and sticks that were in their immediate vicinity, and put together a little fire. It wasn't much, but it would help to keep Alannah warm enough as he took off her clothes and checked her for injuries.

"Can you undress on your own or do you need help?" he asked as he knelt beside her. She was still where he'd set her down, not having the energy to do anything right now.

"Umm." She chewed on her bottom lip for a moment. "I th-think I n-need h-help."

Undressing his best friend had not been on his mind when they got onto that boat. Then again, none of this was something he could have predicted. If he had, they never would have gotten on the boat to begin with.

Trying to be as professional about it as he could, he removed the life jacket, then her leggings and long-sleeved T-shirt. For now, he'd leave on her bra and panties, they didn't have enough material to do too much to lower her body temperature, and she deserved some modesty.

"You hurt anywhere?" he asked as he skimmed his hands over her body in search of any injuries from the explosion.

Before she could answer, she hissed as his fingers brushed over a nasty-looking bruise forming between her right hip and where her ribs ended. It was just high enough that he worried her ribs had been affected.

"I th-think I h-hit it in the b-boat. When it w-was sh-shuddering. B-below d-deck, when I w-was g-getting d-dressed."

Swallowing a curse, he continued his search. The life jacket she'd been wearing had been destroyed, so there had to be at least one other injury he hadn't found yet.

Helping her sit, he rested her against his chest and checked her back, where he found a deep laceration between her shoulder blades.

That had to be the wound from whatever ruined the life jacket.

There was nothing he could do for it right now without a first aid kit. The fire would help warm her up a little, but what they both needed was to find help. Alannah was too weak to move, so he'd leave her there, find help, then come back for her.

Easing her back so she was lying down again, partially propped up against the tree trunk, he palmed one of her cheeks. She immediately tilted her face into his hand, nuzzling against it.

"I'm going to go look for help," he told her. "I want you to stay here." When she opened her mouth to no doubt offer a protest, he touched a fingertip to her lips. "Don't argue, sunshine. You're in no condition to walk anywhere right now. You need to rest and warm up. I won't be long. And when I come back, I'll have help. So stay here, rest, and dream about how good a hot meal, dry clothes, and a warm bed are going to feel."

Even though he could tell she hated the idea of them splitting up, Alannah gave him a small nod. She knew she'd already reached and exceeded her capabilities. If she pushed herself any harder, she would wind up passing out.

"Be safe, grumpy," she whispered.

Leaning down, he rested his forehead against hers. "Always, sunshine."

Letting her go was hard.

Straightening to stand, almost impossible.

"Be back before you know it," he assured her, giving what he hoped was an encouraging smile.

She just nodded, and he could see unshed tears swimming in her golden-brown eyes.

Taking that first step almost killed him.

It was only the knowledge that Alannah was counting on him that kept him going, taking step after step, getting further and further away from her.

He had to do this.

Had to find help.

But what if there was no help to be found?

～

October 18th
    7:14 A.M.

Watching Jake walk away and not calling out to him to tell him to come back had to be one of the hardest things Alannah had ever done in her life.

Safe was with Jake.

Without him ...

It felt like anything could happen.

That was probably a silly way of looking at it since he'd been with her for three of the four fires, and on the boat with her when it exploded, but she'd survived those fires *because* of him.

Jake might have brought this danger to her, but he had also kept her alive at every step.

What would she do without him?

Not just in terms of her physical safety, because he brought so much more to her life than that.

Something ran much deeper. He brought with him a sense of psychological and emotional safety. One her parents had never provided for her. Jake thought he'd failed because her family continued to hurt her and there was nothing he could do to stop that from happening, but the reality was, she lived only because of him.

He was her grumpy, but he was also *her* sunshine as much as she was his.

Because he reminded her that not all people were like her parents. There were good and honorable people in the world, people who took on responsibilities that weren't theirs simply because they cared and they wanted to.

That was the only reason her parents' and sister's mistreatment hadn't destroyed her. It was why she was able to search for the love she'd been deprived of, and why she never gave up hope that one day she'd have a family of her very own who loved her more than words could explain.

What if ...

What if what she'd been searching for had been in front of her all along?

It was wrong to have these thoughts about her best friend only she couldn't seem to stop herself.

As Alannah lay there on the hard ground, curled up in a ball before the fire Jake had built, wearing nothing but her bra and panties, she wasn't even sure she wanted to stop herself from thinking those thoughts.

Surely, they were only wrong if Jake didn't feel the same way in return.

And there lay her biggest fear.

It wasn't that she doubted Jake loved her as a friend, that he cared about her deeply, and he would always see himself as her protector, all those things were true. But could he love her as more than a friend? Could he ever see himself as her partner and not just her self-appointed protector?

If he couldn't and she let slip that something had changed for her, she would lose him forever. Things would become weird and awkward, and then they'd just stop spending time around one another, and sooner or later, the friendship would disappear.

That wasn't something she could let happen.

So she had to keep those feelings to herself.

Had to.

Seconds ticked by into minutes.

Minutes ticked by into hours.

The sun rose, its light shining through the thick clouds that still covered the sky.

Still Jake didn't return.

How long would it take him to find help?

Surely he must have found someone by now. A house, a road, or some shops. The shoreline was beautiful, and there had to be at least some restaurants close by to take in the stunning views. Houses too. People loved to live on the coast. And more often than not, there were roads close as well.

So why didn't Jake come back with help?

Had something happened to him?

Fear for him clogged her mind, filling her with terror. Losing him would kill a part of her she was sure she would never be able to get back.

Maybe she should go and look for him.

While he'd checked her over for injuries, he hadn't taken the time to pause and take stock of his own body. Determination to get her some-where warm and out of the weather where they could eat and sleep had clouded his mind, and there was a very real possibility he had some sort of serious injury that adrenalin had been masking.

Or he could have slipped and fallen, hurt himself too badly to keep going.

If he needed her, she couldn't just lie there in a ball and do nothing. That's not what he would do if their positions were reversed.

Before he left, Jake had laid out her soaked clothes before the fire, and now she pushed wearily to her feet to retrieve them. They were still damp but a whole lot drier than they'd been before. The salt from the water and the sand and dirt from the ground they'd been laying on made them stiff and scratchy, and putting them back on wasn't pleasant.

But she did it.

If Jake needed her, there wasn't anything she wouldn't do.

The wound on her back from where the life jacket had been damaged in the explosion stung as her shirt brushed against it, and she had to leave her leggings resting low on her hips because the bruise on her side, which was continuing to darken to a horrible bluish black, hurt too much to have anything on it.

Somewhere along the way she must have lost her shoes, but that didn't matter. She was walking with or without them.

Adding a few more sticks to the fire to keep it going, she would need a reminder of their location in case she couldn't find Jake and had to try to come back. It would also help him to find the spot where they'd been in case he was okay, and it had just taken longer to find help than either of them had anticipated.

Then with a deep sense of trepidation, Alannah headed further down onto the sand and started walking.

Within the first minute, she heard someone call her name.

Hope and relief flooded her system.

He'd done it. Jake had found help.

Turning around, she saw him sprinting across the sand from behind her.

Alone.

If he was back, where was the help he'd found?

Then it hit her.

He was coming from behind her, the opposite direction from which he'd left. That meant he'd completed a circle. Surely ...

Surely that circle couldn't have been the entire island.

If she had to guess, she would have thought he'd been gone maybe two hours, if he really had circled the entire island, that would make it pretty small.

Maybe she was wrong.

Maybe he'd just gone along a bit, headed inland, and then circled back in the other direction before turning again to hit the spot where he'd left her waiting.

That idea was dashed when Jake reached her side.

"Where were you going?" he demanded, in the hard tone she knew was only used when he was afraid. Jake afraid was never a good thing.

"I was worried you were hurt and was going to go looking for you. Are you okay? Did you find help?" The question was stupid because if he had it would be here with him, but she couldn't let go of that last tiny sliver of hope just yet.

His gaze softened, but the fear hidden in his eyes was far too visible for her liking. "Alannah, I don't know ... I don't know how to say this, but ... there *is* no help here. We're alone on this island."

The words seemed to hover between them for a moment.

Sparing her their impact for a few more seconds.

But when it hit, it hit hard.

They'd fought their way through the ocean all for nothing. They had no food, no means to call for help, no means to get off the island other than to head back into the ocean, no shelter, and no warm clothes.

They had nothing.

That first sob caught her by surprise. She was no more ready for the second or the third. Nor was she prepared for Jake to snatch her into his arms and crush her against his chest, holding her tightly while she wept, every bit of fear and exhaustion seeping out of her in those tears.

Eventually, logic began to edge out the fear. Falling apart wasn't going to help them. In fact, it was going to hurt them because it gave poor Jake another problem he had to solve. They couldn't survive this if she made herself a hysterical burden Jake would have to carry.

Their only hope of surviving was if they worked together.

Somehow, Alannah managed to find the strength she hadn't known she possessed, one born of a deep-seated desire to live, and lifted her wet face to meet Jake's steady gaze. A gaze that gave her strength and confidence.

"We need to come up with a plan because we're not dying on this island." She said the words and meant them, somehow believing that together there was nothing they couldn't do.

Even survive this.

# CHAPTER

## Thirteen

October 18<sup>th</sup>
4:44 P.M.

"Wow," Alannah said, taking a step back to admire their handiwork. "This is a real upgrade from what you used to build in the woods when we were kids."

The smile she gave him was strained. Lines of exhaustion and worry bracketed her mouth, and there were dark smudges under her eyes, but she was holding it together and Jake was so very proud of her.

She'd done everything he'd asked of her today. No complaints, no asking for breaks, although he knew she needed them and made sure they stopped regularly to recharge. They were both hungry, thirsty, and exhausted, but they'd worked side by side for hours, and Alannah was right, at least they had something pretty good to show for it.

"Guess all those years in the military and with Prey taught me a thing or two."

"A thing or fifty," Alannah corrected. "When we used to play in the woods and you and Jax would build those little huts with branches, I used to think they were cute, but this is worthy of being in a magazine."

Her enthusiasm surprised a chuckle out of him. She was exaggerating, that was for sure, the little shelter he'd made for them was big enough for both of them to sit comfortably inside, as well as keep their new fire undercover.

Something they were going to need if the menacing clouds building were anything to go by.

Another storm was coming.

While that was a blessing in the fact that it would give them access to fresh water so long as they had something to collect it in, it was a curse in that it would drop the temperature further, and with them in a weakened state, they would be more susceptible to hypothermia.

"If I had my phone, I'd snap photos so we could post them all over social media when we get home," he told her, only half joking. It wasn't that he thought the shelter was spectacular, but anything that made Alannah smile he would happily do.

An odd feeling for him.

Other people's happiness had never been his top priority. Taking care of his little brother, making sure they were as little a burden as possible on family members who didn't want them, protecting people, fighting for answers, those were all things he'd prioritized in life, but not making someone smile.

Smiling had always seemed so … frivolous.

Life wasn't sunshine and roses, you had to make the best of what you were given. Work with what you had, not what you wished for.

When he had so many other problems in life, it didn't seem worth the time or the effort to focus on making someone feel good when you could put that time and effort into making sure they were safe, protected, or cared for.

Only now, hearing Alannah giggle and seeing her smile become a little bit more real and a little bit less lined with strain, exhaustion, and fear, he realized that sometimes making sure someone was happy was worth more than anything else in the world.

An ominous rumble of thunder broke the spell of the moment, and Alannah's giggle died on her lips as the fear took over again.

No doubt she was thinking about the storm when they'd been out in the middle of the ocean and how close it had come to claiming their lives.

But this time they weren't in the ocean, at the mercy of the waves and the wind, they were on dry land and had a shelter that would protect them from the worst of the weather. The fire would help to keep them warm, and the way he'd positioned it beneath the walls of branches meant it should stay lit no matter how bad things got.

At least that's what he was hoping and praying for.

"Go inside," he ordered gently, giving her a nudge toward their temporary home.

"You're coming in, too, aren't you?" Alannah asked, an edge of panic to her voice.

After finding her on the sand earlier when she'd decided to head out looking for him, she'd been scared to have too much distance between them. Ideally, she liked him within viewing distance.

He got it. They were alone out there. Abandoned on a deserted island that he'd been able to walk the entire circumference of in less than two hours. There were no people, no houses, no roads, no structures other than the small one they'd made themselves, and they had no food, warmth, or change of clothes.

Their situation was serious, and he hadn't come up with a plan yet on how they were going to get out of it. For now, they had a shelter. They'd soon have some water to drink thanks to the two systems, one with leaves and the other with rocks, that he'd built earlier. And that water would last only so long as it rained because he had no means to store it longer term.

They had literally nothing other than the clothes on their backs and whatever they could find on this deserted island.

"I'm going to be right there," he assured her. "Just checking everything is okay with the water collection systems I set up."

Even though she nodded and didn't say another word, Jake could feel her eyes on him as he walked through the trees back down to the beach. He'd decided it was safer to be a little further inland to build their shelter, then they could use the trees more, and benefit from their protection. But that meant not being visible to anyone passing by on a boat.

As much as he didn't like it, their best bet at being rescued was for his brothers to track them to this island. They knew there had been an issue with the boat even if they didn't know exactly what it was, so he knew they'd be looking for him and Alannah. When they found the remains of the yacht, they'd search every island in the area and sooner or later stumble on this one.

He hoped.

He prayed.

After checking everything, Jake headed back to the shelter. Just as he reached it, the clouds opened and a torrent of rain poured down upon them. The wind had picked up as well, but as he settled inside their little makeshift home, he was protected from the worst of it. Taking the space closest to the entrance also helped to block most of the wind for Alannah and the fire.

"So ..." she said slowly, her big eyes blinking up at him in the dim light. The clouds had cut out most of the sun's light, and their little shelter took care of most of the rest of it. At least with the fire it wouldn't be as bad as that complete darkness of being lost out at sea.

"So ..." he echoed back, making her smile.

That smile quickly faded. "What are we going to do, Jake?"

Knowing they had to be smart about this, he'd made the decision to focus on their immediate needs first. As much as he'd love to just pick Alannah up and transport her off the island and back home, that wasn't something he could do. They couldn't just jump back in the water and hope to swim to some other more populated island, there wasn't even anything else within sight. So shelter and water had come first. Tomorrow, after the storm, he'd find them something to eat, then they'd work on figuring out a longer-term plan including how they might attempt leaving the island.

But right now, what Alannah needed was rest not obsessing over a problem with no immediate solution.

"Come here." Shifting slightly so he was a little closer to her in the small space but still blocking most of the entrance with his body, she didn't hesitate. Once he had her in his arms, snuggled against his body, he laid them both down. Curling around her so she wasn't exposed to any wind, and was closer to the fire for its warmth and comfort, he held her snug against him.

Which was nice.

Holding her like this was intimate in a different way than sex would be. Sex could just be sex, it didn't have to mean more, but cradling another person in your arms was deeper. It meant something.

Right now he just wasn't sure what.

"I don't want you to think right now," he told her.

"How do I stop thinking?"

"By closing your eyes and remembering that for now we're safe, and mostly warm and dry. Soon we'll have water to drink, and then we can work on a plan. The best thing you can do for both of us right now is sleep."

"I'm not sure that I can. I'm so tired but ... the fear, it's too much," she admitted in a soft whisper.

His heart cracked at her declaration. He was supposed to be her protector, but all he'd done was fail epically over and over again.

And this might be his biggest fail of all, because there were no guarantees either of them was making it off this island alive.

∼

October 19th
6:07 A.M.

It felt like they'd gotten sucked into a time vortex rather than gotten stuck on a deserted island.

Time just moved so slowly.

Didn't help that the storm had been going on for hours so they were stuck in the little shelter she'd helped Jake to build. Well, he'd done most of the work and she'd just followed his instructions, not that Alannah had minded, it had given her something to do so she didn't give in to the panic threatening to consume her. It had also helped that it reminded her of summer days playing in the woods for hours.

Thankfully, the shelter had been able to withstand the storm, the location Jake had chosen was protected by the trees, and he'd clearly known what he was doing. His calm, steady, sure tone as he'd talked her through what he was doing and what he wanted her to do had also helped keep her from losing it.

Aware of the fact that she'd done nothing but twist and turn all night, Alannah did her best to remain still. She wasn't the only one who was exhausted, and she knew she had kept Jake awake all night.

He was the kind of guy who wouldn't allow himself to sleep until she was asleep. While she'd done her best to fake it, she was guessing she hadn't done a very good job, which meant neither of them had really slept at all.

Why she couldn't just close her eyes and give in to the exhaustion weighing heavily upon her she had no idea. It wasn't like she wasn't tired enough, she felt like she could go to sleep for a month, it was just she couldn't seem to shut off her mind.

Jake told her to leave worrying until the morning, and in theory, it all sounded so simple. He was right, for now they were warm and dry, but that didn't change the fact they were still stuck on an island she had no idea how they were going to get off.

The only times she'd managed to drift off to sleep, that sleep had been ruined by nightmares where she and Jake were trapped there forever, dying a slow death without enough food and water.

Honestly, she'd rather be awake and exhausted than sleep and live out her worst fears.

Because she really had been trying to allow Jake to rest properly even if she couldn't, Alannah hadn't asked about the water they were collecting. If she told Jake how thirsty she was, she knew without a shadow of a doubt he'd head out there to get her a drink. With the howling winds and pouring rains, he'd be soaked and frozen, not that he'd complain about either, but she'd feel even more awful than she already did.

All of this was her fault.

If she'd just agreed to go with him and the rest of his family, none of this would have happened. Jake would be really safe, warm, and dry right now instead of huddling on the hard ground, before a small fire, in a tiny shelter, on a deserted island.

Tears filled her eyes, but she held them back.

Crying would only disturb Jake and make him worry more than he already was.

Maybe if she could sneak over him, she could go and get herself a drink and take those few moments alone to gather herself. She didn't want to be a burden, it was bad enough knowing this was her fault, but she didn't want to make this harder for Jake. He kept saving her over and over again, but he shouldn't have to. She was going to have to be smarter, stronger, tougher, and live up to his example.

"Going somewhere?" Jake asked the second she shifted out of his warm embrace.

"Rain seems to have lightened. I was going to get a drink," she explained, disappointed in herself for disturbing him. It felt like she couldn't do anything right. As much as she wanted to be able to be like Jake, handle all this with his calm confidence, she didn't have the training or the skills to do it.

She was the weak link, and no amount of wishing differently was going to change that.

"If you're thirsty, you should have said something. I would have gone and gotten you a drink." Jake immediately sat up and moved to leave their shelter, but she grabbed his arm to hold him in place.

"That's why I didn't want to tell you. I've already stopped you from getting a good night's sleep, I wasn't going to make you go out in the rain for me as well."

Something close to distress passed through his dark eyes. "Don't you know I would have gotten you as many drinks as you needed?"

Offering her warmest smile, Alannah wrapped her arms around his neck and hugged him hard. "I do know, and it's why I didn't say anything. You've taken such good care of me, but, Jake, this is my fault." Her voice wavered on that last word, and as much as she hated it, she knew there was nothing she could have done to stop it.

"How do you figure that?" Jake asked in a voice that seemed to be genuinely confused.

"I should have listened to you," she said softly, voicing the worry that had kept her awake all night, the one she couldn't escape no matter how exhausted her brain and body were.

"About going with my family?"

Alannah nodded. "If we had you wouldn't be here now. Are you ... are you angry with me?" She couldn't even look at him as she asked the question. He had to be, and it was just like her protective grumpy not to let on.

"Are you angry with me?"

Her brow furrowed. "Course not. Why would I be? If we'd done what you wanted, we'd be safe right now. We wouldn't be lost with no one knowing where we are and what happened to us. If they think we died in the explosion, they won't be looking for us. We could never be found, Jake. We could die here."

"If I'd kept my distance like I knew I should have, these men would never have targeted you. You'd be safe and sound at home, going about your life, not having almost been killed so many times over I don't even want to count them up."

Tears blurred her vision, but she was able to hold them in. "I wouldn't have been safe and sound going about my life, Jake. I was missing you. It had been months and I thought ..."

"What did you think, sunshine?" he asked when she didn't continue.

Holding back the tears was no longer an option. They tumbled freely down her cheeks and she didn't bother to try to wipe them away. "I thought I had finally done something that had pushed you out of my life. I know how selfish that sounds. Like I think the entire world revolved around me and the only reason you could possibly have for not contacting me as much as you usually did was because I'd done something, but I couldn't stop the thoughts. They were always there, taunting me. Every message you didn't answer, every phone call that went to voicemail, I thought it had to be me. If even my own parents didn't want me and weren't shy about letting me know it, how could anyone else ever truly want to have me in their life?"

Speaking her deepest and greatest fears out loud was hard, but what was the point in holding them back?

There was a very real possibility that they weren't going to survive this, so holding onto her secret fears seemed silly.

"Is that what you really thought?" Jake sounded stricken at the very idea.

Reluctantly she added, not wanting to hurt him more but feeling freed by admitting that out loud. "It's what I always think. It's why I don't have a lot of close friends. I purposefully keep them at a distance so that when they eventually leave, I feel justified. It's stupid. I know it. People aren't mind readers, I need to tell them what I'm thinking, I need to face my fears and give them a chance, but knowing it and doing it are two different things."

Jake's large hands lifted to frame her face, and his eyes locked onto hers. "I would never leave you, Alannah. I had to put distance between us to keep you safe. No other reason. And I couldn't even stick with that, even knowing the danger. I brought that danger directly to your door. If anyone should be angry with anyone else, it should be you angry with me. This isn't your fault, it's mine. All of it. Including letting you think that anything you did or didn't do would end our friendship. You're family to me, sunshine, okay? Always have been and always will be, every bit as much as my brothers and Cassandra."

His words should soothe her, make her feel better, but in fact, they did the opposite.

Her feelings for him were changing, growing into something more, and he'd just effectively told her that he saw her as another sister, not as someone who could one day be more to him than just a friend.

# CHAPTER

*Fourteen*

October 19<sup>th</sup>
7:00 A.M.

What he'd said earlier in the shelter hadn't convinced Alannah that he wasn't going anywhere, Jake could tell.

Not that she was letting on. Well, she was doing her best to convince him that she believed him and that she was okay, but he'd known her long enough to recognize the differences between her real smile and her fake one.

It was a subtle difference, and one he doubted anyone else would be able to pick up on.

But he wasn't anyone else, he was her best friend, and he knew when she was faking cheerfulness for the sake of those around her.

What he needed to do was come up with an idea to distract her for a while. She'd been through so much in such a short time that he knew her mind had reached overload. Now everything, no matter how small, was going to seem like another boulder of a problem that she didn't know how to solve.

An idea had already formed, it was a crazy one, and one that he was pretty sure she was going to shoot down as soon as he mentioned it. If she didn't, if she said yes, then it was going to change things between them, maybe in a way that would mean they could never go back.

Was that a risk he was prepared to take?

For such a good cause he had to believe he could go through with it, but he couldn't deny he was glad he had a bit of time to work up some courage.

"Do you really think you can catch us something for breakfast?" Alannah asked, a hint of doubt in her voice as she followed him along the sand and down toward the rocks.

"You doubting me, sunshine?" he asked, shooting her a smirk. "Because that wouldn't be wise. Don't you remember all the times I used to catch you fish when we were kids?"

The smile on her face turned genuine, and he felt a stab of relief. Whatever doubts she fought she was at least trying to fight them, and that was all he could really ask of her.

"I remember, but I think there's something *you're* forgetting, grumpy."

"Yeah, and what's that then?"

"This time around, you don't have a fishing pole. When you and Jax used to catch fish for us to eat, you always had equipment. Now we don't have anything. So how exactly are you going to catch us breakfast?" Although her smile was still there, a thread of worry had tangled itself in her voice.

The rain last night had provided them enough water to drink to satisfy them both with some left over, but now they were starting to really feel the effects of not eating in well over twenty-four hours. His stomach was cramping with hunger pains, and he was sure Alannah's was no different.

"Oh ye of little faith," he teased as they reached the rocks. "Prepare to see a genius at work."

Alannah rolled her eyes at him. "Yeah, you're a real genius, Jake Holloway."

Her sassy tone made him laugh, and the sound of it immediately brightened Alannah's smile, making it a real one again. Laughing wasn't something he did often, and it was usually either his sunshine or his little niece that managed to make him do it.

That was because both of them were special, although in vastly different ways. Essie was such a happy, excitable, energetic little girl that you couldn't help but spend time around her and not feel better about life in general.

And Alannah was ...

His sunshine.

"A real genius," he agreed with a grin. "And I'm going to prove it to you. You're going to have to eat your words, Alannah Johansen."

"I'll happily eat my words along with a fish. *If* you can catch one," she sassed back.

Still grinning as he walked along the rocks, leaving her waiting on the sand, he went hunting. The storm had stopped, the sky was clearing, and the ocean had calmed right down. Now only the occasional lazy wave rolled across it.

Perfect for catching them some food.

It wasn't really their food situation that scared him the most. Jake was confident he could keep catching enough fish to keep them going, and today they would explore the island some more and see what other food sources it provided. The water situation was tougher, he didn't want to have to keep relying on rain to keep them hydrated, so he was hoping they could find a fresh water source as well.

Their biggest problem was how they would get off the island, not how they were going to survive on it.

Didn't take him long to locate the best spot to position himself, and then it was just a waiting game. As soon as a fish came close to the rocks all he had to do was grab it. It took a lot of time and practice to learn to do it right, move too slowly and you missed the fish, move too fast and you startled it away.

Had to get it just right.

Which was exactly what he did.

Patience was a virtue, and in this case, it was going to be the difference between spending the day with a full belly or starving to death.

Wasn't more than a few minutes before he saw a nice-sized fish approach. Shifting so he was in the right position, as soon as it was right below where his hand was, he darted it down into the water and came up with a fish.

That would teach his sunshine to doubt him.

Setting the fish in a small rockpool beside him to keep it fresh, he continued to wait. One fish wasn't enough for a proper meal, he was going to bring back almost more than they could eat. That would definitely have Alannah eating her words.

When he had four good-sized fish for each of them, Jake collected his stash and headed back to where Alannah was standing on the sandy shore, staring out at the ocean. She must have heard him coming because she turned to face him, her eyes going wide when she saw what he held in his hands.

"Woah!" She hurried over to him, her gaze darting between the fish and his face. "When you do something, you go all out. I was thinking you might be able to catch us a fish each if we were lucky, but you have eight. That's four each," she said excitedly.

"Told you you'd be eating your words."

"And I told you I'd be happy to eat my words if I was eating fish as well. You caught so I'll clean and prepare. I still remember how to from when we were kids, though I haven't done it since."

Without hesitating, she took the fish and headed back to the water's edge. That was one of the things he loved about Alannah, she didn't hesitate to get her hands dirty and do what had to be done. She'd been the same as a kid, too. When she was younger, she'd been a bit of a girly girl, preferring to play with dolls or dress ups, but she'd also been willing to run barefoot through the woods, and climb trees, or gut fish, and play in the mud with him and his brother.

"Use a rock to cut them since we don't have a knife," he called after her.

"'Kay."

Leaving Alannah to take care of that, Jake returned to their shelter, pausing along the way to drink some water. It was annoying they had nothing to store it in, every time they were thirsty, they would have to go to the collection points he'd made. If he could find them a proper water source, maybe they could rebuild a shelter close by.

By the time Alannah came back with the fish, he had the fire burning brightly, and a fresh stack of firewood stored inside their shelter. Once they'd eaten and he'd seen if she was willing to try his idea to take her mind off their situation for a while, they'd go exploring.

Using sticks to prop the fish up in the flames to cook, while they waited, he turned and studied his best friend.

Was he completely crazy to be contemplating suggesting this?

What if she said no? She might never trust him again.

What if she said yes? It could ruin everything.

"Why are you looking at me like that?" she asked, catching him staring and brushing self-consciously at the locks of blonde hair that had escaped her tangled ponytail.

"I was wondering something."

"Care to clue me in?" she asked as she reached out and pulled one of the fish out of the fire, pulling off a piece and putting it in her mouth.

No time like the present to jump and pray he was wearing a parachute. "You said you've never had an orgasm. Why don't you let me try to give you one?"

～

October 19th
8:27 A.M.

Alannah choked on the mouthful of fish when Jake blurted out the last thing she expected him to say.

He wanted to try to give her an orgasm?

Was he crazy?

This morning he'd as good as told her that he saw her as another sister, so why on earth would he want to do anything sexual with her?

How could he put her in this no-win situation?

If she said no, she risked hurting his feelings since it was obvious he was feeling guilty that the people after his family had started the chain of events that led to them being here even though Alannah truly believed it was her fault they were on the island.

If she said yes, she risked ruining their friendship both because he would find out there was actually something wrong with her and she just wasn't capable of having an orgasm like a normal person, and because things would be awkward and virtually irreparable if they took this step.

Shifting so he was behind her, Jake gave a moderate slap to her back, between her shoulder blades, dislodging the piece of fish she'd choked on.

"So?" he asked when she stopped coughing and he'd resumed his spot beside her, reaching out to take his own fish from the flames.

"Have I somehow slipped into a parallel universe? If that's what you're asking then yes, yes I have."

Chuckling he reached over and ruffled her hair, making her swat at his hand. "Sometimes you're adorable."

Great. He thought she was cute. Just what every woman wanted to hear from a man who had just offered to make them come.

"Why don't you let me try. I'm sure that you can come with the right person."

Why did those words make her wish that Jake was the right person?

Never before had she thought or felt about this man the way she was beginning to. He'd always been her best friend, her protector, her favorite person, but there had never been anything romantic about it.

Until now.

Now things were changing, and while for Jake this might just be about trying to apologize for the actions of people he had no control over, for her she was afraid this would take these fledgling little feelings and make them into something more.

Something too big for her to come back from.

"Come on, what harm could it do to try?" Jake asked and she wondered why he was being so persistent. This wasn't like her Jake at all. Did he not get that doing this would change things between them?

Nibbling on her fish, Alannah tried to choose her words carefully. She appreciated that he was trying to make things up to her even if she didn't think he needed to, but she wasn't prepared to lose Jake from her life. Besides, she'd lived all the way to thirty-two without an orgasm, she was pretty sure she could live out the remainder of her years never getting what the hype was about.

"I can't come, Jake," she told him. "Can't. As in there's something wrong with me."

"There's nothing wrong with you," he growled, making her smile despite the nerves dancing in her stomach.

"I think there is."

"Then that's your problem. You need to stop seeing yourself as broken, unlovable. Damn your parents for doing this to you," he snarled.

"My parents?" Honestly, she'd never thought about it that way before. They *did* make her feel unlovable, and because of them and their inability to love her she had been left feeling broken.

Was it possible they were the reason she couldn't orgasm?

That their neglect had put some sort of block in her mind that she hadn't been able to find her way around?

A tiny ray of hope shone down upon her, maybe she wasn't broken after all. But that ray was quickly snuffed out. Even if it was her parents' neglect that had caused her problem, she'd still tried to come on her own and with partners and nothing had ever worked. Maybe her parents were the cause but that didn't mean the damage they had done could be undone.

"Give me a chance, sunshine. Let me prove to you that you aren't broken, you're beautiful and bright and everything good in the world."

"You really want to do this?"

"Absolutely."

"Why?"

"Because you're my sunshine and I won't have anything dimming your light."

"But what if it ..."

"What if it what?"

"What if it changes things between us?" she asked, unable to meet Jake's gaze. He was being so sweet, so tender, so soft for what she as used to with her grumpypants, but how could he not see that this would change everything, good intentions or not?

"It can't change anything if we don't let it," Jake replied confidently.

"You really think it's that simple?"

"I don't want to lose our friendship, do you?"

"Of course not."

"Then, yeah, I think it's that simple."

Could it be?

Could they try this and then just go back to the way things were before?

Would she even want that?

Regardless of whether Jake could make her orgasm, her feelings had shifted and although she'd been refusing to think too much about it, she was starting to think that she wanted more from him than simply friendship. What if she let him do this and it proved to her that she did want more, would she be able to be satisfied with all Jake was willing to give her?

Or was she overthinking this entire thing?

"Trust me, sunshine," Jake said as he shifted closer. "Let me do this for you. Believe that I can."

*Simple.*

*Make it simple.*

The words whispered through her mind and she clung to them. Her parents had already taken so much from her, left behind so much damage, did she really want to hand over this piece of herself to them and not even fight for it?

No.

The answer to that was no.

Like a spell had been cast over her, Alannah moved a little away from the fire so she could stretch out on her back. When Jake knelt between her legs, nudging them apart, for a second, she almost panicked and backed out.

Even though she wanted to trust Jake, the fear of doing this and losing him was so strong.

There was no way she could live without him being part of her life.

When Jake leaned over and touched a kiss to her forehead, she melted under his tender ministration. She wanted more kisses like that only not on her forehead but on her lips. Wanted to know how Jake kissed, was it all practical and methodical like he did everything else or was there passion burning under his tight control?

"Just relax, sunshine," Jake said as he moved down her body.

That was easier said than done when his large hands caught the waistband of her leggings and panties and tugged them down her legs.

The second cool air brushed against her bare skin, Alannah realized how stupid this was.

Jake could see her.

All of her.

And he was staring at her core with an almost mesmerized expression on his face, and she felt herself grow wet. How could she not when a man was looking at her like he wanted to devour her?

"You're going to come on my fingers and my face, sunshine." Jake said it with such authority that she believed it to be true.

Never in her life had she seen a more erotic sight than that of Jake's dark head as it settled between her spread legs.

"Keep your eyes on me, sunshine," Jake ordered as he brushed the pad of one calloused finger along her center. "See this?" He held up the finger, which shimmered in the light of the fire with the evidence of her arousal. "This is proof you aren't broken. Hear me?"

She nodded without realizing it.

Jake didn't make her feel broken. He made her feel beautiful and desirable.

When his mouth closed around her aching bud and he sucked hard, her hips came flying off the ground, making him chuckle. The sound reverberated around her bundle of nerves, making her whimper as sensations assaulted her.

While he suckled and flicked at her bud with his tongue, the tip of a finger teased her entrance. Needing more than what he was giving her, Alannah tried to shift to take his finger deeper, and Jake chuckled again, pressing his free hand down on her stomach to hold her in place.

"Stay still for me, sunshine," he ordered, then his mouth was back on her, licking, sucking, and driving her wild.

Bit by bit, he slid a finger inside her, then lazily pumped it in and out. A second finger joined it, stretching her deliciously, and by the time a third was added, she was whimpering, thrashing, and pleading, begging for everything he had to give her.

Hooking his fingers so they grazed the spot inside her that she had been utterly convinced did not in fact exist, Alannah felt something brewing inside her. Much like the storms that had ravaged them in the ocean and last night in the shelter, it grew into something all-consuming.

No longer could she think, all she could do was feel.

Pressure built low in her belly as Jake continued to lavish attention on her willing and receptive body, then as it began to send out tendrils of pleasure to the rest of her, it just fizzled out and died.

Tears of frustration replaced her moans of delight, and her body went completely still. Jake had tried his best, but just like she'd told him, something was wrong with her.

She'd wanted to come.

So badly.

But she couldn't.

Because she was broken.

# CHAPTER
## *Fifteen*

October 19<sup>th</sup>
8:56 A.M.

"I told you," Alannah whispered in such a broken voice that it gutted him.

Jake had been so sure it was working. He could feel pleasure building inside her, it was plain to see on her flushed face and hear in her breathy moans, then all of a sudden it had vanished.

What her parents had done to her had messed with Alannah's head in more ways than he'd realized.

And he wasn't sure he could help her find a way to undo it.

There was nothing he wouldn't do to help her, but in the end, she had to be the one to finally shrug off the way her parents had seen her and truly see herself.

That was her problem. When Alannah looked at herself, she didn't see the strong, vibrant, resilient, sunshiny woman who would go out of her way to help a person in need. Instead, she saw a baby not wanted by its parents, one they were constantly putting up against her sister, and then criticizing all the ways they didn't think she measured up. She saw the girl who could never do anything right, who never got any time or affection, who lived in old second-hand clothes discarded by their golden child. She saw the girl who was made to do all the chores around the house, who was punished for any imperfect grade at school, who wasn't allowed to have hobbies because they cost money that should go to the child they loved.

She saw a failure because even her own parents didn't want to love her.

How did he help her see herself as the woman she really was?

The woman he saw her to be.

"Don't give up, sunshine," he told her, holding her in place by gripping her hips with both of his hands when she tried to move out from underneath him. One of his hands shimmered with the evidence of how close she'd been to letting go and allowing herself to have the pleasure she so badly deserved.

"We tried, it failed. *I* failed," she added as though that was how she truly saw it. Alannah had never been allowed to have time for fun as a child unless she was able to get away from her parents. Their cruel words and heartless attitudes to their second daughter had damaged her deeply, and he so badly wanted to help her heal those wounds.

"We didn't fail," he corrected. "We had a little bump in the road, but that's okay, we can just try again." As far as he was concerned, he'd spend the rest of the day if that was what it took touching her until she finally let go of the barriers she'd built and let pleasure flood in. Those barriers were built with every nasty word her parents had ever said to her, every time they'd denied her comfort when she was hurt, scared, or sad, every time they'd told her she would never live up to her sister and that she would never amount to anything.

Dismantling those thick walls would take time, but right now they had oodles of it.

"Try again?" Alannah gave a derisive laugh that was nothing like her normal, beautiful, light-giving one.

"Why not?"

"Because this is embarrassing enough, I don't want to keep proving to my best friend over and over again that I am truly broken."

Hearing her call him her best friend rankled in a way it never had before. It was true, of course, and he didn't want that to change, and yet at the same time, he would never have offered this if he didn't want something to change.

Tears shimmered in Alannah's eyes. Combined with the glow of the fire, it made them seem like pools of pure gold. That was exactly how he saw this woman, as a precious metal who deserved everything good in the world. It wasn't that she wasn't good enough for her parents, it was that they had never deserved her. She was too good for them. Too good for him.

"No, sunshine," he said firmly as he moved so he completely covered her. While he made sure he didn't crush her with his much bigger body, he did allow a little of his weight to press onto her, reminding her in every way he could that she wasn't alone. He was right there, and he wanted to help her overcome the burdens her parents had unfairly saddled her with.

Wide eyes looked up at him and she sucked in a breath at his proximity. There was no way for him to hide the evidence of how beautiful he saw her, how turned on he was watching her as pleasure built inside her, it was nestled between her legs, and if she was willing to try again, he'd do everything he could to give her what she deserved no matter how hard it made him.

"You are not broken. Say it."

Those wide eyes seemed to somehow widen further. "S-say it?"

"You heard me. Tell me. Tell me everything amazing about you, how you are the complete opposite of broken."

"I'm ... I don't ... what am I supposed to say?"

Balancing his weight with one arm, his hand claimed one of her breasts, tweaking the nipple and making it pebble. "Tell me how beautiful you are, inside and out. Tell me how smart you are, building an entire business on your own. Tell me how much you care for people, that you volunteer at the homeless shelter, that you donate to charities, that you've given people the shirt off your back because they needed it more than you."

"Wh-what does that have to do with anything?"

"How could a woman who does all those things be broken. You are not what your parents tried to make you. They tried to crush you, but you were too strong for that. All you have to do is finally believe once and for all that everything they said about you, to you, it's all untrue. Lies. Can we try again?"

Her tongue dipped out and dragged along her bottom lip, making him groan. At the sound, a small smile quirked up the corners of her mouth. "We can try again."

"Can I make love to you, sunshine? I'm clean, never gone bare before, and I think you're on birth control." That hadn't been his original plan, he'd thought his mouth and fingers would be enough, but she needed to feel all of him so there could be no doubt how hard she made him.

"Y-you want t-to?"

Annoyed that she asked it like there was any doubt, he shifted so he could grind his erection against her bare center, making her gasp. "Any doubts about that?"

When she shook her head, he raised an eyebrow at her, silently asking for an answer to his question. He could tell she was considering it, but he had no clue what her answer was going to be until she gave a small nod.

"Words, sunshine." The only way they were doing this was if she gave her express permission.

"Okay. I'm clean and I am on birth control. I want you to ... make love to me."

Shoving down his pants, he didn't hesitate. Alannah was already wet, ready for him, and the more time he gave her to think, the more she was going to try to talk herself out of this. One thrust was all it took to bury himself deep inside her, and she gasped as he filled her.

"Look at me," he ordered. She needed to see that this was him, see the truth in his eyes, know that he didn't think she was broken. Dinted and damaged, yes, but never broken. Honestly, Jake didn't even think it was possible to break this woman. She was too damn strong for that. Even after everything she'd been through over the last several days, she was still there, trusting him in the most intimate of ways.

Her big, golden-brown eyes locked onto his, and he allowed everything he felt for her, all the admiration and awe, to shine through.

Reaching between them, he took her bud between his thumb and forefinger and rolled it, making her moan, her internal muscles quivering around him.

"Say it," he ordered.

"Say what?"

"That you're not broken. That there is nothing wrong with you. That you're holding yourself back, preventing yourself from feeling the pleasure you deserve, that you were never what your parents told you you were."

"I-I'm not b-broken."

"Like you mean it this time." No longer holding himself still, he rocked his hips, pulling back and then thrusting into her again. "You." Thrust. "Are." Thrust. "Not." Thrust. "Broken. Say it."

"I'm not broken," she said, stronger this time.

"Again." Jake picked up the pace, thrusting harder, faster, his fingers working her bundle of nerves with every single one.

"I'm not broken."

"Again." She was close, he could feel it. Her body was wound tight, now all she had to do was let herself detonate.

"I'm not broken." Alannah roared the words out into the quiet, peaceful little island, and he pressed hard against her bud, and finally got the response he'd been hoping and praying for.

Letting go of the old bonds, Alannah set herself free.

Her internal muscles clamped around him, and she cried out her release as she let herself fly high, taking every drop of pleasure she deserved. Not letting up, Jake continued to thrust and never stopped touching her bundle of nerves, prolonging her orgasm for as long as he could, and then, when he felt it waning, he picked up the pace, working her toward a second.

Crushing his mouth to hers, he kissed her like he'd been dreaming about when they were on the yacht. She tasted sweet, like something he'd never experienced before, and as he shoved her into a second orgasm, succumbing to his own, Jake wondered how he was going to move forward with his life, never getting another taste of her.

Or if he even wanted to.

∾

October 19<sup>th</sup>
      6:42 P.M.


This was crazy.

How could she be stuck on a deserted island, with no means of getting off, scared about the future and what it held for her and Jake, and yet at the same time feeling so amazingly free and light inside?

It was like a burden she had been carrying had suddenly been taken off her, and it was wonderful.

Of course, Alannah had known that the fact that she couldn't orgasm like a normal woman had been a weight on her mind. It had certainly also been the cause of breakups with more than a handful of her boyfriends. They'd taken it as a personal slight against them, like she was implying it was their fault when that couldn't be further from the truth.

Always, she'd placed the blame squarely on her shoulders.

Only sometimes male egos could be a fragile thing, and they hadn't gotten that no matter how hard she'd tried to explain. It wasn't them not being good enough or generous lovers that prevented her from orgasming, it was herself. She was being her own worst enemy.

Jake hadn't taken it as a slight when he hadn't made her come that first time, though. He'd just taken it as a challenge and jumped in even harder to make her do what she had been positive was impossible.

*Harder*.

She snickered at her own joke. He'd certainly been hard, thick, long, and amazing inside her. He had somehow managed to fill her up in a way she hadn't thought was possible. He hadn't just given her amazing orgasms—yes multiple orgasms—he'd filled up a piece of her that had been missing.

Self-confidence.

Self-worth.

Those were the things that he'd given her.

For the first time in her life, she had been completely and utterly vulnerable with another person, and they had made her feel seen. Jake had seen her, not the unwanted burden her parents always made her out to be.

That was a feeling she wanted to hold onto for as long as she could, for the entire rest of her life, no matter how long that turned out to be.

"What are you laughing at over there?" Jake asked, his voice deliciously low and sultry. It washed over her like a wave of desire, and she had to clench her legs together so she didn't do something silly like climb onto him, straddle his lap, and sink down onto his length.

"Nothing," she answered quickly, not wanting him to know what she'd been thinking, although she was sure her bright red cheeks would give her away. The curse of being a blusher.

"Doesn't look like nothing. Are you squeezing your legs together right now?" he asked with a smirk.

"Umm ... no?"

"Is that a question, sunshine?"

She shook her head, sure that if she spoke the words wouldn't be another lie but a plea for him to give her another moment of indescribable bliss.

One thing she had determined this morning when Jake had finally pulled out of her and they had no choice but to return to the reality of their situation, was that for as long as they were on this island, she wasn't going to worry about the future. What was the point in worrying about sex changing her friendship with Jake and irreparably ruining it when they might not even live more than another couple of days, or weeks, or maybe months?

For now, she was just going to take moments of joy when she found them.

If that meant another round of sex with Jake, then so be it. No feeling guilty and no anxiety. Just joy. Just pleasure. They both deserved it.

"You sure, sunshine? Because it looks to me like you *do* have your legs squeezed together. If you do, then that would make you a liar, wouldn't it?" He arched a dark brow at her and hot, needy desire pooled low in her belly. How did he manage to turn her on with just a handful of words and a single searing look?

After the morning, they cleaned up and gone looking for a water source. Thankfully, they found a freshwater lake so packed up the shelter they made and moved it further inland. Moving away from the shore where they could be spotted if someone came looking for them was scary, but she trusted Jake to know their best moves to stay alive.

She also trusted him with her body.

Shocking, but she did.

The last two lots of orgasms he'd given her proved it.

No longer did she find a barrier. Now when he brought her close to the edge, instead of pulling away and backing up, she just jumped right on over it.

"Do you know what I do to liars?" Jake asked, leaning in to feather a quick kiss to her lips, not nearly enough.

"N-no," she said on a breathy moan as her lips tried to chase his and make him kiss her properly.

"I punish them."

His words would sound dangerous if it wasn't for the desire darkening his own eyes. Instead, the words came out sounding erotic, and Alannah squirmed as they did crazy things to her insides.

"P-punish them? H-how?"

"You're about to find out."

In a movement that was far too quick for her to do anything about it, he pounced. In one smooth moment, he had her flipped and lying on her stomach across his thighs. One of his legs was hooked around hers, pinning her in place.

Not that she had any intention of fighting.

This game they were playing, this dance they were engaged in, was far too intoxicating to make it stop. A distant part of her mind screamed at her to protect her heart because if they got off this island, the game would stop and the dance would end, but she couldn't seem to summon any energy to do that.

Instead, heat flooded her system as Jake's large hand began to massage her backside. His fingers were so close to her aching core that she tried to squirm and reposition herself to get them where she wanted them, but he merely tightened his hold.

"How many spanks do you think would be an appropriate punishment?" he asked.

"Spanks?" she squeaked. She'd never done anything like that before, although, the idea didn't sound scary or intimidating in the least.

"Seems only fitting, you did lie after all, didn't you, sunshine?" A featherlight touch against her soaked center had her hips trying to move to find some friction. Jake laughed and withdrew his hand. "Didn't you?"

"Yes." No point in lying about it, his hand could feel how wet she was.

"Then you deserve a punishment, don't you, baby girl?"

This time, it was her heart that fluttered at his words. Had the endearment slipped out accidentally because he was caught up in the moment, or had it been a conscious decision?

"Don't you, sunshine? Don't you deserve a punishment?" His hand stroked her backside, and she shivered, but not in fear, nope, it was all arousal.

"Y-yes."

"Are you going to take it like a good girl?"

This man and his words.

Once again, he had heat flushing her system, making it feel like she was on fire. The good kind of fire, the kind that burned hot and bright but brought only pleasure.

"Y-yes."

"There's my good girl. I think five is a suitable punishment."

Cold air suddenly whispered across her backside as Jake slipped her leggings and panties down to expose her bottom.

The first strike caught her by surprise, and she jolted at the sudden spike of pain.

Before she could think too much about it, Jake's hand was smoothing softly over her stinging skin, soothing away the pain.

"There's one, you ready for the next one, baby girl?"

Now that she was prepared, she nodded, and the next spank didn't catch her by surprise. As soon as his palm connected with her skin, Jake immediately soothed away the sting with featherlight strokes.

Each one had her growing wetter, and wetter, and by the time the final one landed on her no doubt rosy red backside, she was so wet and so turned on that if he didn't do something about it, she was going to take matters into her own hands.

"You did so well, baby girl," Jake crooned softly as he helped her sit up. "Took your punishment like such a good girl. Did you learn your lesson, sunshine? Are you going to lie to me again?"

Was she?

Why did the sting on her backside and the wetness in her panties tell her she was?

He must have read exactly where her mind had gone because he shot her a charming smile. "A brat, I see."

"Jake, please," she begged, her hips rocking, needing something to put out the fire he'd set inside her.

"Please what, baby girl? You need to come?"

"Yes, please," she whimpered, she felt so empty.

"Asking so nicely, sunshine. I think that deserves a reward."

Finally, his fingers were inside her, filling her up. He didn't go slow, setting a fast pace that had her head falling back as pressure built quickly. Each pump of his fingers grazed the spot inside her she was now convinced did in fact exist, while his thumb pressed on her bud with just the right amount of pressure and speed to have her breathing growing ragged.

How had he managed to learn her body so quickly?

It was like he possessed some sort of magical powers.

Who would have guessed her grumpy, stoic, always in control best friend had such passion hidden beneath the surface.

And who would have guessed she would have liked his dominance so much?

Maybe it was because it was easier to fight off her fears and worries when she handed over her pleasure to Jake, knowing he would take good care of her.

Exactly like he was doing right now.

The pressure built, so big it felt like she couldn't contain it a second longer, and then she exploded. Her internal muscles clamped around his fingers and like he always did he kept working her through the orgasm making it last for as long as he could.

When the last shudders of it faded away, she sank down against him, resting her forehead on his shoulders. What was this man doing to her?

Ruining her for any others that was for sure.

"Such a good girl," he murmured as he shifted her and pulled up her panties and leggings, then lying them both down so they were on their sides with her between the fire and his large body. Protecting her like he always did.

"What about you?" she asked looking over her shoulder. "You didn't come."

"Don't need to," he told her, his gaze tender as he leaned in to touch a kiss to her temple. "I have exactly what I want."

Guiding her head down to rest on his forearm, Jake held her snugly against his body. Ruining her for sure for any other men. But did she even want another man? Jake gave her everything she had ever wanted or needed, and even though she knew the risks, when they were snuggled together like this, those risks didn't seem to matter.

Alannah was beginning to figure out what she wanted. The thing was, what did Jake want?

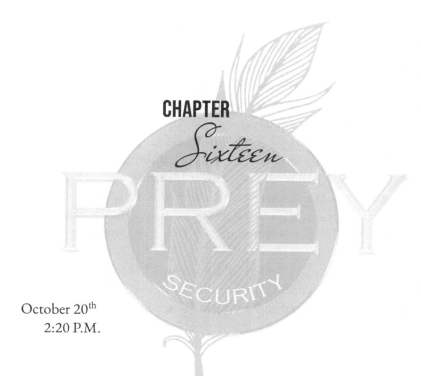

# CHAPTER
## *Sixteen*

October 20th
2:20 P.M.

"There doesn't seem to be any animals on the island," Alannah said as Jake held out his hand and helped her climb up and over a fallen tree trunk blocking their path.

"Birds, probably rats, snakes, insects—"

"Okay, okay, okay," Alannah cut him off, shuddering and scrunching up her face, making him laugh.

"I know, you're not a fan of bugs."

"Or snakes, or rats," she added.

"Spiders are your least favorite if I remember correctly," he teased. It was strange, but ever since he and Alannah had had sex, things felt even easier between them. It had always been easy with her, they'd gotten along from that very first day, and she knew him in a way that not even Jax and his stepbrothers knew.

But now it had changed again.

There was a lightness inside him that hadn't been there before. She always brought light into his life, helped keep the anger and darkness at bay, but this light wasn't just in his life it was inside him somehow.

Like she had transferred a little flame of it to him.

Now that flame sat inside him, and it was growing. The anger had abated even more, and even though he was afraid that he would fail her and not get her off the island, there was peace there as well.

It was weird but in a good way.

However, he was doing his best not to examine it too deeply. They were still trapped there, and even if they got off the island and got back home, that wouldn't eliminate the danger his family faced. The future was uncertain, but in the utter peace and quiet of the island, that didn't seem to matter. Here was for living in the moment, and what happened after that would happen whether he spent his time worrying about it or not.

"Did you see one? A spider?" Alannah shrieked, abruptly yanking backward and almost sending them falling down to the ground.

Laughing, he managed to keep their balance and jumped down the other side of the large tree trunk and then lifted her down beside him. When he went to keep walking, Jake found himself held in place by the expression on Alannah's face.

"What?" he asked self-consciously.

"You never laugh like that at home. You're always so in control, or being all grumpy, but here ... you're different. Freer. Lighter."

Maybe she wasn't the only one who needed to learn how to set themselves free from the bonds of the past. Jake knew he was always going to feel some measure of anger at his father for not making any attempts to change his lifestyle when he became a single dad, and to all the relatives who made him and Jax feel like a burden. There would always be anger about his dad being set up as a traitor, and everything that was done to his stepmom.

But he was starting to realize that the anger didn't have to rule him.

There was a way for that side of him to coexist with a side of himself that found moments of joy, not just found them but actually went looking for and embraced them.

Anger didn't have to be his defining characteristic.

"I feel different," he admitted. "Lighter. Freer."

"It's this place," she said, looking around them at the beautiful scenery. "There's something about it that just allows you to let go."

"It's because there's nothing else, we've been stripped down of all the things that we're usually surrounded with, left naked and bare to the truths we run from."

A blush crept up Alannah's cheeks, and because he knew her so well, Jake knew exactly where her mind had gone. His best friend was unlocking a side of herself she hadn't even known existed. A side of her that was made for him. She loved his dominance last night, loved her punishment, loved being called a good girl, loved letting him take control so she felt safe to let go and feel rather than think.

Every moment he spent with her like that was taking his feelings for her and twisting them a little more. What were they going to look like by the time he found a way to get them off the island and back home?

If they did get back home, would the spell be broken?

Was it this place that stripped away your armor to leave you nothing to hide behind really magical?

Of course, he knew it wasn't, there was no magic there, but in a sense there was. Not the witches and warlocks kind, just being immersed in nature, no modern conveniences, alone with someone he cared about. That was the magic.

But it couldn't last.

He had no idea what Alannah wanted, she hadn't said anything about the future, and he hadn't either. Fear of being rejected, that he wasn't good enough to be her life partner, was holding him back.

It made him a coward, he knew that. And sooner or later, they were going to have to talk things through. They'd crossed a line, and there was no going back to the way things had been before. Things had changed whether he liked it or not.

He just wasn't sure if that was a good thing or a bad thing.

One thing he did know, though, was that he wouldn't give Alannah up. If she wanted to stay best friends when they got home, he'd deal with that. And if one day she fell in love and got married, he'd find a way to handle that too. Because living without Alannah's sunshine was not an option.

"When we get back to our shelter, I'm going to strip you bare again and take everything you can give me," he told her, brushing his lips across her ear and then nipping lightly at her earlobe.

Alannah sucked in a breath, and he wasn't sure if she was aware of it but her body drifted closer to his, making him smile. This woman had captivated him from day one, and how strong and brave she'd been these last few weeks was only making him fall harder for her.

Just as he was about to capture her lips in a kiss, he heard something.

Voices.

Was it?

Straightening, he cocked his head to the side and listened. It could have been nothing more than the wind rustling through the leaves, but he could have sworn he heard two distinct voices talking.

"Jake, did you—?"

Cutting her off with a hand to her mouth, Jake pulled her closer and then lifted her off her feet and moved them so they were hidden behind a couple of trees. Those were voices, he was sure of it, but this island had been empty for the last two days, and he couldn't just assume that whoever had stumbled upon it now were innocent civilians.

People were hunting him, and thus Alannah since she was his best friend. He had to assume the worst-case scenario until he knew better.

"Stay quiet till we know who they are," he whispered, his voice low so it didn't carry, his lips back by her ear, only this time not in a sensual and playful way.

Her big eyes widened with fear, the spell of just seconds ago when they were both so relaxed gone, as the reality of their situation came crashing down around them all over again. The island had been a reprieve, but one that was about to come to an end.

"We stay here until we catch a glance at them. Then if they're just fishermen or explorers, we can go to them and ask for help."

What he left unsaid didn't need to be said out loud.

If they weren't just people out exploring the island for fun, then they were here for a purpose. To search for him and Alannah. If they were part of the team the remaining rapist had sent after them then sooner or later they would find the shelter and the fire. Once they found it, they'd know for certain that he and Alannah were on the island. It wasn't big, it wouldn't take them long to search it. There was only so long the two of them could hide before they'd be found.

And when they were found ...

That didn't even bear thinking about just yet.

Holding Alannah close, he brought her with him to their knees and then tucked her between his body and a tree trunk. It wouldn't offer her much protection, but it was all he could do.

Then they had no choice but to kneel there and wait.

It didn't take long.

The voices grew louder, although it seemed like the men were actually making an attempt to be quiet since he couldn't make out the words, just that at least two of them were talking, since one man's voice was deeper than the other's.

Then he saw them.

Two men dressed all in black, with assault rifles slung over their shoulders.

Definitely not people out for a day of fun. They were hunters, and they were hunting him and the woman he had long ago vowed to protect.

~

October 20th
   2:32 P.M.

Those were not fishermen.

Or explorers.

Or anyone who just happened to be out for the day and decided to stop at an island they passed to walk around and have some fun.

Those men were hunters.

And she and Jake were the prey.

The two men dressed in black had big guns slung over their shoulders, and as they walked, they scanned the landscape around them.

Searching.

For her and Jake.

There was not a single doubt in Alannah's mind that these men were working for the last person involved in Jake's stepmom's rape. The man who was so determined to protect himself and his secrets that he would go to any lengths he had to.

Including murder.

That was what would happen if they got caught.

She and Jake would be killed.

Maybe not right away. Maybe they'd be tortured first, maybe they'd be leveraged to try to get Jake's brothers to back off. Maybe they'd even try to trade them for Cassandra, because the remaining rapist was Jake's stepsister's biological father. She was living proof of what had happened.

Not that any one of the Charleston Holloway brothers would ever trade their baby sister for anything or anyone.

Not Jake.

Especially not her.

So possible torture and death were all that was in her future if those men caught sight of them.

And how could they not?

The island wasn't very large. It took only a couple of hours to walk it. After a few days there she could find her way fairly easily from any point back to their shelter. Even if the men walked past them now, it wouldn't mean they were out of the woods. Sooner rather than later, the men would find their little shelter, and once they did, they'd know that the two of them were there.

All they had to do then was scour the island until they caught them.

Pressing her body tighter against Jake's, Alannah found she could no longer watch the men approach. She didn't want to know the second they were spotted, didn't want to see those weapons aimed at her and Jake, didn't want to watch the men stalk toward them.

Against her, Jake's body was strong and steady. She had no doubt he would fight, might even get the upper hand. But it wouldn't last. Not only were there two armed men against them, but she was sure more of the men in black were scattered on the island, or at least close by.

Jake might fight, but he couldn't win. The odds were stacked too high against them.

Sooner or later the magic of this island had to end, the bubble they'd been living in would pop, Alannah just hadn't thought it would be this way. She'd thought they'd either try to make it off the island and perish at sea or slowly waste away and die. If they were lucky, she thought his brothers might find them before either of those scenarios could take place, but she hadn't thought they would be captured.

Why didn't the men just believe they'd perished in the explosion?

It was totally plausible that even without bodies it could be assumed that they were dead, and their bodies had simply floated away or been eaten by ocean wildlife.

The voices grew louder, and she held her breath as though her subconscious actually believed so long as they couldn't hear her breathing then they wouldn't see her at all.

Waiting was the worst.

Knowing each breath she took could be her last.

They didn't know what orders these men had been given. Perhaps they weren't interested in torturing them or capturing them, perhaps they just wanted them dead. The orders could be to kill on sight.

If that was the case, these were her last seconds on earth.

Clinging to Jake, she buried her face in his chest, dragging in lungfuls of his scent, wanting to imprint it on her mind so it was the last thing she would experience before death came for her.

Only it didn't come.

The voices grew louder until she was sure the men were mere feet away from them, but then there were no shouts or gunshots, instead the voices began to recede.

Was it possible ...?

Had the men walked right past them without spotting them?

Terrified to move in case she was wrong, and the men had spotted them but just hadn't done anything about it yet, Alannah just crouched there and held onto Jake, needing his presence to ground her. There was nothing he could do to save her from those men, but that didn't matter, Jake had always been her safe place, and he was now as much as he ever had been.

"They're gone," Jake's low voice whispered, and the hand that had been cradling the back of her head rubbed lightly, his fingers stroking through her tangled locks.

"G-gone?" she repeated, not moving, unwilling to believe they'd been spared.

At least for now.

"We have to move, now, we won't have long. They're heading toward our shelter, and once they find it, they're going to call in rein- forcements if there aren't already more men on the island looking for us."

"Why are they looking for us? They should think we're dead," she whimpered, still not lifting her head from Jake's chest and keeping her eyes squeezed firmly closed. After all, if you couldn't see the monster then it couldn't see you either, wasn't that the way it worked when you were a child?

"I don't know. Maybe they're just being thorough, wanting to make sure we didn't survive. Whatever their reasons, we have to get out of here."

"There's nowhere to go," she protested as he stood, dragging her up with him, and she had no choice but to open her eyes so she didn't slow him down when he started moving.

"There wasn't anywhere to go," Jake corrected. "There is now."

"What?"

"Those men didn't swim here like we did, sunshine," Jake said, already moving and towing her along with him.

Right.

Of course.

Her mind was so clogged with panic that it couldn't think clearly.

The men hadn't been lost at sea and washed up on the shore, they hadn't struggled to get around the rocks blocking the way, they weren't soaked like she and Jake had been when they finally got onto the sand. The men had come on a boat.

A boat.

If they could get to it …

Was that too much to hope for?

Doing her best to keep up with Jake's much longer stride, Alannah ran as fast as she could alongside him. While he seemed to be able to run without making much of a sound, she did not possess that same skill.

When she ran, it sounded like a herd of elephants was traipsing through the woods.

With each step they took, she kept expecting the men with the guns to come jumping out, but nobody came.

While she was simply following along, Jake seemed to be moving with a purpose like he suspected he knew exactly where the boat would be.

Finally, they reached the tree line, and he froze. Alannah immediately recognized where they were. This was the same beach where they'd first landed when they reached the island. She hadn't walked all the way around the shore, they'd mostly explored inland, but she knew Jake had said there was only one way through the rocks. They'd been lucky they'd approached that way because if they'd been on the other side of the island, they would have been dashed to pieces on the rocks and never made it to safety.

Maybe that would have been better.

What was the point in surviving the ocean only to die a couple of days later at the hands of violent men?

At least these last few days had given her something wonderful, a piece of herself she'd thought lost, and some healing of old wounds. That was worth something, maybe even worth dying a horrible death at the hands of the men with guns.

"There," Jake said triumphantly as he pointed to the small motor-boat sitting on the shore.

Escape.

Freedom.

Life.

All represented in the small craft.

*If* they could get to it.

You didn't need the same training and experience that Jake had to know that as soon as they left the trees they were exposed. They didn't know if there were more than the two men on the island, for all they knew, another was hiding just out of view, ready to pick them off once they were flushed out of the protection the woods offered.

Still, it wasn't like they were drowning in options.

They either waited to be spotted or for their shelter to be found and the hunt for them to start in earnest, or they made a run for it.

Put like that, there wasn't just a lack of options, there was only one.

They *had* to try to get to that boat.

Otherwise, they were already as good as dead.

"You're going to go ahead of me," Jake said, grabbing her shoulders and leaning down so they were eye to eye. Gone was the playful man he'd been just minutes ago, this Jake was the serious, stoic, always in control man she knew and loved.

Yes loved.

Loved as a friend and was starting to love as something more.

"I'll be right behind you, but I want you to run and not stop. Not for anything." The fingers gripping her shoulders tightened almost painfully. "You hear me, Alannah? You don't stop for anything. You keep running until you're in that boat, and then you get yourself the hell off this island."

"But—"

"No buts. I'm going to be right there with you, I have no plans on dying, but if we're spotted, I will do whatever I have to in order to make sure you survive."

Tears blurred her vision, as much as his determination to always be her protector made her love him even more, she didn't want to lose Jake, not for any reason.

"You ready?"

No.

There was so much she wanted to say, so much she wanted to make sure he knew, so much they had to talk about, but they didn't have the time so she merely nodded.

"We got this, sunshine."

Since there was no time for words, she merely leaned in, brushed her lips across Jake's, and then started running for the boat. The sand was soft against her bare feet, and she became aware of the soles of her feet stinging. She must have cut them up a little while they were running through the woods.

Nothing she could do about it, so no point in worrying or letting it slow her down.

With about twenty yards of sand between the tree line and water, they were almost halfway there when gunshots suddenly filled the air.

# CHAPTER

*Seventeen*

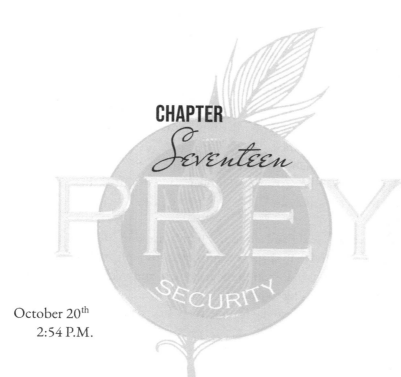

October 20th
2:54 P.M.

So close, and yet not close enough.

At the sound of the gunshots, Alannah cried out, turned around, tripped, and went down.

At least Jake hoped she only went down because she'd tripped because the alternative was that she'd been hit.

Diving toward her body, he covered it with his own, offering the only protection he could.

While he'd hoped they would both make it into that boat, he was prepared to give his life to save Alannah. Or even just to give her a chance. It wasn't even about being prepared, he would gladly do it. Even if things hadn't changed between them over the last couple of weeks, he would be more than willing to sacrifice his life for hers.

She was his best friend, and the vow he'd made as a five-year-old was one he had honored into adulthood. Alannah was his to protect, his best friend, but maybe there had always been more there and he just hadn't seen it.

"Are you hit?" he asked, trying to keep the panic from his voice.

"No. At least I don't think so. I just tripped. Are you hit?"

"No. Just worried about you."

"They're shooting at us." Alannah said it like she couldn't quite grasp it, even though they'd both known the risks when they made a run for it. She was in shock, but as he glanced over his shoulder, he could see the men shooting at them were still quite a way down the beach.

There was still a chance.

At least for Alannah.

"Get up, sunshine, get onto the boat and get out of here, I'll hold them off for as long as I can."

"No."

The word was said firmly, and her hands fisted in his shirt, gripping him with a ferocity that surprised him even though it shouldn't. His sunshine had learned to be tough the hard way, and even though she was terrified, she wasn't going to just give up.

"I'm not leaving you to die for me, there has to be another way."

Was there?

Was there something they could do?

If he could get his hands on one of those weapons, they would at least stand a chance. The boat was tiny, so he didn't think there could be more than six people searching the island. If he was armed, he liked those odds.

But trying something meant allowing Alannah to stay in the line of fire.

"Jake, we're in this together," she said firmly. "A team. I won't let you sacrifice yourself."

Running through scenarios in his head, he knew he had to come up with something fast, their window of opportunity was quickly diminishing.

For now, there were only the two men, but if more were on the island the gunshots would have them zeroing in on this location. If they were going to do something, it had to be now.

"We're going to get back up and run for the boat. When we get to it, you're going to jump in, and I'm going to push it into the water. Then I'm going to fake being hit and go under. You're going to stay in the boat until they get close. When they're distracted, I'll make my move."

This was risky.

The riskiest thing he'd ever done.

He'd been in more dangerous situations in his career, but none of them had involved his best friend putting her life on the line.

"Are you sure you want to do this? I can probably buy enough time for you to get away."

Her gaze was clear and shining with determination. "I'm positive. Let's do this."

With a single nod, he grabbed her wrists and dragged her up with him. Then they both started running again. The gunshots had temporarily stopped while they were both down, but they started up again, plowing into the sand as he and Alannah sprinted the last of the distance to the boat.

Like he'd told her to, she jumped right into it, then turned her big trusting eyes on him. She had no idea what her trust did to him. After what her parents had done to her, she had every right not to ever trust another person again, and yet here she was putting her life in his hands and believing that he could protect it.

Pushing the motorboat out into the water was easy enough, and when a bullet pinged right into the water beside him, Jake knew that was his chance.

Giving the boat one last shove toward the ocean, he dropped and went under. While he'd been in Delta Force and not a SEAL, he'd grown up playing in the ocean. He was confident in the water and a good swimmer. Holding his breath was easy enough and without moving too much to alert the men chasing them that he was alive and well, he maneuvered himself around to the other side of the little boat.

This was still a risky plan, but he was starting to feel better about it.

Above him in the boat, Alannah let out an ear-splitting howl of pain, that if he didn't know better, he would have thought she believed she'd just witnessed the death of her best friend.

Thankfully, the gunshots stopped, and he had to assume that the men hunting them believed that not only had they killed him, but they had easy prey to do whatever they wanted with.

Keeping low in the water, allowing just the top of his head to his nose out so he could breathe, he kept still and waited.

Didn't take long until he could hear the splashing sounds of the men approaching the boat.

"Don't think about doing anything stupid, darling," one drawled, and he wondered what Alannah was doing.

"You killed him," she whimpered, and even though he couldn't see her, he knew she was crying. She didn't have the skill to cry on command, but given how afraid she likely was, he wasn't surprised that she was crying or that the tears were real. They just weren't because she thought he was dead.

"He didn't have to die yet, he shouldn't have tried to run," the other man said, his voice lower, deeper, bordering on bored.

"Why are you doing this?" Alannah whimpered. They hadn't had much time to talk through a plan, so he was glad she had figured out enough to know that keeping them talking was helpful.

This was only going to work if he got the timing absolutely perfect.

Even one second off and he'd be dead for real, leaving Alannah at the mercy of these two men who didn't even know the meaning of that word.

"Your boyfriend didn't tell you that his family is trying to ruin a man over something that happened over twenty years ago?" bored man asked.

"He told me what happened to his stepmom, and why you're after him, but I don't understand what that has to do with me. I didn't do anything, I'm not part of this," Alannah wept.

"You weren't until he made you part of it. Now you're right in the middle of it, darling," the other man drawled.

The splashing had stopped, and he was sure the two men had reached the boat. If he was standing right now, the water would probably come up to his chest, the men were likely about the same height as him so it would give him a clear shot at taking them down.

Once he had one down and his hands on the weapon, he could eliminate the other. As much as he'd love to keep them alive, try to get some answers out of them, this wasn't the time. This little boat was more the kind that came with a bigger one than the kind you took out to travel long distances.

Chances were a whole army of these men was somewhere close by, and now that he had the means to get Alannah off the island, he was going to take it.

"D-don't," Alannah's panicked voice hit his ears. "Don't touch me."

"What're you going to do to stop it?" the drawler asked and then chuckled in a way that made Jake see red.

He knew exactly what these men had planned for Alannah, and there was no way he was going to allow it to happen. She'd only just learned that her body belonged to her, that the past and the way she'd been treated didn't have to affect how she saw herself, no way was he was going to allow her to lose that freedom so quickly.

This brave, strong, sunshiny woman deserved the world, and while Jake didn't know if he could be the one to give it to her, he did know that he wasn't going to let anyone hurt her. He was her protector, and he took that job very seriously.

It was now or never.

There wasn't going to be a better opportunity. The men were distracted by Alannah and the sick things they wanted to do to her. They were completely unaware of his presence, and they would remain so until he struck, and it was too late for them to do anything about it.

Taking a deep breath, Jake dropped completely below the surface and made his move.

~

October 20th
   3:03 P.M.

*Come on, Jake.*
  *Where are you?*
  *Please do something.*
  *Soon.*

Alannah pressed herself into the very back of boat as the men standing in the water before her reached out to try to grab her.

The looks on their faces told her exactly what they were going to do if they got their hands on her.

"Don't be shy, darling," the man with the startling blue eyes said as he managed to get a hold of her wrist and yank her toward them.

"Stop! Don't," she cried, hitting at him and trying to pull herself free. Even though she knew these men weren't going to get a chance to follow through on what they had planned, the terror she felt was real.

*Jake will stop them.*

*He won't let them hurt me.*

Reminding herself of that didn't seem to be helping. What if Jake really had been shot? She was assuming he'd done what he said he was going to do, but maybe that last bullet had hit him and he was already dead. It had been a couple of minutes since he went under, and he hadn't come back up, which meant if he had been hit he was already dead.

Or maybe he'd been shot on the beach.

When he'd asked her, she'd said she hadn't been hit, and he'd said the same when she asked him, but at the time, adrenaline had been buzzing through her veins, and she hadn't really been completely sure that she wasn't shot because she couldn't feel anything. It had been like her body was numb, too focused on survival to worry about anything else.

Now she could feel, though.

The fingers wrapped too tightly around her wrist for her to break the hold felt like tentacles. If she felt this repulsed just by his hand touching her, how was she going to feel when he did so much worse?

*Come on, Jake.*

*Now.*

*Please.*

Apparently, this time her plea was heard by the universe, because the other man who was watching her with almost bored light brown eyes, suddenly howled and let go of his weapon as his hands went under the water, and he hunched over as though in pain.

Relief hit her hard.

Jake.

He was alive and making his move.

Unsure what she should do that would be the most helpful, Alannah yanked hard on the arm that was still being held by the other man.

Distracted by his friend's howl of pain, she was able to break her hold this time, and since the last thing she wanted was to be used to manipulate Jake in any way, Alannah threw herself overboard and into the water.

It was cold on her skin, and her clothes were immediately soaked through, reminding her of the fear of those hours spent at sea, wondering if they would survive.

Fighting through the memories, she kept under the water and swam herself a small distance away from the boat. She didn't want to be in the way, and when she came up for air and turned to look, she was amazed at what she saw.

Like he was Triton or some other god like sea creature, Jake had gotten his hands on the weapon that had floated off when he must have hit the bored man. He rose out of the water, which streamed down around him, and lifted his weapon, firing at bored man and hitting him several times.

Bright red blood bloomed on bored man's chest, and he seemed to hover in place for a moment before he collapsed into the water, which immediately turned red around him.

Blue eyes let out a frustrated roar and lifted his weapon, aiming it at Jake.

Fear for her best friend chilled her more than the water ever could.

Despite her intentions of staying out of the way, Alannah couldn't help a small scream falling from her lips before she could stop it from happening.

Her strangled scream had blue eyes turning in her direction.

That one moment of distraction was all Jake needed.

A few more shots echoed through the air, and the next thing she knew, blue eyes dropped down into the water as well.

Was that it?

Was it over?

Were the two men dead?

As much as she wanted to believe they were safe now, Alannah was having a hard time trusting what her eyes had just seen. What if the men were faking death? What if they were going to pop back up and start shooting? Blue eyes still had his weapon even if Jake had bored man's.

And what if there were more of them on the island?

Or in a boat nearby?

Even if these two were dead, it wasn't like she and Jake were safe. At best, they'd had a reprieve, but she wanted the threat against them to be gone completely not just temporarily.

"Sunshine."

Another scream fell from her lips when she blinked and saw a figure standing before her. It took her shock-addled brain a moment to process what it was seeing and realize that it was only Jake.

Throwing herself at him, when his arms closed around her, she finally felt a semblance of calm wash over her. Jake was there so she was okay. Jake, her hero, had just killed two men and given them at least a chance at surviving.

How many times did that make now that he'd saved her life?

"Are you okay? Did they hurt you?" he asked, and she could hear the worry in his voice. It grounded her and reminded her that she had to stay strong. Jake was counting on her to be able to hold it together.

"You stopped them before they could hurt me," she assured him. "Are you okay?"

"I'm fine."

"Are you sure? For a moment, I was worried one of the bullets had hit you for real and you weren't faking being dead," she admitted, tightening her hold on him to assure herself that he was there and real.

"I didn't get hit, just had to wait for the perfect moment to strike."

"What did you do to him?"

"Got him where no guy wants to be hit," Jake said with a smirk.

"They're both dead, right?"

"Both dead."

"And we have the boat."

"We have the boat."

"Which means we have a way off this island," Alannah said, excitement shoving away most of the shock. Sooner or later, she was sure they would have discussed building a raft to try to leave, but this was so much better.

"We sure do." Jake's smile had her smiling back and relaxing further. "I'm going to put you in the boat, then I'm going to get the bodies and hide them in the trees. Don't want anyone to see them too quickly when someone comes in search of them."

Carrying her through the water along with him, Jake paused at the boat and lifted her up, setting her inside. Then he set the gun beside her. Its presence made her feel a little better, because now they at least had a way to protect themselves.

Jake retrieved the other weapon and passed it to her, then he found one of the bodies and dragged it out of the water and along the sand to the trees. Alannah felt a moment of panic when he disappeared into the woods, but he was out of her sight for barely a few seconds before returning.

After locating the other body and dumping it along with the first, Jake was back in the boat with her, and they were finally ready to leave. The memories she had of the island weren't all bad, in fact, some of them could be considered to be the highlights of her entire life, but she was still glad to leave.

Alannah wanted to get back to civilization. She wanted clean, dry clothes, a warm bed to sleep in, and a nice hot meal of comfort food. Then she wanted to join the rest of the Charleston Holloway family. As badly as she needed to keep her business going so she could support herself after this mess was finally cleared up, the cost of staying close and putting her gym above anything else was too high.

Risking Jake's life wasn't an option.

He'd been ready and willing to make the ultimate sacrifice for her, and she would never forget that. If she had to rebuild her livelihood from scratch once the threat was eliminated, she'd find a way to do it. She'd much rather do that than lose the very best friend anyone could ever ask or hope for.

"Ready to get out of here?" Jake asked as he leaned over to get the motor started.

"More than ready. I can't stop thinking about how amazing a

steaming hot shower will feel, and wearing clothes I haven't worn for days that are all filthy and salty. And the food ... mmm ... I don't even know what I want to eat first, I just know I'm going to eat way too much, and when I finally climb into a cozy bed, I'm going to lie awake for ages because I'm too full."

As wonderful as sleeping in a bed with soft pillows and warm blankets sounded, she couldn't deny she'd miss the feel of Jake's body snuggled against hers. When you compared the two, maybe sleeping on the hard ground with Jake won out a little above the cozy bed.

"Why aren't we going?" she asked, looking over at Jake, confused as to why he hadn't got the motor running so they could get moving.

"Because the motor must have been hit by a stray bullet and won't start. Looks like we won't be going anywhere after all."

# CHAPTER
## *Eighteen*

October 20<sup>th</sup>
3:19 P.M.

*Damn it.*

Once again, Jake had been so close to getting Alannah out of this mess only to fall short at the last moment.

He had weapons, they had a means of transport, and yet it wasn't enough.

The damn motor had been destroyed by a bullet.

Feeling the weight of failure and defeat resting heavily on his shoulders, Jake looked over at Alannah who was watching him with an expression he couldn't read.

"I'm sorry," he told her, wishing she knew just how deeply. He was supposed to protect her. Why couldn't he for once in his life actually follow through on that vow?

Crawling across the bottom of the boat, Alannah rested a hand on his knee. "Jake, you don't have to be sorry. You literally saved my life. Again."

"I keep failing you, sunshine." Not allowing himself time to think about it and second-guess his instincts, Jake reached out a hand and palmed her cheek. "I always fail you."

"How do you figure that? Because you couldn't stop my parents from being the terrible human beings that they are? That is not your fault. You were there for me. Always. No questions asked. If I called, you came. When I was sad, you cheered me up. When I needed advice, you gave it to me honestly, no beating around the bush, telling me what you thought I wanted to hear, or sugar-coating things. When I started my business, you were my biggest cheerleader, making me believe in myself even when I doubted I had what it took to make it work."

Alannah shifted closer, and her other hand reached out to grab hold of his.

"When I've made bad choices in relationships, you've always helped me pick up the pieces. When you thought I might be in danger because of the people after your family, you stayed away to protect me. You saved me in the fire at my gym and again in my building's parking lot. It was because of you we weren't on my yacht when it blew up, and without you, I would have drowned in the ocean in the storm. You found this island, made us shelter, found us food and water, and kept us alive. And you saved us again right now, killing two people before they could hurt me. How can you possibly think you've failed me? From where I'm standing, I'm basically the mess you somehow manage to keep alive and functioning."

The smile she shot him and the teasing tone of her voice eased some of the weight crushing him down. While he wasn't sure he believed what she'd just said, it helped to know that *she* believed it.

"And, Jake, you gave me a precious gift on this island, you made me see that I wasn't broken, only banged up a little. You helped me smooth out those dented pieces and heal a little more of my childhood trauma. Thank you."

Moving up onto her knees, she rested her hands on his shoulders, squeezed lightly, and then feathered her lips across his before rocking back onto her heels and shooting him that determined look that he recognized.

"Now, the Jake I know doesn't give up that easily. I know we're both exhausted, worried, and scared, but we have a boat. Who cares if it doesn't have a motor? At least it's seaworthy. If we'd wound up building a raft it wouldn't have had a motor either. I say we grab ourselves some branches for oars and we get the heck out of here."

She was right.

Giving up wasn't in his vocabulary.

These feelings of failing Alannah couldn't be allowed to dictate the decisions he made.

Building a raft had been his intention if they weren't found by his brothers in a couple of days, and they would have had to use oars to row it away from the island. This was a whole hell of a lot more stable and safer than anything he could have made, so they were definitely in a better position, even if they could have been in an even better one if the motor hadn't been damaged.

"Thank you," he said, leaning in to brush a kiss to her lips. "You're right. This can still get us out of here, just a lot slower. Stay here, I'll grab us some branches."

"I can help."

"You could, but I'd rather you stay here. Won't take me long," he assured her.

Leaving both weapons with her in the boat, Jake jumped out and quickly swam the short distance back to shore. No one had ever spoken about him the way Alannah just had. Sure, plenty of women were impressed with his body and his military service, who might go so far as to call him a hero. But they didn't speak in that same impassioned tone, like he wasn't just a hero but a superhero.

Was that how Alannah saw him?

Had she been saying those things just to break him out of his moment of panic, or did she really see him as the person in her life that she turned to to seek whatever it was she needed?

As he crossed the sand to the nearest trees and began to break off a couple of branches that were the approximate size of an oar, he realized he'd always thought he brought nothing but his promise of protection to their friendship. She was the one who brought light, joy, happiness, energy, and a sense of balance. Without her, he was sure he would have succumbed to the dark anger that raged inside him.

Looking back at the boat as he picked up the branches, he saw her watching him. When she noticed him looking, she waved at him, and even though he couldn't properly see her face he knew she was smiling at him.

Warmth spread throughout him, and he was suddenly filled with the need to be closer to her, to have her by his side where she belonged.

Belonged.

Never had he thought of it that way. They were best friends, and they spent a lot of time together, but they'd also had separate lives in a lot of ways. He kept his romantic interludes to himself, and Alannah never shoved her boyfriends in his face.

Maybe that was because they had both felt something neither had dared to speak aloud.

Splashing through the water as quickly as he could, he tossed the branches into the boat, then planted his hands on the side and boosted himself in. By the time he was sitting in the boat, Alannah already had two of the four branches he'd brought with him in her hands.

"I'm glad you didn't act all silly and macho and only bring branches for you," she said, shooting him one of her brilliant smiles.

Despite the fear still lodged firmly in his gut, he smiled back at her. "I didn't want to listen to you complain with no way to drown you out."

For a second she just stared at him, her mouth hanging open in shock. Then she snapped it closed and shot him another smile. "I like this new side of you. You've always been my grumpy, but these last couple of days you've been different. Making jokes and being all sexy." Her cheeks blushed as she said that final word, but she didn't break the hold her gaze had on him. "I know it's crazy because we've both been terrified about the future, and we're both exhausted, but I like it. I like seeing you learn to be more relaxed."

It was her.

She was the reason he felt lighter.

Something about connecting with her on a deeper level had unlocked some as yet unnamed emotions inside him.

"I'll try to keep that in mind for when we get home," he told her.

"When," she said with a nod.

The last thing he wanted to do was burst her bubble and rid her of the enthusiasm she was feeling because she was going to need that energy. But he also couldn't allow her to hold onto false hope.

"We're going to do our best to get home, sunshine, but we still have a long road ahead of us. Yes, we have the boat, and it's going to help us a lot, but we won't be able to move all that fast across the ocean. We have no protection from the sun or the weather if another storm rolls in. We don't have any food, and more importantly, we don't have any water."

"You make it sound so hopeless."

"Not hopeless, sunshine. Never hopeless. I just want us both to have realistic expectations. I also want you to know I won't give in to the fear again like I did earlier." Jake knew he couldn't afford to when Alannah's life rested in his hands.

"Oh, Jake." This time when she leaned over, she touched a tender kiss to his cheek. "The whole world isn't on your shoulders. You're allowed to be human. Allowed to have emotions. Even allowed to panic once in a while. When you slip, I'll be here to hold you up. I might not be as big and as strong as you, but I can steady you and let you rest for a while."

Alannah was right.

She wasn't as big and as strong as him.

She was bigger and stronger.

Not physically, but emotionally.

Despite being treated badly by her parents all her life, Alannah still sought love and happiness, whereas growing up being made to feel like a burden had led to him closing himself off emotionally to everyone outside his family.

Had his determination to protect himself from potential pain cost him a chance at healing and happiness?

Or was that chance sitting beside him so determined to work with him as his partner regardless of the consequences?

And if Alannah was his chance, was he brave enough to reach out and take it?

~

October 21<sup>st</sup>
   2:14 A.M.

Part of her wished they were back on the island.

As Alannah lay on her back inside the small motorboat, staring up at the vast expanse of sky above her, she couldn't help but think back to that night on her boat. Back then, she'd felt so optimistic, she thought that she and Jake were safe, they'd left the threat behind, and everything felt fresh and exciting.

With her feelings for Jake already beginning to change, the wide sky above them, littered with a million sparkling stars, had felt like a wealth of possibilities. With his body warm and strong beside hers as they sat under that blanket watching the sunset and the night sky come to life, everything had been perfect, and now ...

Now they were once again lost at sea.

While the other part of her knew they had to try to get off that island at some point, at least back there they'd had shelter, fire, and food and water. Here in this little boat, they had none of those comforts.

As November slowly approached, the weather continued to get colder, and although they'd been blessed with sunshine all afternoon and evening instead of pouring rain and howling winds, there hadn't been enough warmth in the sun's rays to fully dry her clothes. They were damp, and after wearing them for days, and with all the hours she'd spent in the water and the sand, the material felt scratchy and irritated her skin.

Plus, she was freezing cold, her stomach grumbled with hunger, she would sell her soul for a glass of water, and the soles of her feet throbbed from the dozens of tiny cuts she'd gotten running through the woods. After they'd rowed for a while, Jake had used a little seawater to clean away the blood and bits of dirt and sticks embedded in the wounds, and while so far none of them seemed to be infected, they both knew that could easily change.

Despite rowing for hours, all that surrounded them was the ocean.

Miles and miles of ocean.

All the way out to where the ocean met the sky.

Whatever boat the two men Jake had killed had come from, they hadn't spotted it, and if they'd come from another island or even the mainland, if it was nearby they were yet to find it.

The longer they drifted aimlessly in the wildness of the ocean, the more the optimism she'd had when they first left the island began to dwindle.

It was hard to stay positive when death felt like it was creeping ever closer.

"I can hear you thinking ... and worrying." Jake's voice suddenly rumbled through the otherwise quiet night.

One thing she'd always loved about being out on the water was how quiet it was. It was like being in another world. Now, though, the silence broken only by the lapping of water against the sides of the motorboat just seemed to torture her, reminding her of how alone and vulnerable they were.

"Can't sleep," she said, rolling over so she was facing Jake. The boat was long enough only for her to stretch out completely flat. Jake was much taller than her and had to keep his knees bent. He must be so uncomfortable, and after everything he'd done to keep her alive these last few days, he should be relaxing in a huge, comfortable bed, with his belly full, safe and sound.

Tears sprang to her eyes and Alannah fought not to let them fall.

She'd been the one to talk up the idea that they could do this, and she'd vowed to herself not to fall apart and give Jake another problem to worry about.

"Hey, what's wrong? What are these tears for?" One of the calloused pads of his fingers touched her cheek, catching a stray tear that wouldn't follow her orders and stay put.

"Guess everything is just catching up with me," she whispered.

Tenderness shone in his eyes, visible even in the thin light of the moon and stars. When he opened his arms, she didn't even hesitate to snuggle into his embrace. Slowly, warmth seeped back into her body. How Jake managed to be so cozy when he'd been on the boat as long as she had, Alannah had no idea, but she wasn't complaining.

She could lie against his big body forever, soaking up his warmth and strength.

Forever.

Was that really what she wanted with Jake?

Her feelings were changing, of that she was sure. What she felt for him now was different than what she'd felt before that first fire at her gym.

Or was it?

Had this attraction always been there and she just hadn't let herself see it?

Of course, she's always seen how hot Jake looked, you'd have to be blind not to notice all those muscles, but it had never affected her before because he'd just been Jake, her best friend since she was four. He'd always been more than a hot body as well, she'd seen through his grumpy exterior to the big heart he hid underneath. He was loyal and protective, he would do anything for the people he loved. Just because he didn't always show how he felt didn't mean that she didn't see it anyway.

Now she had to decide if she was willing to take the biggest step of her life.

Decide if she was willing to risk losing the best friend she would ever have by admitting that she no longer saw him as just that best friend who had always been there.

Whether they made it off this boat or not, Alannah knew she had to tell him. If they were going to die alone at sea, she didn't want to take her last breath holding onto that secret. And if they were rescued and got back home, she didn't want to spend the rest of her life wondering what could have been, if she'd let the best thing to ever happen to her slip through her fingers.

There was never going to be a perfect time to shake up her entire world and potentially turn it on its head in either the best or the worst way possible, so she may as well just do it.

"I know now isn't the best timing, but—" her words died abruptly when a bright light suddenly cut through the darkness, and the unmistakable sound of an approaching boat had them both jerking up into sitting positions.

A boat was coming.

But was it help or death that approached?

"What do we do?" she asked, turning to Jake. As much as she wanted to support him, help him, and work as his teammate, he was the one with training and experience, she brought nothing to the table except a willingness to do anything he asked of her.

Clear indecision marred Jake's handsome features as he stared at the light growing steadily closer. As they both watched, they saw that it was a search light, roaming backward and forward across the water in a slow, even, methodical pattern that said whoever the people on that boat wanted to find they were invested in it.

Jake's family or the people out to kill them?

There was no way of knowing without letting themselves get found.

If it was Jake's family, then they were only minutes away from the clean, dry clothes, hot meal, and warm bed she'd been dreaming about. If it was the people who wanted to silence the Charleston Holloway family, it was suffering and certain death.

Two sides of the coin.

Good or evil.

Rescue or death.

Hope warred with fear inside her.

"We have to take the risk, sunshine," Jake finally said, and she could tell by his tone he was already second-guessing the words the moment they were out of his mouth. "If we don't, we're just going to remain lost out here. We could find our way to help, but we just as easily could not. We have no food and no water, no protection from the weather. If we don't take this chance, we might not get another."

"You don't have to convince me, Jake. I trust you," she assured him. It was true, she did. Even if this wasn't help they had to give it a try. Their choices were severely limited, and they were already living on borrowed time. If this was help, they were saved, and if it wasn't then they were only speeding up the inevitable end anyway.

"I don't know that I deserve your blind trust in me, sunshine."

Managing a genuine smile, she pulled Jake in for a tight hug. "Too bad, grumpy, because you have it. I know this could be the people we're running from, I'm not naïve and I'm not stupid. I get that we're risking our lives, but you're right, we're out of choices."

"So lucky to have you in my life, sunshine," Jake whispered before crushing his mouth to hers in a fiery kiss.

Then side by side they stood and shouted and waved their arms to attract attention, unsure whether they would face family or a deadly foe.

# CHAPTER

## Nineteen

October 21st
2:28 A.M.

The bright rays of the search light hit them.

This was it.

They were about to find out if they'd just been rescued by his brothers or somebody they'd hired, or by the men who had been hunting his family for months.

Life or death.

What awaited them on that boat?

For about the millionth time in the last ten or so minutes since they'd first spotted the other vessel, Jake second-guessed himself.

Alannah said she knew what they were getting into, understood the risks involved, got that they didn't have a lot of choices, and their chances of stumbling across land in what amounted to a rowboat were slim. But it didn't matter that she said she was on board with this plan, he couldn't help but feel that she didn't truly understand just how dangerous these men were and what they'd do if they got their hands on her.

She knew what it felt like to believe she was going to die in a fire, but the last thing he wanted was for her to know what it felt like to be tortured. To be unable to get away from the pain that others inflicted not just willingly but joyfully.

Men like the ones hunting them were sadists. They enjoyed other people's suffering, got off on it. If they weren't, they would have found a legitimate way to put their skills to use without working for someone like the man determined to keep his identity a secret.

Still, it was too late to back out, too late to try to come up with a different plan or just cross their fingers and pray for a miracle. Even if they hadn't started waving down the boat, the chances of them not being spotted were slim. They had only makeshift oars so they couldn't move very fast while the other boat had an engine. It would have found them sooner or later, they'd just sped it up a little.

"We're in this together, Jake," Alannah said as the light stayed fixed on them and the boat drew closer. "If it's them and we're captured now, I don't blame you. I agreed with this plan. Don't blame yourself, okay?"

As if he wouldn't if the worst was about to happen.

When the boat reached him, he knew. This wasn't his brothers out searching for them.

If it was, the first thing they would have done was yell out to let him know it was them, aware of the fact that he'd be uncertain if it was friend or foe.

But there was no sound from the boat other than its engine running, and his fingers curled into fists as he resisted the urge to grab his weapon and open fire. The only thing stopping him was the knowledge that if he started shooting, they'd shoot back, and with their positions it was him and Alannah who would likely get shot.

While the light stayed fixed on them, a rope was dropped down, but still no one spoke.

"I'm sorry, sunshine," he whispered as he forced himself to reach out to the rope that would soon be delivering them to their enemies. To pain and suffering. To death.

"It's them?"

"Yeah. If it were my brothers, they would have let us know before now. I'm sorry. We should have tried to hide from them, get away."

Regret pressed heavily against him, and his mind scrambled for a way to undo this. Only there was no way. Even if they jumped into the water, it wouldn't take them long to be found. There were likely a dozen or more men currently sitting on that boat.

"Together. We're together in this. I agreed, stop blaming yourself." A hint of irritation was in her voice this time, like she was annoyed with him for trying to shoulder all the responsibilities, and it was so very brave of her that he couldn't help but smile.

"I'm not giving up. We'll figure something out, find a way," he vowed.

"Course we will."

Knowing that if they didn't let themselves be pulled up the men would simply come down and get them, Jake guided Alannah's hands to the rope and then gave it a tug. Immediately, they were pulled upward, out of the minimal safety the broken motorboat had offered and into the unknown.

Seconds later, hands reached out and grabbed hold of them, hauling them over the side of the boat and tossing them down onto the deck. Alannah stayed close to him, her fingers reaching out to grab his and holding onto him tightly, but she didn't cower under the leering stares of the men surrounding them, and for that, he was so very proud of her.

Bravery wasn't the lack of fear, it was simply doing what you had to do despite being afraid. Which was exactly what his sunshine was doing, and it made him love her so much more.

There was no point in denying it.

Staring certain death in the face made being scared of his feelings pretty redundant.

Right or wrong, somewhere along the way these last couple of weeks, he'd fallen in love with his best friend.

"Seems this time you lose and we win," a voice sneered as a man stepped closer. A faint hint of smoke surrounded him, and Jake deduced this was the man who had been setting the fires.

Arching a brow at the man, Jake merely studied him impassively. "Yeah? You think? Because all the other teams your boss sent after my family are either dead or in custody. What makes you think you're going to be any different?"

Smoke man merely laughed like that was hilarious. "Look around you, my friend. This time we're in the middle of the ocean, in a boat, and the odds are stacked quite firmly against you."

"Odds have always been stacked against us since your boss is the one with all the knowledge, and we're walking around blind. Didn't stop my brothers from taking out every single team sent after us," Jake reminded him. The odds might be against him, but he was fighting for something more important than the money and ability to hurt others that had led to these men taking the job. To them, this was just a job, but for him, the life of the woman he loved was hanging in the balance.

Failing wasn't an option.

So he *had* to figure out a plan.

"Don't forget we have another beautiful person in the mix," smoke man said as he took a step closer to Alannah, squatting down beside her and making her shrink closer against his side. "A stunning one. Being lost at sea hasn't taken from your beauty at all, my dear."

Gasping, Alannah looked from smoke man to him and back again. "It's you. He's the one, Jake. The one who got me out of the fire in the park. I don't understand. Why did you try to kill me and then save me? If you hadn't stepped in, I would have died that day."

A brief look of something crossed the man's face. "You reminded me of someone, your screams ..." he trailed off and shook himself as though trying to let go of an unwanted memory. "I left a note in your car. I thought you would see it, give it to them, and they would back off. I believe I was misinformed. I was told you were his girlfriend, and when he went to you I thought it must be true. But given that he and his family wouldn't back off to save your life, I suppose I was wrong, you're not that important to him after all."

The words made Alannah flinch slightly, not noticeable to the others, but since she was pressed against him, Jake felt it. Smoke man's declaration had him clenching his teeth together to refute it. Alannah was important, she meant everything to him, but if he said that he was painting an even bigger target on her back. Better if these men believed they were just friends even if that no longer felt true to him.

"Bring them inside," smoke man said to the other half dozen men standing around watching them.

Well, watching Alannah was a little more accurate. It didn't take any special training to read their expressions. They wanted some time with her, to be given permission to take whatever they wanted from her, and the sick feeling in his stomach told him that it was no doubt what would wind up happening after they tried to extract some information out of him.

"We have a room prepared for you," smoke man continued. "Probably not the kind you were hoping for. There's no steaming shower and comfortable bed waiting for you. No hot meal and clean clothes. But at least you'll be inside, I'm sure that will be nice after your time on the island. That was you, wasn't it? Who had the cute little shelter? Who killed two of my best men and stole their boat?"

There was no real anger in the man's voice, though, and Jake doubted he cared that two of his men were dead. However, a thread of excitement worried him more than anything else. Smoke man was looking forward to this. He might have spared Alannah's life once, but it wouldn't happen again.

And as the men grabbed them both, dragging Alannah away from him, Jake was forced to acknowledge there was likely nothing he could do to stop the inevitable from happening.

He hadn't saved his sunshine, hadn't fulfilled his long-ago promise to her.

He'd failed.

∼

October 21st
2:36 A.M.

The wounds on her feet stung as she and Jake were led through the boat.

Well, *led* was being more than generous. They weren't being led, they were being pulled along faster than she could keep up. Which was probably a good thing so that her feet didn't take too much more punishment. None of the wounds were deep, but Alannah wanted to be prepared to make a move whenever Jake gave her an indication that it was time.

They weren't giving up.

They were going to fight until their last breaths if necessary.

Of course, she didn't want to die there, especially not when things were changing between her and Jake, and it felt like a world of possibilities stretched out in front of her so long as she was brave enough to reach out and take them. But if they couldn't fight their way out of this, at least she wanted to die knowing she'd done every single thing within her power to live.

Down two flights of stairs into what looked like the lowest deck, they were led along the short hall and then into a room.

As they entered, it felt like she slammed into a brick wall even though no such wall blocked the doorway.

It was a mental wall.

Because the room was something out of a horror movie or an episode of Criminal Minds or Dexter.

This wasn't just any room, it was quite obviously set up for one very specific purpose. Plastic sheets were strung up across the walls and covering the floor. A single chair sat to one side, and a bed was pressed up against the adjacent wall. The only other piece of furniture in the room was a table that held what could only be described as instruments of torture.

That's what this room was.

A torture chamber.

Nausea swelled in her stomach, and she was suddenly glad she hadn't eaten anything since the fish Jake had caught for lunch. After eating it for breakfast, lunch, and dinner all the previous day and then twice already yesterday, she'd been starting to get sick of the taste, especially when they had no seasonings or sauces to go with it, but she'd still been grateful for food to put in her belly so she didn't starve.

"Put the beautiful lady in the chair," the fire man said. His tone was creepy because it was so normal. It didn't sound evil, angry, or scary at all, just like a regular tone you would use when talking to your friends.

The two men holding her arms immediately shoved her into the chair, using the leather restraints already attached to it to secure her arms in place.

"Those are leather, my dear, so you'll find that it won't abrade your skin like plastic would, and it won't leave bruises like metal might," fire man told her, then stood there staring at her expectantly.

Did he expect her to thank him for that?

As though banging up her wrists was her biggest problem right now?

When Jake gave her a discreet nod, she assumed he was telling her to play along so she looked at fire man and offered a weak smile. "Thank you."

"You're welcome." He beamed at her as though she'd made his day. "I think we'll keep Mr. Holloway where he is for now. You two are dismissed."

The two men who had just bound her to the chair gave small nods and then disappeared from the room, leaving her, Jake, fire man, and the two remaining guards holding onto Jake and shooting him wary looks like they weren't sure he wouldn't start fighting them at any second.

He would.

She could see it in his eyes.

But she also knew Jake well enough to know that he was also going to try to gather some intel before he made his move.

Fire man moved toward her, and Alannah braced for pain. Instead of touching her, he merely knelt at her feet and reached out to circle his hand around her ankle. It took every ounce of self-control she had not to flinch or kick out at him. He deserved whatever meagre pain she could inflict and so much more after everything he'd put them through, but Jake had a plan, and she wasn't going to mess with it.

"You have beautiful feet, my dear," fire man told her as he lifted one of her feet off the ground. A furrow creased his brow when he saw the small cuts dotting her skin. "Did you get these running from my men?"

There didn't seem to be any point in lying so she nodded.

"I always liked feet. I'm sorry you were hurt." Trailing a fingertip lightly across the myriad of scratches, he then leaned in and touched a kiss to the sole of her foot.

While it didn't help with the nausea, it did give her an idea.

Earlier, when she'd asked why he had set the fire at the park and then saved her from it, he'd said that she reminded him of someone. Could he have had a previous girlfriend or wife who he had worshiped the way he was currently touching kiss after kiss to her feet, whose screams he had heard in a fire?

It couldn't hurt to push a little, right?

"Did you lose someone?" she asked softly, and his gaze darted up to meet hers. Swallowing down the fear that she was going to make things worse, she kept talking. "Before you said that my screams ... that they reminded you of someone. Was it someone you loved?"

"It was my entire world I lost that day," fire man replied. "The woman I loved and planned to marry, and the career I worked hard for. I was in the military, too, you know. Explosives." Fire man flicked a glance over to Jake. "I tried to save her. Failed. Watched as she died inside that house, unable to get inside. They said her death made me lose my mind. I think they were right. It also made me lose my heart. It died along with her. So, if you're expecting mercy, my dear, I'm afraid I have none to give."

The look he gave her was almost apologetic as he reached into his pocket and pulled out a lighter.

Of course.

What else would this guy choose to torture her with except some sort of fire?

"My boss needs to know if you have his name, or if you're close to figuring it out," fire man said, again his gaze over to Jake, the question for him and not for her.

When Jake didn't provide an answer, fire man tutted. Then he flicked the lighter, making its tiny flame appear. The grip he had on her ankle tightened when instinct had her trying to tug her foot away from what her brain recognized as coming pain.

Her ragged breathing was the only sound that filled the room, but when fire man held his lighter to the bottom of her foot, somehow, she managed to contain her gasp of pain.

"You understand, I'm sure, why it's imperative I know anything your family knows before you both die," fire man continued, talking to Jake. "We can do this the easy way or the hard way. The easy way is you just tell me what I need to know, and we can move on, otherwise, we can do this all night."

The lighter was brought close to her skin again and held there.

For a tiny flame, it caused a whole lot of pain, and the longer it burned against her skin, the harder it got to hold in her cries.

At last, a whimper fell free, and she heard Jake growl.

"It's so easy to hurt others when you have the upper hand, isn't it?" Jake sneered. "Would you come at us if you didn't have a couple of dozen men at your disposal?"

"A couple of dozen?" Fire man snorted like the idea was ridiculous. "I had only a dozen and you killed two of them on the island. Ten men is more than I need to get the answers I require. In fact, I could do it on my own. All I need is to hurt your girl for long enough, and you'll tell me what I want to know."

"I'm not his girl," Alannah whispered.

This time fire man gave her an almost pitying look. "Don't lie to me, dear. I don't like it. Now tell me, Mr. Holloway, do you have a name, or can I assure my boss he's safe?"

Burning pain in her foot as he touched the flame to one of her open wounds had Alannah crying out before she could help it, and Jake growled again.

"We don't have a name. Satisfied?"

"Perfectly." Immediately, the pain withdrew, and fire man stood. "That wasn't so hard was it?" Sending another apologetic look her way, he reached out and patted her head like she was a dog to be played with. "Now I'm sorry, my dear, this won't be pleasant for you, but my boss did promise us some time to enjoy you when we caught you. Personally, I won't be partaking in it, no need, I will forever only love one woman, and the thought of touching another feels like a betrayal. But I can't say the same about my team. They're quite looking forward to it."

There was no way to stop the fear that churned in her stomach.

This was always what she had been most afraid of, and now it was about to happen.

Ten men or twenty, it didn't seem to matter. It was still too many.

Her breathing increased to the point where white dots danced in front of her eyes as she hyperventilated.

"I'll be waiting upstairs. When my men are finished with their fun, I will come and end your suffering." Fire man ran his hand down her cheek almost tenderly before moving out of her line of sight. "I'll leave you to watch, Mr. Holloway. As punishment for all the trouble you've caused my employer."

Behind her, she could hear the door opening, footsteps, and then a moment later, a different man appeared before her. This one didn't look apologetic in the least, in fact he looked the opposite, he was everything evil embodied and he was about to rape her.

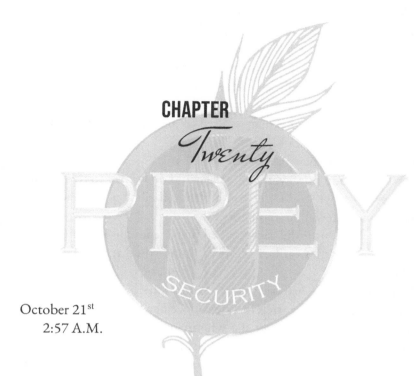

# CHAPTER

## *Twenty*

October 21st
2:57 A.M.

Every muscle in his body tensed.

Every nerve ending stood at attention.

Every sense heightened as he bided his time.

Jake was ready to pounce, could feel the energy surging inside him, every bit of anger and fear he'd felt these last few weeks as he watched Alannah's life get put on the line time and time again was now being channeled into something constructive.

As soon as his opportunity presented itself, he was ready to make his move.

Still, nothing was harder than hanging still in the arms of the two guards flanking him as he watched another man enter the room and walk straight to the chair where Alannah was bound.

Open hunger was on the man's face, and because he knew it would look suspicious if he didn't at least try to get to her, Jake made a half-hearted attempt at fighting out of the men's holds.

"Don't touch her," he growled.

"What're you going to do to stop me?" The man sneered as he began to unbuckle the leather straps from around Alannah's wrists.

"I'm going to kill you," Jake replied simply as he strengthened his efforts to get free. Freedom wasn't his goal yet, but he needed the guards to think he was giving it his all so they were unprepared when he actually did unleash on them.

"Course you are," the man scoffed as he snatched Alannah up, throwing her over his shoulder.

For one second, their gazes met.

Since he couldn't use words, all Jake could do was try to reassure her with his eyes, let her see that he had a plan and all he needed her to do was hold on for a few more moments.

Tossing her onto the rickety bed hard enough that her body bounced, the man was on her before Alannah could try to crawl away from him.

Nothing in his life had been as traumatic as this moment.

Watching as the man stretched out above her, pinning her in place, crushing his mouth to hers as she whimpered and fought. When the man reached between them and freed his length from his pants, then shoved Alannah's leggings and panties down enough to bare her to the room, he saw red.

But it wasn't until the man nudged her thighs apart and settled between them, lining up to shove himself inside her, that Jake sprang into action.

Both men holding onto him were distracted, their arousal heavy in the air, one of them reaching with his free hand to palm his erection. There was never going to be a better moment to do something to give him and Alannah a chance of living.

Tearing himself free from the men who had no idea of the strength coursing through his body, Jake grabbed both their heads, one in each hand, and slammed them together.

The blows stunned both of them but caught the attention of the man on the bed, who lunged toward him. With his pants around his knees, he stumbled and fell, and Jake laughed as he stomped on the neck of the man closest to him, crushing his windpipe, then reached for the one who had been about to rape Alannah.

"Told you I'd kill you," he said with another cold laugh as he snapped the man's neck.

That left one alive in there with them, and he was fumbling for his weapon, blood smeared all over his face, and swaying slightly.

Tearing the weapon from the man's hands was like taking candy from a baby, and he'd snapped his neck before he was able to put up a fight, leaving them alone with three dead bodies. With three dead, that left another seven to go plus the smoke man. They could wait in the room until whoever was next in line for a turn with Alannah came looking and then kill him, that would eliminate another of smoke man's team and even the odds to seven to two.

Definitely doable.

Now, though, he needed to take a moment to check in on his girl.

Spinning around, Jake found her huddled against the wall on the bed, her knees pulled up to her chest, her clothes still in disarray, her eyes wide, and her breathing still much too fast.

Tucking the weapon into the waistband of his pants, Jake held up his hands like he would approaching any other traumatized victim, because he couldn't count on Alannah being cognizant enough to recognize him right now. Then he walked slowly toward the bed.

"Hey, sunshine, it's me, Jake. Grumpy," he added as he knelt on the bed before her.

"You killed them," she whispered.

Since he knew she'd seen him kill before, he didn't think she was scared of him or upset about what he'd done. She knew they were in a kill or be killed situation.

That was confirmed when she launched herself at him, almost knocking him off the bed as she threw her arms around his neck. "You saved me. Again. Thank you."

A small growl rumbled through him. "Don't thank me for that. As long as I'm breathing, I'll always be there to save you."

Planting a kiss on his lips, she gifted him one of her sunshiny smiles. "I believe you."

As much as he'd love to drag this moment out and keep Alannah in his arms where he wanted her, they still had a long way to go if they wanted to survive. So reluctantly, Jake stood, bringing Alannah with him, and set her on her feet. She winced slightly and he wished he could baby her feet for her, let her stay off them so the fresh burns didn't cause her pain, but in this moment their lives were more important than a bit of pain.

Righting her clothes, he felt her stiffen and knew it was going to take a long time for her to heal from this whole ordeal. Even then, there would be scars.

"We're going to wait for the next guy to come looking for his turn and kill him, then we'll start making our way upstairs," he explained, positioning her so she'd be behind the door when it opened. "After that, they'll realize something is wrong and we don't want to be trapped in here when they do. Ideally, we'll find them all alone and kill them as we go. I have a gun, but I'll only use it if it's strictly necessary. I don't want to alert anyone that we're free."

Still wide-eyed, Alannah nodded and stayed where he left her as they both waited.

About ten minutes later, he heard it.

Someone was approaching.

From what he could hear, it was only one man, and he tensed in preparation.

As soon as the door swung open, Jake spun into action.

Catching the man by surprise, before he could do anything about it, Jake had an arm locked around his neck and was pinning him against his body. Although the man fought, Jake had a steady hold and pulled tighter, cutting off air to the man's lungs and blood flow to his brain, until he finally stopped fighting. When he was dead, Jake dropped his body to join his colleagues.

Without hesitating, he grabbed Alannah's hand, tugging her along with him as they stepped out into the hall. Thankfully, she came without protest, and he angled her behind him, while still maintaining his hold on her hand.

The boat wasn't huge, three decks plus the top one, and not more than a handful of rooms on each level.

They found one man in the engine room, but he was so busy with the magazine full of naked girls that he was reading—likely to get himself ready for his turn with Alannah—that he didn't even know they were behind him until Jake was on him.

Five dead, six to go.

With the bottom deck cleared, they moved up one. This level was the bedroom suites, and all of them were empty.

Not good for them, because that meant the others were likely congregated on either of the remaining two decks.

If he could get them to the top deck unspotted, he'd have Alannah jump off the boat and wait for him in the water. While they could find her that way, she'd at least be harder to spot which should hopefully buy them both enough time for him to kill the remaining men without having to worry about her.

Reaching the next deck, he heard voices, and as they crept closer he could see four men drinking and lounging around a table. That meant there was still smoke man and one other somewhere else.

Killing these four men without the gun was unlikely, which meant he needed Alannah out of the way.

"I want you to get up on the top deck and as soon as you hear me start shooting, jump into the water," he whispered, holding his lips above her ear.

"I don't want to leave you," she whispered back, her fingers tightening around his.

"Don't want to leave you either, sunshine, but this is the best way. Go. They're drunk, I can take them out before they get to their weapons, then there are only two to go. Please, sunshine, go, be safe."

Indecision was still warring in her eyes, but she stood on tiptoe to feather her lips across his. "Be safe," she said softly and then she was gone, limping up the final flight of stairs.

Giving her time to get up, he readied himself. As soon as he started shooting, he would alert the two other men. While these ones laughing and drinking wouldn't have time to get to their weapons before he started killing them, smoke man and the other one left of his team would.

His position would be blown, so he'd have to move quickly. With one last deep breath, he threw open the door to the living room where they were hanging out, and as they all turned he started firing.

Four shots, four dead bodies.

Trusting his abilities, he didn't stop to double-check that they were dead, just ran for the stairs Alannah had just gone up, praying she'd jumped like he told her to.

Just as he reached the top, someone fired on him.

Dodging to the side, ignoring a burning sting across his shoulder, he returned fire and heard a thud that he hoped was the sound of a body hitting the deck.

Firing into it a couple more times to ensure it was dead, Jake jumped over it and scanned the top deck in search of the final man.

When he spotted him, his heart dropped.

Smoke man emerged from the darkness, with Alannah pressed against his chest, the smell of gasoline heavy in the air, and a lighter in his hand.

~

October 21st
3:21 A.M.

Cool air hit her skin as she reached the top deck.

Leaving Jake behind felt like leaving part of herself behind.

It felt wrong.

They were partners, a team, she should be there with him.

Alannah believed that even as she knew there was nothing she could contribute right now. She'd be a liability to Jake, splitting his focus and putting him in danger. This might be what he needed her to do, but that didn't mean she liked it.

Jumping back into the water was the last thing she wanted to do. In fact, Alannah would be perfectly happy to never go back in the ocean again for as long as she lived. But if Jake thought that was where she'd be safest so he didn't worry about her, that was what she would do.

Running to the closest railing, she was just lifting her foot over it when she heard footsteps.

Before she could even turn around, she heard a soft whooshing sound, like someone was throwing liquid. For a second, she wondered if she was imagining that the sound was coming from behind her and was in fact nothing more than the sounds of the ocean below her.

Then something sloshed all over her.

Drenching her.

Only it wasn't water.

It felt thicker and the smell ...

She would swear that it was gasoline she'd just been covered in.

Desperate to get the potentially dangerous liquid off her, Alannah was going to throw herself over the edge and into the water, when whoever had thrown the gas at her spoke.

"I wouldn't do that if I were you," fire man said, and she heard the slight click of the lighter. "You might survive, but the fire mixing with the gasoline would still do tremendous damage in the seconds it would take you to fall and hit the water."

Those seconds might be barely a couple, but he was right. The flames would still eat at her skin, and by the time she hit the water and hopefully doused them out, they would leave lasting damage.

"Turn around. Don't be stupid," fire man ordered, and since she didn't see that she had another option, it would be too big a risk to try jumping and hope for the best when she could feel how close behind her he was, she did as she was told.

Right as she faced him, gunshots echoed from below deck.

Perfect.

Jake was taking out more of fire man's men right this very second. There had been four in that room, and another five dead before that, which meant only one more of them was up here somewhere.

Not somewhere.

There.

Running toward them.

"Kill him," fire man ordered, and with a nod, the man took off for the stairs she'd just come up. "I don't know how he did it, but even if your boyfriend kills him and survives, you won't, my dear."

"He's not my boyfriend," she whispered automatically, the smell of the gasoline on her clothes, hair, and skin making her feel a little dizzy.

"Don't lie, dear. I see how he looks at you."

It was stupid to be taking relationship advice from a man who had clearly lost his mind when he lost the woman he loved, but she was doing it anyway. "How does he look at me?"

"The same way I looked at Wendy. Like she was the sun of my world, like everything revolved around her, like I couldn't live without her. I'm glad I'm going to go out the same way she did, burned alive."

With that, he lifted the plastic container sitting on the deck beside him and doused himself with the remaining gas. She tried to dodge around him, but he was too quick. His arm snapped out to wrap around her neck, pulling her up against his body, the lighter still in his other hand.

Maybe he was glad to be burned alive, she guessed as self-imposed punishment for not saving his love, but she certainly didn't want to die this way. Nor did she want her screams as the flames consumed her to be the last memory Jake would have of her.

Jake was at the top of the stairs, firing shots at the remaining man, who dropped while he stayed standing. Firing a few more shots into the body on the deck, Jake jumped over it, and she knew the exact second he saw her.

The horror on his face as he took in the situation had her heart sinking.

Jake knew there was no way to save her.

Both she and fire man were doused in gas, and he was holding a lighter. If Jake shot at them, the bullet could do the same thing as the lighter and set them on fire. If he tried to jump at them to get control of the lighter, he'd never cross the short distance between them before fire man could set them alight.

It was hopeless.

"I guess you get to live after all," fire man said to Jake. "But she doesn't. I hope you all learn your lesson. Nothing is more important than the people you love, certainly not answers from a two-decade-old crime, when the victim isn't even alive to enjoy any justice they might get. When you get home, tell your family to back off, leave the past where it belongs, and live for the future. Live for those you love because you never know when you're going to lose them."

Those words weren't for her because fire man thought she would be joining him in death, but they resonated nonetheless.

For so long, she *had* been living in the past. Allowing her parents' lack of love and care for her to dictate everything she did, and because of that, she hadn't realized everything she'd ever wanted had already been sitting there staring her in the face.

Jake.

She wanted him to be her future, but to make that happen, she had to have a future.

No way was she just giving up and accepting her death.

Just because Jake's hands were tied didn't mean hers were.

"Don't, please," Jake begged. "Don't take her from me."

"It's the only way you'll learn," fire man said, lifting the lighter, his gaze locked on it, and she knew if she didn't try something right this second it would be too late.

Lifting her foot, Alannah rammed it down on fire man's, at the same time she slammed her head back into his chin, and her elbows into his gut.

While she might be smaller than fire man and not as strong, she'd caught him by surprise, and his hold on her loosened, giving her the chance to scramble away.

"Shoot," she screamed at Jake as she slid across the deck, putting some distance between her and fire man so she didn't get set alight along with him.

"Sometimes love really does win," fire man said as his lighter flickered to life at the same time Jake fired at him.

There was no way to know which set the man on fire, but he was suddenly engulfed in flames. The sounds of his screams would haunt her forever. They were inhuman, something she hoped to never hear again.

Coughing as the smell of smoke and burning flesh mixed with the gas that still covered her body, she jerked when Jake was suddenly beside her.

"Hold on, sunshine," he urged as he scooped her up and started running with her.

Where she wasn't sure, nor did she care. Jake was there so she was okay, he'd take care of her. The fumes were making her dizzy and giving her a headache, and she sighed in relief as she was suddenly pressed up against something cool.

"Keep your eyes closed," Jake ordered gently, and she realized she had closed them.

Happy to do what he ordered, she was exhausted anyway and finally her body felt like it was ready to let go and get the sleep it needed, she kept them closed and cool water began to flow over her.

Focusing on her head first, Jake rinsed it off before stripping her out of the gas-soaked clothes and washing every inch of her body. His touch was soft and steady, and he scrubbed at her skin. While she'd thought if she was ever blessed with a shower again, she'd be able to stand for hours washing herself over and over again, Alannah decided this was better.

This was the man she had fallen in love with taking care of her.

His love for her felt echoed in every touch, how thorough he was, how careful not to hurt her, how he made sure to lean her against the shower wall so she wasn't putting all her weight on her cut and burned feet.

They did hurt, she realized somewhat absently as the weight of exhaustion crushed down upon her.

Actually, she ached all over.

"It's okay, sunshine, let go, sleep, I've got you."

Those words put a smile on her face, and trusting Jake to watch over her as he called his brothers and got them both help, Alannah gave in to the exhaustion and got washed away to sleep.

# CHAPTER
## Twenty-One

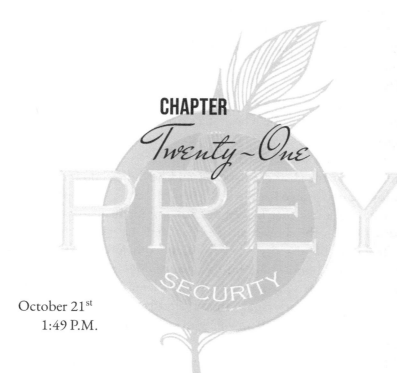

October 21st
1:49 P.M.

Sitting in a hospital room in clean, dry clothes, with a full stomach, showered, and warm felt surreal.

Jake couldn't quite believe that he and Alannah had survived and were back home, safe and sound. Well, safe for now. They'd survived this attack, but that didn't change the fact that one more rapist was still out there, who was no doubt going to make some other attempt to silence them.

In reality, his best bet would be to lie low and not stir them up further. They were still working to find out who he was, but it was the fact that these men had kept coming after his family that kept giving them more clues as to their identities.

Three down and one to go.

They would find this man he had no doubt about it, but for the moment, figuring out who he was wasn't Jake's priority.

The woman lying sleeping in the hospital bed was.

Alannah had been through hell because of him. She'd been targeted over and over again, and if it hadn't been for her own actions would have died an excruciating death.

That was the hardest pill for Jake to swallow.

He hadn't saved her.

She would have died.

And he would have been forced to watch it happen.

"Safe, she's safe. Alive, she'll heal, she's strong, she can survive this," he whispered aloud.

The real question was, could they?

Things had changed so dramatically, and he didn't know if it was possible for them to just go back to being best friends.

What he did know that he wanted was for Alannah to wake up. She'd passed out in the shower on the boat while he was washing the gasoline from her body and was yet to regain consciousness. Once he had her clean, he'd bundled her into a towel and gone searching for a radio. Alerting the coast guard and then his family, it had been his brothers who arrived first since they'd already been in the ocean searching for him and Alannah unwilling to believe they were dead.

Both had been taken immediately to the hospital and checked out, and neither of them had any serious injuries, although they were both dehydrated and suffering from some minor cuts and bruises. The bottoms of Alannah's feet were messed up, but they'd heal so long as she mostly kept off them for the next few days.

Still, knowing Alannah was okay and her waking up and telling him herself were two different things, and he was desperate for the latter.

"Come on, sunshine, I really need you to wake up now," he whispered into the silent room. His brothers were all at the hospital, but they'd understood without him needing to say it that he needed some time alone with Alannah as he watched over her. "You can go back to sleep right after, I just need to hear you say you're okay."

Maybe what he also needed to hear her say was that she didn't hate him for almost getting her killed. She'd asked to stay with him, and he'd told her no, sent her away, thinking he was sending her to safety when instead, he was sending her right into the heart of the danger.

How could he ever forgive himself for that?

"Jake?"

The whispered word had his heart rate picking up. Finally. His sunshine was awake. "Hey," he said softly, reaching out to brush a lock of hair off her forehead.

"Was it all a dream? Are we still on the boat? Or the island?" Alannah's brow was furrowed with anxiety, and the pad of his thumb couldn't help but reach out and smooth it away.

"Not a dream, sunshine. You're safe, back home. We're in the hospital."

"Are you okay? Did you get shot?"

That the first words out of her mouth after confirming that it was all real were asking after him warmed him in a way he could get all too used to. After his mom died, no one had really cared how he was doing, no one had put him first, and while he knew he had a family who adored him and would move heaven and Earth for him, it wasn't the same as knowing that this sweet woman cared about him in a way he'd never allowed himself to hope for.

"No, sunshine, I didn't get shot. We're both okay. Exhausted, dehydrated, banged up, especially you with your feet, but we are both okay."

"I was lucky you came with me. If you hadn't been there, I'd be dead a dozen times over."

Jake was shaking his head vigorously by the time she finished her sentence. How could she say that? If it were solely up to him, she would be dead. There had been no way for him to save her when the smoke man doused her in gasoline and threatened to set her alight.

She'd saved herself.

Reaching out a hand, she took one of his and laced their fingers together. A look of tentative hope on her face made his stomach drop. He knew where this was going, and he wasn't sure he was ready—or ever would be—to have this conversation.

"Before the boat found us, I had something I wanted to tell you. Something important," Alannah said, a fine tremor to her voice that told him she, too, was nervous about having this conversation.

Just braver than him because she was going to push for it, whereas he would have just moved forward, pretending the last couple of days had never happened.

"Things have changed, Jake," she said softly, her fingers tightening around his.

"What are you saying?" he demanded, slightly too harshly if Alannah's flinch was anything to go by. "Are you saying we're still just best friends, or are you trying to tell me you want more?"

For a few seconds, she just looked at him, and he got the uncomfortable feeling that she was actually looking all the way inside him and down to his soul.

"It would be easier to just say I don't want things to change, that we should pretend we didn't have sex several times, but I can't do that," she told him. "I don't want to lie. I know we never talked about it, that when we were on the island it felt like we were in another, somewhat simpler universe, but my feelings for you have changed. I want more. I want a future where maybe we explore this new development, see where it goes."

His pulse pounded in his ears.

Everything she'd said was everything he was afraid of.

What if they tried and it turned out he wasn't enough for her?

Never in his life had he been enough for someone.

If they did what Alannah wanted and it didn't work out, there would be no going back. He'd lose his best friend.

That wasn't a risk he was prepared to take.

"Look, Alannah, I don't want things to change, I'm sorry. I just want to be your friend." The lie tasted bitter on his tongue, but now that he'd said the words, he couldn't take them back. "It's not that I don't care about you or don't want you in my life, of course I do. You're my best friend and you always will be, but I don't want to risk messing up our friendship. Can you understand that?"

"I understand," she whispered, pulling her hand away from his. "It's because I'm not worth the risk," she said softly, doing her best to hide her devastation but failing miserably.

That wasn't it at all, although he had no idea how to convince her of that.

It was because *he* wasn't worth the risk. Jake wasn't sure he had what Alannah deserved, and if he didn't, and she wound up dumping him, there would really be no going back.

Hurting her sucked and he hadn't wanted to have this conversation right now, but he also couldn't offer her false hope. He wasn't good enough for her. Sooner or later he'd fail her like he had on the boat.

"Hey, nothing has to change," he said, forcing a smile he certainly didn't feel, and reached out to ruffle her hair like he would any other time. "We're still best friends. You're still my sunshine, and I'm still your grumpy."

Because Jake was afraid that if he stayed around her any longer he'd confess his true feelings, his fears and insecurities, he pushed to his feet. It was running away like a coward, but it was all he could handle when his emotions were so fresh and raw.

"I'm going to let you get some rest, but we'll talk later, yeah?"

"Yeah," Alannah echoed without any conviction.

As he gave her a quick kiss on the cheek then hurried out of the room, he wondered if he'd already done exactly what he was afraid of.

Had lying and turning her down done exactly what he was afraid of anyway?

It felt like there was no good answer. Either he didn't give them a chance and lost her, or he gave them a chance and lost her.

Either way, he lost.

～

October 21ˢᵗ
6:35 P.M.

Being anywhere without Jake felt weird.

Wrong.

It had only been four days since they'd sat out on the deck of her yacht watching as the sun set and stars blinked on one by one, but it felt like she'd lived an entire lifetime in those four days.

For four days, he'd been her everything, the only thing standing between life and death, the person making sure she was provided for, the person who taught her more about her body and what it was capable of than anyone else ever had.

Now Jake was just ... gone.

It hurt.

A lot.

Alannah kept rubbing at her chest because it felt like something sharp and prickly had lodged in there. It wasn't like she was asking for a ring and a proposal, all she wanted was a chance for them to explore the changed feelings she had been so sure they were both experiencing.

Only now she was doubting everything.

Maybe things hadn't changed for Jake. Sometimes his ability to be so stoic about everything meant it was hard to tell if he was lying to her. Usually, she assumed he wasn't, because they were both adults and best friends, so why should he have to lie to her about anything? But today she wasn't so sure.

She *wanted* him to be lying.

Because if he wasn't, then he truly did only feel friendship for her, and she'd gone and stupidly fallen in love with him.

How very *her* of her.

Falling in love with men who would never love her back seemed to be her curse. She just never thought it would include Jake.

Despite what he'd said about still wanting to be friends and not wanting anything to mess that up, it had already been messed up. They'd had sex, kissed, and she'd caught feelings, things could never really go back to the way they'd been before.

"I'll be staying with you tonight, Alannah, you won't be alone," Jax said from the driver's seat of the car as he parked across the street from her building. She appreciated that, she hadn't been back to the underground parking garage since the incident, and she wasn't ready to face that yet.

She also appreciated Jax stepping up in his big brother's absence.

Jake just walking away wasn't what she'd expected him to do regardless of whether he'd been willing to give them a shot.

*You're not worth it.*

*Not worth it.*

The insidious little voice kept whispering those words, and she was afraid that the more she heard them, the more she would believe them.

With everything else she had on her plate to deal with, the last thing she needed was for her self-worth to take another plummet.

"Appreciate it, Jax," she said, fighting a yawn. Apparently, she'd slept for almost twelve hours after passing out in the shower on the boat. She shouldn't be so tired, but her body felt as though she hadn't slept at all.

"Look, about, Jake, he—"

"I'd rather not talk about it." Alannah added a smile to soften the words, but right now she was holding onto an avalanche of emotions by a thread. One single thread. It wasn't going to take much to make her lose her grip on that thread.

"Okay, honey, but I'm here if you change your mind."

With a nod she hoped conveyed her appreciation, they both climbed out of the car. Her body felt heavy as they crossed the street and headed into the lobby. Normally, she'd make sure to spend a little time chatting with the doorman, but today all she could manage was a watery smile.

Trudging alongside Jax, they headed into the lift to head to her floor. Usually, she took the stairs, they were a good little workout to start or end her day, but there was no way her legs could handle six flights with how she felt.

When they stepped out of the lift, Alannah felt like she was in a fog, all that hope she'd felt when she realized fire man was dead and they'd survived had vanished like a puff of smoke when Jake rejected her.

Rejected her.

Like everybody else in her life.

*Because you're not worth it.*

*Why would you ever think you were?*

Lifting her head to tell Jax that she realized she didn't even have her keys, they'd gotten blown up along with her purse and all her identification on her yacht, Alannah froze.

Someone was standing outside the door to her apartment.

Not someone. Jake.

Jake was standing there.

Only he didn't quite look as put together and in control as she usually saw him.

As soon as he saw her, he straightened, his eyes locking on hers like a heat-seeking missile and refusing to look away.

"Wh-what are you d-doing here?" she stammered. Jake was the last person she expected to see tonight. Her plan had been to get home, take another hot shower, change into something more comfortable than the hospital scrubs she'd been given to wear home, order takeout, then fall into her bed for much-needed sleep.

Nowhere had she factored Jake into her night.

"Telling you I'm an idiot," he replied.

"An idiot?"

"You're worth it. You're worth the risk. You're worth everything."

Those words were exactly what she needed to hear ... four hours ago in her hospital room. Now ...

Now they didn't feel real, they felt like he was just panicking and telling her what he knew she wanted to hear. How was she supposed to believe that he'd changed his mind in a matter of hours?

"You two should talk inside," Jax said, giving her a nudge.

Talking was the last thing she wanted to do. Shower, food, bed. That was what her body needed, she didn't have the emotional energy left for a conversation, but Jake was looking at her with hopeful eyes and she found she couldn't say no.

After all, how long could this conversation take?

"Fine," she muttered.

Her worry about keys was unfounded since Jake seemed to have a set. He unlocked her door and held it open for her. Somewhat reluctantly, she entered, dropping down onto her huge, fluffy, leather couch. It cocooned her like a soft cloud, and while not quite as good as her bed would be, it felt nice to be sitting on something comfortable instead of the sand and dirt on the island.

"I'm sorry I hurt you," Jake said without preamble as he dropped to his knees in front of her. "It's not you who isn't worthy, it's me."

"What do you mean?" she asked totally confused.

"I didn't save you."

"I'm sitting right here."

"But if you hadn't gotten yourself out of the smoke man's hold, I wouldn't have been able to save your life. You would have died. A horrific death. And it would have been my fault. I would have failed you."

Jake had a real thing about failing.

Just like she did about not being worthy of love and affection.

Together, their problems could tear them apart, drive a wedge between them, or they could help each other heal. Learn to see themselves the way the other saw them.

"It wouldn't have been your fault, Jake," she said softly. Reaching out with tentative hands she grasped his, relieved when he quickly held onto her like a lifeline. "I know you promised to protect me when you were five, but I never, not even at four, thought that meant you could shield me from all pain. I just thought it meant you'd always be there. That I'd never have to be alone again. You've given me that every day since."

"I'm worried I'm not worthy of you," Jake admitted, his gaze drifting away before steadfastly returning to meet hers.

"Because you think you have to protect me from everything, but that's never what I needed, Jake. I just needed you. I just want you. But I don't think I can go back to just being best friends." Jake had been honest with her, so she owed him the same.

She owed him the truth. The entire truth.

No holding anything back.

"I realize that we're taking a big risk, I realize that if it doesn't work out then our friendship could be ruined. But I don't care. I want to take that risk. I don't want to live with regrets, and I certainly don't want to live without you in my life."

"I told you on the island we'd find a way to make it work no matter what happened. I should have held to that promise instead of bailing on you out of fear."

"At least you came back, at least you're facing your fears instead of running from them. I don't want to run from my feelings, Jake. I want to embrace them. I understand that maybe you don't feel the same way."

"Feel what way?"

It was time to say the words and pray she wasn't about to get rejected. "I'm in love with you, Jake Holloway."

# CHAPTER
## *Twenty~Two*

October 21st
6:57 P.M.

She loved him.

*She* loved *him*.

Alannah loved him.

Jake couldn't quite believe that it could be true.

That voice in the back of his mind kept reminding him that Alannah would be dead right now if it wasn't for her own quick thinking. Although she didn't seem to see it the same way.

Maybe if she could see past it, he could learn to as well.

The hands he clutched like a lifeline—because that was exactly what they felt like to him—trembled slightly, and Jake realized Alannah was looking at him with something close to panic in her eyes. Fear and regret as well.

It was then that he realized he hadn't said the words back.

Instead, he'd just been sitting there staring at her like she'd suddenly grown two heads.

To him that was because she was so impossibly amazing, he could hardly believe that he was lucky enough to have been blessed with having her in his life, but Alannah was no doubt convincing herself that he didn't feel the same way.

Leaning in, he crushed his lips to hers. His hands moved, one to cup the back of her neck so he could ravish her mouth, and his other curled around her back, tugging her toward the edge of the couch so she was balanced half on it and half against him.

When he finally pulled back to take a gulp of air, he found Alannah's golden-brown eyes searching his.

"Jake?"

That she didn't trust him hurt a little, but he had no one to blame but himself. If he hadn't panicked and fled the hospital that afternoon, so afraid of failing her and losing her that he'd almost lost her anyway, then she wouldn't have a single doubt about him.

"I love you too, sunshine," he said the words he knew she needed to hear, and that maybe he needed to as well. While he knew his dad had loved him and Jax, he never said the words to them, and as two little boys who had lost their mom, they'd needed that from him. The relatives who had cared for them when his dad was away hadn't loved him, if they had, they wouldn't have made him and Jax feel like burdens. His stepbrothers and Cassandra loved him, but it wasn't like they went around saying those words to each other, they all just knew that they were family.

Hearing those heavenly words fall from the lips of the woman who was the center of his world was an almost magical experience.

"You do? You're sure?" she asked, tentative hope lighting her eyes.

At least he'd had a mom for the first six years of his life who never missed an opportunity to tell him and his brother how much she loved them, so while it had been a long time since someone had said it to him, for Alannah this was all brand new.

Her parents had never told her they loved her because they didn't. And the men she'd dated over the years, desperate to find someone who could love her the way she deserved hadn't loved her even if they might have said the words.

Right here and now, Jake vowed that never again would Alannah doubt that she was worthy of love. Framing her face with his hands, he held it still, so she had no choice but to meet his gaze and read the sincerity in his eyes. "Twenty-eight years ago, I found you crying in your backyard and I made you a promise. I promised that no one would ever hurt you again. I know you told me I haven't, but I can't help but feel I've failed in that vow. I won't fail in the one I'm making to you today. I love you, Alannah Johansen, more than I thought I was capable of loving another person. I'm not the easiest guy to get along with, and yet you never seem to mind. You accept me, faults and all, and I can't imagine not having you in my life."

Tears trickled down her cheeks, but since she was smiling, he assumed they were happy tears. Catching them with the pads of his thumbs, he leaned in and held his lips a millimeter from hers.

"Never again will you doubt your worth. You're everything anyone could ever want and you're mine. If you don't want forever, sunshine, then now is the time to back out." Just because he'd panicked earlier didn't mean he wasn't one hundred percent ready to commit to a future.

"Forever?" Her voice wavered, but her smile grew bigger.

"I think it was written in stone from that first moment, we just had to work through our personal issues enough to see it."

"Forever," she said again, and this time she closed the small distance between them and pressed a soft kiss to his lips. "I want forever, too."

Warmth rushed through his system knowing that they wanted the same thing, that they had the same goals, hopes, and dreams. That didn't mean everything would be easy, Alannah had a lot of trauma she was going to have to work through, but they'd do it together. As a team.

"So what did you have planned for tonight?" he asked, as much as he'd love to ravish her delectable body, if she was too tired, he'd be content to just curl up at her side and hold her while she slept.

"Shower, food, bed."

"Hmm, as long as you're willing to be flexible on the meal, I think we can make that happen." Nipping lightly at her bottom lip, he scooped her into his arms and stood, heading for the bedroom.

Alannah giggled as she wrapped her arms around his neck. "How flexible do I have to be?"

"Flexible enough to let me feast on you," he said, trailing a line of kisses from her temple, down her cheek to her jaw.

A shiver rocketed through her and desire darkened her golden eyes. "Do I get to feast on you, too?"

A groan tumbled from his lips as it felt like every drop of blood in his body congregated in one particular appendage. "If you want to, baby girl."

"I want to." The tip of her tongue darted out and ran along her bottom lip, making him groan again.

In the master bathroom, Jake set her on her feet. "Strip," he ordered as he leaned into her walk-in shower to turn on the water and get it heating. Any other time, he'd love nothing more than to take his time and tease her as he stripped her out of her clothes, but today he just needed to have her shaking in his arms as wave after wave of pleasure cascaded through her system.

By the time he'd removed his own clothes, Alannah was standing before him, gloriously naked. There were bruises still marring her skin, and the gash on her back from the explosion was an angry red color, even though it looked clean and not infected. But despite all of that, she looked perfect, and she was his.

"Mine," he murmured as he backed her into the shower.

"Yours," she readily agreed.

Nodding his approval, he positioned her under the warm spray and grabbed a bottle of her shampoo. Pouring a generous amount into the palm of his hand, he set the bottle down on the shelf and proceeded to wash her hair. He took his time, massaging her scalp, then working the soap down her long locks.

"Close your eyes, baby girl," he ordered as he shifted her slightly so he could rinse out the shampoo.

When the suds were all gone, he grabbed the conditioner and again squeezed a generous amount onto his palm. Making sure he got every single strand of hair coated, he then worked the comb through the tangles until it could move smoothly without catching on any knots.

Again, he rinsed her hair, and the smile she gave him, the warmth and appreciation in it, the love, had his heart swelling in his chest. Taking care of his girl felt wonderful, even if it was only in small ways.

Loofah and body wash were next, and Alannah stood there and let him work his way down her body, starting with her arms and shoulders, and finishing with him sitting on the tiles before her as he washed each dainty little toe.

With his girl fresh and clean and taken care of, it was time for feasting.

Curling his fingers into the soft globes of her backside, Jake pulled her closer. Nudging her feet apart, he spread her legs and settled his between them, leaving her spread open and ready for him.

"Hands on my shoulders," he ordered.

When her small hands settled on his shoulders, he dragged his tongue along her center, savoring the taste. Teasing her entrance he then closed his lips around her bundle of nerves and sucked hard.

Alannah gasped, her hands tightening their grip on him, and he hummed his approval, making her hips thrust against his mouth.

"Uh-uh, baby girl, I'm in charge here," he warned. "You'll come when I'm ready for you to come, and you'll come as many times as I want you to. Understand?"

Giving a shaky nod, her eyes dark with arousal, she stood still and he leaned in again, taking a deep breath and inhaling her scent.

Then he was on her, licking, nipping, and sucking, alternating between thrusting his tongue inside her and lavishing attention on her bud until she was writhing in his hold, pleas falling from her lips.

"Now, sunshine," he ordered, then scraped his teeth lightly across her bundle of nerves and she fell apart.

It was only his grip on her hips that kept her standing, and she was leaning heavily against his shoulders as she rode out the wave of pleasure. As soon as he could feel her coming down from her high, he started up all over again.

"Jake, I can't," she said, trying to pull away from him.

"What did I tell you?" he asked, swatting at her backside.

"Th-that you're in ch-charge here," she stammered, subconsciously rocking her hips closer to his mouth, seeking more of his touch.

"That's right, baby girl." Smoothing his hand over the cheek he'd just tapped, he gripped her hips once again and buried his mouth between her legs.

Suckling on her bud had her coming apart again, her cries filling the steamy shower, and making him impossibly hard.

But it wasn't enough.

"One more," he told her, and again her hips rocked toward him even as she shook her head. "One more," he repeated, then his tongue was thrusting into her at an almost frantic pace as he shifted his hold on her hips so he could take her bundle of nerves between his thumbs.

It didn't take much to make her come a third time, and after she'd ridden out every drop of pleasure he could get from her, he allowed her to sink down so she was straddling his thighs, his erection standing alert between them.

"My turn?" she asked, eyeing him hungrily.

"Nope. Bed was next," he told her as he stood with Alannah in his arms.

"But I didn't get to feast." Her pouty expression made him grin, and he nipped at her bottom lip.

"I'm in charge here, baby girl, those are the rules," Jake reminded her as he grabbed a couple of fluffy mint green towels on his way into her bedroom. "Besides, there's no need to pout. You'll get your turn, after all, we have the entire rest of our lives to get our fill of one another."

The rest of their lives.

He liked the sound of that, and as he spread out a towel, and then laid his girl out on it, he realized just what a lucky man he was to be able to call Alannah his.

~

October 22nd
7:20 A.M.

Something wet touched her inner thigh, and Alannah moaned as warmth pooled low in her stomach.

Blinking open sleepy eyes, she smiled when that same hot, wet thing brushed her other thigh, and she saw it was Jake's dark head between her spread legs.

"May I?" he asked, quirking a brow as his tongue darted out right above her bud which was somehow already throbbing with need despite the fact she'd woken up barely three seconds ago.

"Can't think of a better way to wake up," she answered, voice husky from sleep.

Couldn't think of a better way to go to sleep than what they'd done at bedtime either.

After washing every inch of her body so tenderly in the shower, then making her come on his tongue three times in a row until she thought her death certificate was going to have the embarrassment of being listed as death by orgasm, they'd made love in her bed. Only after they'd eaten dinner with Jax and come back to her room did Jake let her finally taste him. Then they'd made love again, and she'd lost count of how many times Jake had made her come before it was finally too much and she'd sunk into an exhausted slumber, secure in the knowledge that she was safe in his arms.

Forever.

That's what he'd told her he wanted, and even though she couldn't deny she was still a teeny little bit hurt that he'd bailed at the hospital, at least he'd worked through his fears almost immediately and been waiting for her when she got home.

Never again did she want to feel that sense of loss that had filled her soul when she watched Jake walk out of the hospital room door. That emptiness had to be a thing of the past because she was pretty sure if she had to go through it again, it would break her.

"I'm obviously not doing this right," Jake's voice said, pulling her from her thoughts.

"What?" she asked, totally confused, then realized that his mouth had been teasing her needy bundle of nerves and she'd been too lost in her own head to even realize it. "Oh, sorry," she said sheepishly, feeling her cheeks heat with embarrassment.

"Want to tell me what you were thinking about so hard that you couldn't even feel what I was doing?" Jake asked. There was no anger in his tone, no annoyance or irritation, just a little bit of concern and a lot of tender affection.

"Just thinking about how glad I am that you're here," she replied honestly.

Understanding filled his dark eyes. "I'm sorrier than you'll ever know for walking away yesterday. I shouldn't have left your side, not even for a minute."

"I know you're sorry, Jake. I'm not angry, maybe just a little bit hurt still, but I get it, we talked it through and we're good."

"I just need to prove to you I won't leave again."

"I know you won't."

"You want to believe that, but you still have a tiny bit of doubt." When she opened her mouth to protest, Jake took her bud between his lips and sucked hard, making her words turn into a breathy moan. "It's okay to have doubts, sunshine. It just means I need to work harder to prove to you that I'm serious when I say I want forever."

Most of her doubts weren't even Jake's fault. A lifetime of being unwanted and unloved by the people who made you and brought you into this world had messed so deeply with her sense of self that Alannah suspected she would always carry that thread of doubt.

But it didn't have to rule her mind or her life.

Jake loved her, he wanted to be with her, and she loved him too. They could build their own family where neither of them would ever doubt their worth again.

That was what she wanted for them.

Then one day, when they were ready and this threat against the Charleston Holloway family was eliminated, they could think about bringing some new little lives into the world. Children who would be loved unconditionally and would never for a single second feel the pain that she and Jake had experienced growing up.

"Forever," she said, and made a conscious decision to let go of all the negative thoughts and feelings inside her. It would take time, and she knew that she was going to need a lot of counselling to handle everything she'd been through, but in this moment, she only wanted one thing to exist.

Her and Jake and their love.

"Mine," Jake said before his mouth descended on her, finally stealing her ability to think.

His tongue seemed to be in two places at once, thrusting into her and tending to her bundle of nerves simultaneously. And then his fingers were inside her, grazing that magical spot that had stars dancing behind her closed lids.

Spreading her open with his fingers, his tongue delved deeper, those stars shone brighter, and sensations flashed through her body at warp speed. Then his fingers were pumping in and out of her, and his mouth latched onto her bud, suckling it hard, the tip of his tongue swirling over it again and again until it shoved her off the edge.

Right into the most intense orgasm of her life.

She cried out Jake's name as her head thrashed on the pillow, and her hips rocked frantically as Jake drew out every single drop of pleasure from her that he could.

When her eyes finally fluttered open again as all that remained of the earth-shattering orgasm were a few flutters, she saw Jake smiling smugly.

"Bet you weren't thinking of anything then, sunshine."

"Only about how good you make me feel."

"Happy to hear that, because I'm ready to make you come again."

Alannah giggled. "I don't think I can. After last night and then that, I think I'm all orgasmed out, used up my quota for the week."

"Oh, baby girl, you have so much to learn. Who are you?"

"I'm yours," she answered without hesitation.

"And who am I?"

"You're mine."

"So what's my job?"

"Umm, to be my partner?"

"No. Well, yes, but that's not what I meant. My job is to make sure you know your worth. I can't think of a better way to do that than with unlimited orgasms."

"What you're really saying is you have a plan to kill me by orgasm overload," she sassed.

Jake laughed, then his hand swatted lightly at her still tingly bundle of nerves, making her yelp. "Who knew you could be such a little brat. If you're mine then that means your pleasure is mine, and I'm going to make you come over and over again until you think you can't take it anymore, and then I'm going to make you come again."

Why did those words have her insides clenching, and a fresh wave of desire crashing over her?

"Now come again for me, baby girl." Jake's fingers plunged into her without warning, making her hips rise off the bed.

When his thumb brushed across her overstimulated bud, Alannah cried out, and Jake just chuckled and shifted his position, lifting her legs so they were thrown over his shoulders and she was spread wide open for him.

Taking advantage of this new position, his fingers thrust harder, faster, and he teased her bud with soft swipes of his tongue that weren't nearly enough to push her over the edge.

"Please, Jake, please, please," she babbled, unsure if she was telling him to give her more and make her come or telling him it all felt like too much.

"You can do it, sunshine. Your body was made for pleasure, made to be worshiped and adored. So come again, baby girl."

Switching his fingers to her bundle of nerves and his mouth to her entrance, he applied just the right amount of pressure on her bud to have her writhing, her pleas no longer coherent as pressure built inside her. His tongue thrust deep, so hot, so wet, and when he captured her bud between his thumb and forefinger, tweaking it hard, she fell apart.

The sounds that fell from her lips as she rode out the powerful wave of pleasure that crashed over her were pure euphoria. This was love-making like she'd never known it could exist, and she got to do this every day if she wanted for the rest of her life. Finally, knowing that she wasn't broken, that her body was capable of the same things as everybody else's was like living in a dream that was actually reality.

"That was ... that was ..." she babbled as she managed to pry open her eyes to find an even smugger-looking Jake smiling at her.

"Incredible, indescribable, phenomenal, mind-blowing, extraordinary," he supplied for her.

"All of that. But, Jake, I don't think I have more than one more in me, seriously, and I want it with you inside me."

Jake just chuckled and grabbed her under the arms, pulling her up as he shifted onto his knees and settled her so her back was to his chest, her knees on either side of his. In this position, his thick, hard length nestled against her center, and she ground against it on pure instinct, making Jake chuckle again.

"I see you have a short memory, sunshine, let's see if we can do something about that. See if we can remind you who's in control here."

One of his hands claimed her breasts, teasing one nipple and then the other, rolling them between his fingers and tweaking them, while his other rested on her stomach, his fingers slipping between her spread legs and delving into her soaked center.

This man was pure magic, and her head tipped back to rest against his shoulder as he worked her quickly toward her third orgasm of the morning. As she rocked her hips, savoring the feel of his body against hers Alannah had to wonder, was death by orgasm really such a bad way to go when the man delivering them was both her best friend and the man she loved?

# CHAPTER
## *Twenty~Three*

October 22nd
7:47 A.M.

Sliding inside Alannah felt like coming home.

It was like putting the jigsaw puzzle pieces together and no longer having parts missing.

It was belonging.

It was acceptance.

It was perfection.

And the breathy moan that fell from her lips made it that much better. Jake loved that she was a moaner, loved that it was his name falling from her plump lips. Loved the blissed out look on her face as he prepped her for orgasm number four.

Keeping his pace slow and steady, he rocked his hips ignoring the burning need inside him and the fact that his length felt hard enough to break concrete. Watching his girl come was better than any brief rush of pleasure, knowing he was the one who was making her come so easily, time after time, when she'd spent all her adult life believing something was wrong with her and she couldn't orgasm.

That was what loving someone was about.

"How are you doing this," she said on another moan as his fingers played with her bud. "I thought I was broken and now you have me coming over and over again. Magic. Gotta be magic."

Laughing seemed to come so easily when he was with Alannah. She offered him a freedom nothing else ever had and he lapped it up like he was starving.

Because in a lot of ways he was.

The scared little boy who learned to do everything for himself, who so desperately wanted to be loved, was one he'd locked away out of necessity. His dad and stepmom had needed all of them to be strong, to work together to find answers that would clear both their names. But being with Alannah was a safe place to just be.

He hoped that was what he offered her in return.

"I-I'm going to come a-again," Alannah cried out.

Her internal walls fluttered, and he felt himself reaching his own high when someone spoke on the other side of the bedroom door.

"Sorry to interrupt, lovebirds, but you're needed in the living room," Jax called out.

"Oh, I forgot he was still here," Alannah said, cheeks brightening in embarrassment as he felt the pleasure that had been building inside her begin to recede.

Unacceptable.

He'd also forgotten Jax was still there, but with the threat not eliminated and their flight out to Delta Team not until today his little brother had volunteered to stay and watch over them so he could be there for Alannah.

"Come," he ordered his sunshine. No one was stealing this bit of pleasure from her, she deserved only good things.

"I can't," she whispered.

"So easily you forget. You come as many times as I want you to because you're mine," he growled, doubling down on his efforts and working her bud the way he'd already learned had her writhing and pleading.

His own pleasure had receded, but as he watched his ministrations bring Alannah back up to the edge, he felt his own pleasure return. Nothing was more of a turn on than his girl breathless and needy beneath him.

"Come for me, baby girl," he ordered as he thrust deep into her and pressed against her bundle of nerves.

Just like that she combusted for him.

When her internal muscles clamped around him it set off his own orgasm and the world ceased to exist as a rush of ecstasy flooded his system, consuming him in fiery passion and pleasure.

"That had to be the most embarrassing thing ever," Alannah muttered, but her eyes were still dark with desire and she rocked her hips against him as little aftershocks hit both their systems.

"Just sex, sunshine. Jax has had it before and he knows we have too. Nothing to be embarrassed about."

"But he heard us. He was right outside the door while we were right in the middle of things."

"And if he makes you feel embarrassed about it then I'll make sure he only does it once."

A smile lit up her face. "My hero." Reaching up, she framed his face and tugged it closer to hers so she could kiss him.

Hero.

Something he still felt like he had failed at too many times to count when it came to the girl he had vowed to protect. But he was working on catching those feelings any time they popped up and wrangling them under control before they could settle in his mind like a cancerous tumor.

"We better get cleaned up and into the living room," he said as he reluctantly pulled out of Alannah's heat.

"I thought we weren't catching the plane until lunchtime," Alannah said, sitting up as soon as his weight was no longer pressing into her.

"Nuh-uh, stay there," he ordered when she went to stand, then left her on the bed as he headed into her bathroom to grab something to clean her up with.

A few minutes later they were both clean and dressed, and he had her in his arms, carrying her down the hall to the living room so

Alannah didn't put too much pressure on her injured feet. It wasn't just Jax who was there waiting for them, all four of his stepbrothers were there as well.

Even though they hadn't been in relationships all that long it felt kind of weird to see them without their other halves. As he set Alannah down on the empty couch and she nestled in to his side and rested her head on his shoulder when he sat beside her, he realized how glad he was to have found his own other half.

Wishing he'd realized he was in love with his best friend earlier was easy to do, but in the end, they'd found their way together even if it had taken them almost losing their lives to do it. Everything had worked out the way it was supposed to.

Almost.

Because there was still one more rapist who was desperate to keep his identity a secret, and until they found him and brought him to justice his family would never be truly safe.

Which meant all the plans he had for a future with his sunshine had to be put on hold. Not something he was happy with. Their lives already felt like they'd been on hold and were only now just really starting.

"You guys look happy," Jax said with a teasing grin.

"Jax," he warned. No way was he letting his little brother embarrass Alannah about enjoying sex after she'd spent half her life thinking something was wrong with her in that regard.

"What?" Jax's grin grew wider. "I'm happy for you guys. We all are," he added, indicating the rest of their brothers who were watching him with warm smiles as he slipped his arm around Alannah's shoulders and brought her closer against him.

"We are, man, and the girls are dying to get Alannah out there with them so they can find out every little detail of how you got together," Cooper told them.

"But before we leave, we all need to talk," Cade added, always the logical one who brought them back to the task at hand. Jake knew how much of a burden the pressure of responsibility had been to Cade, which was why he'd tried to shoulder as much of it as he could.

"You found something?" Jake asked. Irresponsible of him maybe, but he'd checked out of anything that wasn't Alannah when he came to her place the previous night. She deserved his full attention and he'd been determined to give it to her, but that had obviously meant they'd missed out on a revelation.

"We found *it*," Cole corrected.

He hardly dared to hope. "Does that mean ...?"

"It means we finally know what goes with an Egyptology professor, a principal of an elite private school, and a transplant surgeon," Connor answered.

"You got his name," Jake said as energy flooded his veins. They'd been searching for these names since they were teens, and it felt surreal to have finally got to this place.

"Look familiar?" Cooper slid a photograph across the coffee table.

Snatching it up, Jake nodded immediately. "His features are similar to Cassandra's, the hair color is the same, and he even has a little birthmark at the bottom of his chin just like she does. Who is he and how did you find him?"

"It was the boat," Cade explained. "It took a bit of work, but Prey's cyber division were able to find out who owns it."

"His name is Samson Kennedy," Connor said.

"He was the Ambassador to Egypt while mom was working for the CIA," Cole added.

"He's now the Ambassador to France," Jax told him, a darkness on his face that said there was still something that his brothers hadn't shared and whatever it was Jax didn't like it. "We have a plan to bring him down but it's not going to be easy. We need more than a DNA match to Cassandra to prove paternity because he can just lie and say it was consensual and everyone else who could corroborate that is dead. He already filed a report to say his boat was stolen so we can't use that either."

"Then what are we going to use?" Jake asked as he leaned in to kiss Alannah's temple, needing to feel her close as the culmination of almost twenty years of searching came to a head.

"His daughter," Jax replied.

**What should be an easy way to bring down the man responsible for destroying his family becomes anything but for Jax Holloway in the sixth and final book in the action packed and emotionally charged Prey Security: Charlie Team series!**

Traitorous Lies (Prey Security: Charlie Team #6)

# Also by Jane Blythe

Detective Parker Bell Series

A SECRET TO THE GRAVE

WINTER WONDERLAND

DEAD OR ALIVE

LITTLE GIRL LOST

FORGOTTEN

Count to Ten Series

ONE

TWO

THREE

FOUR

FIVE

SIX

BURNING SECRETS

SEVEN

EIGHT

NINE

TEN

Broken Gems Series

CRACKED SAPPHIRE

CRUSHED RUBY

FRACTURED DIAMOND

SHATTERED AMETHYST

SPLINTERED EMERALD

SALVAGING MARIGOLD

River's End Rescues Series

COCKY SAVIOR

SOME REGRETS ARE FOREVER

SOME FEARS CAN CONTROL YOU

SOME LIES WILL HAUNT YOU

SOME QUESTIONS HAVE NO ANSWERS

SOME TRUTH CAN BE DISTORTED

SOME TRUST CAN BE REBUILT

SOME MISTAKES ARE UNFORGIVABLE

Candella Sisters' Heroes Series

LITTLE DOLLS

LITTLE HEARTS

LITTLE BALLERINA

Storybook Murders Series

NURSERY RHYME KILLER

FAIRYTALE KILLER

FABLE KILLER

Saving SEALs Series

SAVING RYDER

SAVING ERIC

SAVING OWEN

SAVING LOGAN

SAVING GRAYSON

SAVING CHARLIE

Prey Security Series

PROTECTING EAGLE

PROTECTING RAVEN

PROTECTING FALCON

PROTECTING SPARROW

PROTECTING HAWK

PROTECTING DOVE

Prey Security: Alpha Team Series

DEADLY RISK

LETHAL RISK

EXTREME RISK

FATAL RISK

COVERT RISK

SAVAGE RISK

Prey Security: Artemis Team Series

IVORY'S FIGHT

PEARL'S FIGHT

LACEY'S FIGHT

OPAL'S FIGHT

Prey Security: Bravo Team Series

VICIOUS SCARS

RUTHLESS SCARS

BRUTAL SCARS

CRUEL SCARS

BURIED SCARS

WICKED SCARS

Prey Security: Athena Team Series

FIGHTING FOR SCARLETT

FIGHTING FOR LUCY

FIGHTING FOR CASSIDY

FIGHTING FOR ELLA

Prey Security: Charlie Team Series

DECEPTIVE LIES

SHADOWED LIES

TACTICAL LIES

VENGEFUL LIES

CORRUPTED LIES

TRAITOROUS LIES

Prey Security: Cyber Team Series

RESCUING NATHANIEL

RESCUING TOBIAS


Christmas Romantic Suspense Series


THE DIAMOND STAR

CHRISTMAS HOSTAGE

CHRISTMAS CAPTIVE

CHRISTMAS VICTIM

YULETIDE PROTECTOR

YULETIDE GUARD

YULETIDE HERO

HOLIDAY GRIEF

HOLIDAY LOSS

HOLIDAY SORROW


Conquering Fear Series (Co-written with Amanda Siegrist)


DROWNING IN YOU

OUT OF THE DARKNESS

CLOSING IN

# About the Author

USA Today bestselling author Jane Blythe writes action-packed romantic suspense and military romance featuring protective heroes and heroines who are survivors. One of Jane's most popular series includes Prey Security, part of Susan Stoker's OPERATION ALPHA world! Writing in that world alongside authors such as Janie Crouch and Riley Edwards has been a blast, and she looks forward to bringing more books to this genre, both within and outside of Stoker's world. When Jane isn't binge-reading she's counting down to Christmas and adding to her 200+ teddy bear collection!

To connect and keep up to date please visit any of the following

Made in United States
Cleveland, OH
14 June 2025

17741372R00152